NIGHTMARES
OF AN ETHER-DRINKER

JEAN LORRAIN (1855-1906) was the pseudonym of Paul Alexandre Martin Duval. He was one of the leading figures of the Decadent Movement and the author of numerous novels, volumes of poetry and short stories. At one point he was probably the highest paid journalist in France. Though mostly remembered today for his famous duel with Marcel Proust, he might be seen as the true chronicler of the *fin-de-siècle*.

BRIAN STABLEFORD has been publishing fiction and non-fiction for fifty years. His fiction includes a series of "tales of the biotech revolution" and a series of metaphysical fantasies featuring Edgar Poe's Auguste Dupin. He is presently researching a history of French *roman scientifique* from 1700-1939 for Black Coat Press, translating much of the relevant material into English for the first time, and also translates material from the Decadent and Symbolist Movements.

JEAN LORRAIN

NIGHTMARES
OF AN ETHER-DRINKER

Translated and with an Introduction by
BRIAN STABLEFORD

THIS IS A SNUGGLY BOOK

Translation and Introduction Copyright © 2002, 2016 by
Brian Stableford.
All rights reserved.

This Snuggly Books edition is an unabridged, slightly amended version of the translation first published by Tartarus Press in the United Kingdom in 2002 in a limited edition of 350 copies.

ISBN: 9781943813025

Contents

Introduction *vii*

Early Stories:
The Egregore   5
Funeral Oration   15
The Locked Room   24
Magic Lantern   32
The Glass of Blood   40
Beyond   49
Glaucous Eyes   58

Sensations:
One of Them   69
An Undesirable Residence   76
A Troubled Night   91
A Posthumous Protest   100
An Uncanny Crime   109
The Holes in the Mask   117
The Visionary   126
The Possessed   134
The Double   140

Souvenirs:
The Toad   149
Night-Watch   155
The Spirit of the Ruins   161

Récits:
Dolmance   181
One January Night   190
The Spectral Hand   197
Prey to Darkness   206

Contes:
The Princess of the Red Lilies   217
The Princess at the Sabbat   223
Narkiss   231
The Princess aux Miroirs   252

Introduction

NONE of Jean Lorrain's biographers has contrived to discover exactly when or why Lorrain began taking ether, or how much of it he took before realising (too late) that it was an extremely bad idea, but the rumours he encouraged when he classified a series of his short stories as *contes d'un buveur d'éther* were almost certainly exaggerated. He must have had Thomas de Quincey's *Confessions of an English Opium-Eater* (1822) in mind when he used that title, but he must also have known that there was a world of difference between ether-drinking and laudanum-drinking. Although various English writers—Samuel Taylor Coleridge and Algernon Swinburne prominent among them—had produced brilliant visionary fantasies under the influence of laudanum, Lorrain knew too many *morphinés* and *morphinées* to be under any illusion as to its long-term effects on literary production.

Long before he squeezed his first ungenerous drop of ether into a glass of wine or a carafe of water Lorrain knew perfectly well that it was a killer; he could only have risked it in the hope that doses small enough to be harmless might help combat the symptoms of his other maladies. He must, alas, have realised very soon how misguided that hope was, and he probably gave it up within a year—

easily enough, given that the *étheromanes* to which his writings on the subject often refer were not addicts but lunatics unhinged by a strictly temporary recklessness.

Ether is by no means the only hallucinogen to which Lorrain's fiction makes reference, but his references to such old favourites as opium and hashish are mostly tokenistic. He was, after all, a dutiful member of the Decadent Movement, more conscientious than most in his pursuit of the Decadent lifestyle as well as the ideals of Decadent literature. One reason for his fascination with ether was certainly the fact that it had not previously been widely featured in Decadent prose, and he was always ambitious to be a pioneer. He had certainly drunk a good deal of laudanum in the attempt to quell the recurrent fevers and headaches to which he was subject, and it is likely that the nightmares he associated with ether had at least as much to do with the legacy of that usage as with the chemical effects of ether itself, but there was little literary scope left for "revelations" of the effects of opium and hashish since Théophile Gautier and Charles Baudelaire had offered their accounts of the experiments undertaken by the Club de Haschichins in the 1830s and 1840s.

Lorrain's "tales of an ether-drinker" are, in one important sense, set firmly in the tradition established by the Club de Haschichins, whose exploits had provided one of the foundation-stones of Decadent lifestyle fantasy. The pose he adopted in order to set them down and organise them into a series has a mock-scientific aspect; the principal reason why it is the narrator's friends who experience the worst effects of ether under his observation is not that Lorrain did not wish his readers to think that the tales were not based on personal experience but because he wanted to preserve the clinicality of his catalogue of the drug's effects. In this he was following an august precedent. The hallucinatory adventures of Théophile Gautier and his friends had been supervised and guided by a doctor named Joseph Moreau, who liked to style himself "Moreau de Tours". Moreau's study of *Hashish and Mental Alienation* (1845), based in these experiments, reprinted the whole of an article on "Hashish" that Gautier had published in 1843.

Gautier's account of the effects of hashish has little in common with modern reports of the effects of cannabis, and the phenomena he describes presumably had at least as much to do with his own anticipations as with the actual physiological effects of the drug. Lorrain's accounts of the hallucinatory effects of hashish, contained in such novels as *Monsieur de Phocas. Astarté* (1901; tr. as *Monsieur de Phocas*) are so similar to Gautier's that there can be little doubt as to where he researched them, and the legacy of that research seems to have been carried over into his accounts of the effects of ether, suggesting that his experiences under the influence of the drug were prejudiced by expectation. The chief difference between Gautier's musings on the effects of hashish and Lorrain's account of the effects of ether is, in fact, an inversion that had already been suggested by Baudelaire. Although Baudelaire was the great pioneer of the Decadent lifestyle, he was sceptical from the very first of Gautier's attempts to find ecstasy through hallucination, and his own essays on the search for "artificial paradises" concluded that hallucinogens flattered only to deceive, and were far less likely, in the long run, to guide a man to Heaven than they were to deliver him to Hell.

Jean Lorrain knew this before he ever touched a drop

of ether, and he was probably set from the very beginning to find the dark side of the coin whose brighter face Gautier had described so enthusiastically:

"Never had such beatitude flooded me with its waves: I had so melted into the indefinable, I was so absent, so free from myself (that detestable witness ever dogging one's footsteps) that I realised for the first time what might be the way of life of elemental spirits, of angels, and of souls separated from their bodies. I was like a sponge in the midst of the ocean: at every moment floods of happiness penetrated me . . . my whole being had been transfused by the colour of the medium into which I had been plunged."[1]

Given this, the real mystery of Lorrain's ether-drinking is why he did it at all. It would not have been atypical of Lorrain's character and method to have faked the whole thing, merely posing as an ether-drinker for notoriety's sake, but even though we do not known how much he took and when, we can be certain that he did indulge, for the simple reason that it killed him. It did not kill him swiftly, and it certainly did not kill him mercifully, but it did kill him. The ulcers it left in his gut were so bad that he had to have a section of his small intestine surgically removed, and it was while attempting to soothe those in his large intestine with an enema that he blew a hole in his colon and perished—alone and unattended, ignominiously as well as horribly—of fecal peritonitis. We may presume that he did not expect this to happen, but he did know the risks. Why, then, did he take them?

---

1. Théophile Gautier, "Hashish" in *Hashish Wine Opium* by Théophile Gautier and Charles Baudelaire, translated by Maurice Stang. London: Calder & Boyars 1972. p.60.

Although there is no reliable documentation to prove the point, it seems probable that Lorrain first took ether some time after the fateful day in 1886 when he realised, following the death of his father, that his long-anticipated inheritance had all been spent and that he would have to earn a living. He was already well-established as a writer, but while he had lived on the allowance whose eventual dramatic increase he had confidently expected, he had been more than content to adopt the voguish pose of the dilettantish dandy, for whom writing was a vocation rather than a profession. He had published three collections of poetry and a couple of conspicuously literary novels, but these items could hardly be considered a sturdy foundation for a commercial career. As soon as the necessity of making a living by his pen became clear, however, he set to his task with a furious will.

Within a year of his father's death Lorrain had become a prolific newspaper columnist and short-story writer, and the character of his work was utterly transformed. He retained too many pretensions to be thought of as a mere muck-raker (although the enemies he made were not slow to accuse him of it) but he embraced the controversial and the scandalous with a determined will, if not a whole heart. Within ten years his short fiction had chronicled every perversion he could think of—which included a considerable number that no one had ever thought of before—and it was in that spirit that his first tale of etheromania, the cautionary "Oraison funèbre" (1887; tr. herein as "Funeral Oration") was written. It does differ from some of his other tales of perversion in employing a first-person narrative voice—when he went to extremes, as in his pioneering tale of vampiric lesbian paedophilia "La verre du sang" (1891; tr. herein as "The Glass of Blood") he tended to employ a more distanced third-person viewpoint—but the narrator reacts with thoroughly respectable horror and sadness to the realisation that his friend has fallen victim to the demon drug. The story does, however, pay homage to the alleged power of the drug as a stimulant—the one property that distinguished its reputation very sharply from that of laudanum.

It was this property of the drug that Lorrain must have found tempting. A dilettantish dandy can easily tolerate long periods of enforced idleness, and being a "career invalid" only added to the reputation of such writers as Swinburne. While Lorrain had expected to inherit a fortune his persistent bouts of ill-health had been testament to the delicacy of constitution and temperament expectable in a literary prodigy, but once he was a newspaper columnist grinding out copy day by day they became exceedingly inconvenient. The pen-portrait he paints of a literary hack in "Au-delà" (1891; tr. herein as "Beyond") is characteristically vicious, but there is an element of envy in its frank admission that such work requires a strong constitution. Lorrain's physical frailty became extremely inconvenient after 1886, and the medications to which he had become used—including laudanum—were no help to him, because in dulling the pain they also had an anaesthetic effect that made work impossible. In late nineteenth century Paris there was only one drug available whose reputation claimed a remarkable restorative effect, and that was ether.

The reputation was, of course, undeserved, and the toxicity of the substance is so great that even a single drop dissolved in a glass of wine was far from harmless, but by the time Lorrain had figured that out the damage was done. He certainly knew that he had made a mistake long before he sat down to write the first of his ether-drinker's tales, and it seems very probable that he only took the drug for a matter of months, but the initial mistake is not beyond comprehension. Such was the haphazard nature of nineteenth-century medical theory that he may well have taken the drug on medical advice, or at least with medical sanction, and it was certainly only one of several quack cures he employed in the hope of relieving his lifelong proneness to mysterious fevers.

The other early story in which Lorrain makes a brief reference to ether is "La chambre close" (1890; tr. herein as "The Locked Room"). This was only his second experiment in supernatural fiction, and the association of the faint odour of ether with the appearance of a phantom is surely significant, even though it is understated. The story offers clear testimony to the difficulty Lorrain had in bringing himself to take ghosts seriously, but he soon learned that the rather embarrassed ambiguity of the story was something that could be turned to advantage. "The Locked Room" is not entirely satisfactory as a story, but it did enable Lorrain to find a template for the ether-drinker's tales that he would begin to write a couple of years afterwards, which brought the fine line separating subjective and objective experience into much sharper and more strikingly nightmarish focus.

※

The influence that his experience as an ether-drinker had on Lorrain's work is distinctly equivocal (as he would certainly have judged himself, *équivoque* being one of his favourite words). The tenor of his ether-drinker's tales strongly suggests that he was never sure whether to forgive himself or despise himself for the temporary weakness that made him take the drug, but that is hardly surprising. The same work testifies eloquently to the fact that he was never sure whether to forgive or despise himself for his other, far more enduring, "weaknesses": his lifelong ill-health and his homosexuality.

Lorrain, like many nineteenth-century writers, was never certain of the extent to which his ill-health was self-induced. He knew that he was something of a hypochondriac and was quite content to describe himself as a neurotic, and he was slightly less inclined than some of his contemporaries to take refuge in then-popular protopsychological theories which suggested that one could not qualify as a literary genius unless one suffered from "neurasthenia". His symptoms were undoubtedly real, but in a world where Pasteur's germ theory had yet to receive universal assent and epilepsy was popularly thought to be caused by excessive masturbation, he could hardly be blamed for doubting that their reality made him any less culpable.

The fact that Lorrain was so very uncomfortable in regard to his homosexuality confused the situation even further. He never made any real attempt to conceal it from his friends and acquaintances, although he never formally "came out" to his readers, but he did try to keep a firm division between his social life and his sex-life, confining the latter to clandestine excursions into suburban red-light districts. He did this partly for the sake of his mother, who lived with him during the last thirteen years of his life—and survived him, thus adding sad proof to her long-held conviction that his lifestyle would be the death of him—but there can be little doubt that he could never quite reconcile himself to the fact that his particular taste was for what would nowadays be called "rough trade", and that he descended in consequence into an awful morass of shame and self-loathing.

In psychological terms, therefore, Lorrain was certainly a mess, and one is inevitably tempted to speculate that his experiments with ether might have been as much self-punishment as self-stimulation. It would, however, be a mistake to regard his use of the drug as quasi-suicidal. Not only did he stop using it when he found out how much damage it was doing, but he also set out to redress the balance of harm and profit as best he could, by deriving some literary benefit from the failed experiment. However convoluted the reasons for Lorrain's drug-use may have been, the fact remains that his use of ether made significant contact with his attitude to the supernatural, prompting him to produce horror stories of several intriguingly peculiar kinds, of which the ether-drinker's tales were only one.

When he set out to write the ether-drinker's tales Lorrain was already a writer fascinated by ghost-seers, even though he did not believe in ghosts. He was firmly convinced that all apparitions were delusional, and it is not surprising that he interpreted his own experiences under the influence of ether in that light. He was convinced from the outset that all sightings of ghosts and monsters had to be construed in terms of anxiety and guilt, especially sexual anxiety and sexual guilt. The first such story he ever wrote, "L'Égrégore" (1887; tr. herein as "The Egregore"), might still be reckoned his most original, and also his most influential—George du Maurier probably read it before writing *Trilby*, which began serialization in Harper's in 1894, and George Viereck surely had it in mind when writing *The House of the Vampire* (1907)—but its originality resides entirely in its addition of an explicitly homoerotic gloss to a formula that had previously been fuelled and delimited by its heteroerotic subtexts. "Beyond" and "Les yeux glauques" (1892; tr. herein as "Glaucous Eyes") both employ supernatural devices that are exceedingly trivial as well as highly ambiguous, but they do so in order to exaggerate the psychological component of their supposed "sightings", and both contrive a remarkable intensity by virtue of their persuasively misanthropic psychological analyses.

Lorrain's use of ether did not lead straightforwardly to a further exaggeration of this intensity—indeed, it also exaggerated the playful sarcasm of many of his accounts of ambiguous apparitions—but it does appear to have caused him to re-examine and re-evaluate his own psychological development, and it is arguable that its more profound effects are seen in those stories written after the ether-drinker cycle that pose as memoirs and as fairy tales. In order to obtain a better insight into the subtleties of all these works, however, it is necessary to review in greater detail the pattern of his early life.

※

Jean Lorrain was born Paul Alexandre Martin Duval in 1855, in Fécamp, a small seaside town in Normandy. His father, Amable Duval, was a ship-owner whose vessels were involved in trans-Atlantic trade. His love of fiction was fostered at an early age and fervently encouraged by his mother. He was very fond of fairy tales, and fascinated by the idealised princesses who were often their central characters. He was also very fond of dressing up, although it is impossible to gauge the extent to which his affection for silk and velvet was fetishistic. Having been educated at home for a while, Paul was sent to complete his schooling in the charge of Dominican monks, which left him with a lifelong detestation of the clergy. He never formally renounced the Catholic faith, but he gave little evidence of firm belief.

The Normandy shore was a favourite refuge of English exiles, who had crossed the channel to avoid the fiercer strictures of Victorianism. The path had been beaten long before Victoria ascended to the throne, by the unlucky George "Beau" Brummell, whose legendary status became far greater in France than it had ever been in England. Swinburne, who had lived near Fécamp for some years, remained the very model of notoriety so far as Lorrain's home town was concerned; the exotically lurid decor of Swinburne's house, and the scandalous things that were rumoured to go on there, remained common knowledge long after his return to England, and Lorrain paid ironic homage to the suggestive tenor of that kind of gossip in "Dolmancé" (tr. herein as "Dolmance"). Paul never had the chance to meet Swinburne but he did become acquainted while he lived in Fécamp with the similarly colourful Lord Arthur Somerset, a dilettante painter with whom he maintained a correspondence for some years.

Somerset tried to persuade Paul Duval to become a painter like himself, but that influence was far outweighed when the adolescent met Théophile Gautier's daughter Judith while she was on holiday in Fécamp in 1873. Judith, who was ten years older than Paul, was separated from her husband, Catulle Mendès, one of the co-founders of the "Parnassian Movement" whose anthologies provided publishing opportunities to the poets who were later to become icons of the Decadent Movement, including Baudelaire and Arthur Rimbaud. So far as Judith Gautier was concerned, her brief acquaintance with the future Jean Lorrain was a trivial matter—she made no mention of him in her autobiography—but he was profoundly affected by it. He continued to wax so lyrical about the change it had wrought in his life that his firmest friend, Edmond de Goncourt, became convinced that it had been the ruination of him. Goncourt believed—falsely, one must presume—that Lorrain's homosexuality was some kind of traumatic response to his doomed infatuation with Judith, and that everything that happened to him thereafter was little more than a painfully-protracted moral and physical suicide.

After his son had completed a year's military service, Amable Duval sent him to study law, but Paul soon began to suffer from the burning fevers and chest-pains that would afflict for the rest of his life. When he announced that he was giving up the law in favour of a literary career his father agreed to provide a modest allowance, on condition that the family name was veiled by a pseudonym. In 1880, therefore, Paul Duval became Jean Lorrain. Lorrain set himself up in the Montmartre whose image has been strikingly preserved by the artwork of Henri de Toulouse-Lautrec: a world of cheap furnished rooms in which impoverished members of the literary *avant garde* rubbed shoulders with cheap prostitutes and formed enthusiastic cliques in cafés—and launched himself into the standardized lifestyle of a literary Bohemian.

The particular café in which Lorrain elected to spend most of his days was Le Chat Noir. Its *habitués*, who included the key members of Émile Goudeau's literary club, the Hydropathes, and also played host to short-lived groups such as the "Zutistes," included all the most colourful members of the Decadent Movement, and various fringe members of the *fin-de-siècle* Occult Revival, some of whom assisted the Zutistes in testing the limits of public tolerance by means of a wide-ranging celebration of moral perversity.

The poems Lorrain wrote under the influence of the Hydropathes and the Zutistes were reprinted in *Sang des dieux* (1882) and *La Forêt bleue* (1883). *Sang des dieux* was fortunate enough to be published with a frontispiece by Gustave Moreau, whom Lorrain had met in 1880, immediately becoming a devout admirer of his work. Moreau's art became a considerable influence on Lorrain's world-view, equipping it with a gorgeous and gaudy symbol-laden vision of a world dominated by *luxure* and *luxe* (lust and luxury), where eroticism was intricately and inextricably linked with cruelty and death. Following the publication of *La Forêt bleue* Lorrain began to frequent the salon of Charles Buet, where he made his most significant literary acquaintances, including Jules Amédée Barbey d'Aurevilly, Joris-Karl Huysmans and Marguerite Eymery.

Barbey d'Aurevilly is remembered today primarily as the author of the misogynistic classic *Les diaboliques* (1874; tr. as *Weird Women* and *The She-Devils*) but he was far better known in his own day for his non-fiction. He was one of the most prolific and influential literary critics of his day, and the leading exponent of the philosophy of "dandyism," whose manifesto he had provided—ten years before

Lorrain was born—in *Du dandyisme et de G. Brummell* (1845). Although Lorrain had neither the means nor the breeding to compete with such notorious homosexual dandies as Comte Robert de Montesquiou and Pierre Loti, he always did what he could to maintain his own appearances—to the extent that Remy de Gourmont was later to describe him as "the sole disciple of Barbey d'Aurevilly".

In 1883 Huysmans was working on his own handbook of dandyism, *À rebours* (1884; tr. as *Against the Grain* and *Against Nature*): the book that became the Bible of the Decadent Movement. Lorrain's fourth collection of poetry, *Les Griseries* (1887), consists of material explicitly inspired by *À rebours*, and *Monsieur de Phocas* is an explicit homage to it, partly pastiche and partly subversion. Lorrain and Huysmans became fast friends, although their association was weakened somewhat when Huysmans turned to religion in search of a more comfortable lifestyle fantasy.

Marguerite Eymery had only just begun to call herself "Rachilde" in 1883 and her literary career was yet to begin in earnest, although she had already started to cultivate a reputation as an *enfant terrible*. She shared Lorrain's passionate fascination for masked balls, which were then in their last period of great fashionability, and he became her regular escort, enthusiastically competing with her in the outrageousness of his costumes.

While he cultivated these acquaintances, Lorrain was gradually making a name for himself with the outspoken reviews that he wrote for the *Courrier Français*. It was in the *Courrier* that he honed the scathing rhetoric that served him so well when he had to make a living from his pen, and for which he became notorious. His negative reviews were poisonous, and surprisingly indiscriminate, while his favourable ones tended to the opposite extreme. Among the books on which he lavished praise were the three cornerstones of Decadent prose fiction: Elémir Bourges' *Le Crépuscule des dieux* (1883), *À rebours* and Rachilde's *Monsieur Vénus* (1884; tr. as *Monsieur Venus*). Lorrain's advertisement of Rachilde—entitled "Madame Salamandre" (1884)—became her launching-pad, cementing her scandalous reputation. (Rachilde was, however, the wisest of all the Decadents in confining her fantasies of reckless perversity entirely to her work while privately retreating into the respectability of marriage to Alfred Vallette, the staid editor of the *Mercure de France*. Unlike Lorrain, she lived to the ripe old age of ninety-three.)

In 1885 Lorrain added to these acquaintances that of Edmond de Goncourt. Goncourt was thirty-three years older than Lorrain but the age difference did not inhibit their friendship; they remained close until Goncourt's death in 1896. Goncourt took the younger man under his wing, apparently seeing something in him that reminded him of his younger brother and collaborator Jules, who had died in 1870. Lorrain was heartbroken when he found that Goncourt had not included him among the members of the "Goncourt Academy," apparently feeling that his inclusion would have been too controversial.

In 1886 Lorrain met the actress Sarah Bernhardt, and became one of the most fervent of her many admirers, but that was just before the disastrous reversal of his fortunes. Bernhardt was the central figure of the Parisian *monde*, holding the key to social acceptance in the circles in which Lorrain desperately desired to move, and he might well have thought that he had come to the very threshold of paradise before disaster struck. It seems probable, however, that the devastation of his expectations made little difference to her attitude. She accepted his adoration, but like Judith Gautier before her she much preferred the company of his two *bêtes noires*, Loti and Montesquiou. Lorrain wrote several plays tailor-made for Sarah Bernhardt, but she refused to appear in any of them. That was the final sum and definitive symbol of the frustrations that he carried forward into his journalism and short fiction when Amable Duval died in 1886, leaving his estate to be liquidated in order to pay off the debts that he had kept secret from his family.

※

Lorrain's mother had kept control of her dowry and was not reduced to penury by her husband's clandestine profligacy, but she could not possibly maintain her son's allowance. When his father died Lorrain had already published two novels, *Les Lépilliers* (1885) and *Très Russe* (1886), and his reviews had won him a reputation of sorts, but they had earned him more enemies than friends, and even his friends were wary of him. Even so, it was not too difficult for him to change gear and begin a career as a newspaper critic and short story writer.

It is hardly surprising that his journalistic work cashed in on his talent for abuse, nor that his targets reacted angrily. Even before Lorrain set out to make a career of sarcasm and parodic excess, Guy de Maupassant—whose aristocratic family had been near neighbours and slight acquaintances of the bourgeois Duvals—had been sufficiently incensed by resemblances between himself and one of the characters in *Très Russe* to send his seconds round to seek reparation from the author. No duel actually took place then, but this was only the first of several challenges. In 1887 Lorrain was called out by the journalist René Maizeroy, and in 1888 Paul Verlaine sent his seconds round after Lorrain erroneously reported that he had been committed to an insane asylum. In 1897 Marcel Proust, incensed by Lorrain's scathing reviews of his first book, *Les Plaisirs et les jours* (1896), insisted that the pistols brought to their meeting should actually be fired—a decision that might have had considerable import for literary history had the guns not been discharged harmlessly, after which the two men shook hands. Unfortunately, the most damaging of all these disputes was later to be settled in a far deadlier fashion.

After leaving Montmartre in 1887, Lorrain installed himself in an apartment in the Rue de Courty, which he furnished in a calculatedly bizarre fashion that took aboard—to the extent that he could afford to do so—all the lessons he had learned from Lord Arthur Somerset, Barbey d'Aurevilly and *À rebours*. Under the hallucinogenic influence of ether, however, this apartment eventually came to seem rather discomfiting, and he began to refer to it as his "haunted house". When he moved to Auteuil in 1890 he stated that he was doing so in the hope of recovering his health and composure, which strongly suggests that his ether-drinking days were already over by that time. They had certainly been at an end for some time when his mother moved in with him in 1893, but it was only then that he began producing the *contes d'un buveur d'éther* that were reprinted under that subtitle in his most important collection, *Sensations et Souvenirs* (1895).

It is not impossible that Lorrain set out to produce these mock-anecdotal tales in a cynical frame of mind, in order to turn his experiences in the haunted house into hard cash, but it seems far more probable that they were an attempt to come to terms with those experiences and to put them into proper perspective—and however they started out, that is certainly what they eventually became. There are nine tales in all but only eight of them are included here because a translation of the ninth, "La main gantée" (tr. by Iain White as "The Gloved Hand") can found in the Atlas Press anthology *The Book of Masks* (1994).

Although the first of the ether-drinker's tales, "Le mauvais gîte" (tr. herein as "An Undesirable Residence") employs a first-person narrator, thus masquerading—as so many of Lorrain's newspaper stories do—as anecdotal reportage, the narrator is carefully distanced from the observed effects of the ether, which are credited to an imaginary friend, Serge Allitof. When the story was reprinted, a second and subtler distancing move was made by a dedication to Joris-Karl Huysmans; Lorrain frequently added dedications to his short stories but this one, unusually, added to the name the words "*qui l'a connu*", slyly implying that the tale was based on Huysmans' experiences. Allitof, in the story, is working on a Jules Michelet-inspired Satanist history that contemporary readers could hardly have helped associating with Huysmans' already-notorious *Là-Bas* (1891).

The narrator of "An Undesirable Residence"—who, like all Lorrain's seemingly self-based narrators, is a fiction—maintains a determined scepticism, perhaps insisting a little too hard that Allitof's troubles are all in the mind. The second story in the sequence, "Une nuit trouble"

xxiv

(tr, herein as "A Troubled Night"), represents itself as an anecdote told by another imaginary friend, thus allowing it to invert the sceptical insistence. Here, de Jacquels is permitted to conclude—with far less reluctance than the luckless guest in "The Locked Room"—that although he had certainly been dreaming, his dream was not just a dream, but an actual insight into the metaphysical framework of human life closely akin to the visionary quality of art. In this story, the careful preliminary citation of a poem by Maurice Rollinat is not a dutiful acknowledgement of the story's inspiration but a recruitment of further evidence suggesting that de Jacquels experience, however carefully it is dressed with sardonic lightness, has something profound within it. As the sequence progresses from "Réclamation posthume" (tr. herein as "A Posthumous Protest") and "Un crime inconnu" (tr. herein as "An Uncanny Crime") to "Le possédé" (tr. herein as "The Possessed") and "Le double" (tr. herein as "The Double") the flippancy of the tales decreases by degrees and their nightmarish quality becomes more deeply felt. When the final story evokes the spirit of Hans Christian Andersen it does not do so to deflate the narrator's hallucination but to reassure and console him that it is, after all, resistible and ultimately harmless.

One story in *Sensations et Souvenirs* that Lorrain did not include in the ether-drinker sequence, "L'un d'eux" (translated herein as "One of Them"), might be regarded as a useful key to the understanding of the whole sequence. This piece begins—again, as many of Lorrain's newspaper stories do—as an apparent item of commentary on current affairs, to which an exemplary anecdote is added. This makes it all the more remarkable that Lorrain poses as a narrator whose ideas and opinions are definitely not his. This narrator finds masked balls oppressive, depressing and deeply puzzling. Unlike Lorrain, who loved to dress up and disport himself at the Opéra on the nights leading up to Mardi Gras, this fictitious voice has no idea what makes people do that, although it is uneasily certain that their motives are perverse. From the narrator's point of view, the masked figure that he encounters in the street and then again—seemingly impossibly—at the railway station is an utterly mysterious apparition. What, if anything, can be going on inside that costume?

The hypothesis that there is actually nothing inside the mask but a void is soon set aside in "One of Them"—although it was to be reconsidered at much greater length as the central motif of "Les trous du masque" (tr. herein as "The Holes in the Mask")—but much more is made of the fact that the flesh outlined and emphasized by the black silk tights is disturbingly androgynous. Whoever—or whatever—is inside the costume is completely obscured by it. It is, in the end, merely "one of them"—but one can hardly avoid suspecting that it is Jean Lorrain himself, under clinical and critical examination from a purely hypothetical viewpoint, just as Serge Allitof and Maxime de Jacquels are Jean Lorrain himself, under clinical and critical examination from a not-so-safe distance.

All the ether-drinker's tales are tales of apparitions, and all the apparitions are ambiguous, even when the supernatural interpretation is clearly intended to be rejected. All of them are hallucinations, but even when the characters actually wake up to find that they have been dreaming the implication is clear that their dreams were not just dreams. "A Troubled Night" is unusual in ramming the point home by using the already-ancient device that Lorrain had first tried out in "The Locked Room", but it is obvious in the other tales that even the dreams that are nothing but dreams are not without meaning.

All the members of the Decadent Movement were obsessed with symbolism—to the extent that everyone who ever disapproved of the word "decadence" insisted on calling it the Symbolist Movement—and Lorrain was already convinced, some years before the publication of Freud's *The Interpretation of Dreams* (1900), that dreams were symbolic and that their symbolism cried out for interpretation in sexual terms. The apparitions in many of Lorrain's tales are not even illusions, let alone ghosts, but the hallucinatory aura that surrounds them lends them a significance that is more profoundly emotionally-charged than those manifestations that remain stubbornly inexplicable. "An Uncanny Crime" is the most melodramatic of the mock-voyeuristic *contes d'un buveur d'éther* because it carefully complicates and clarifies the central mystery of "One of Them" in its dramatization of the guilt experienced by a gentleman who masquerades as a butcher in order to check into a cheap hotel on the eve of Mardi Gras for a night of homosexual passion with his lower-class pick-up, and is then overcome by shame and fear of discovery.

A similar intensification of feeling—perhaps even more remarkable in context—is manifest in the stories that belong to the Souvenirs sector of *Sensations and Souvenirs* (the ether-drinker's tales are, of course, chief among the sensations). The three that are reprinted in this volume include one that is explicitly non-supernatural—"Le crapaud", tr. as "The Toad"—and two that are ambiguous—"Nuit de veille", tr. as "Night-Watch" and "L'âme des ruines", tr. as "The Spirit of the Ruins"—but it is "The Toad" that is the most obviously and most revealingly symbolic, as well as the most strikingly horrific.

None of these stories is, of course, an actual "memoir"; no matter how many trivial biographical details their narrators may share with Lorrain they are all works of pure fiction. They are, however, deeply felt; Lorrain obviously had no difficulty in imagining that he might indeed have had such traumatic experiences. The most obviously fictitious is "The Spirit of the Ruins", which takes great care to associate itself with the highly artificial nostalgia of the Occitan poet Frédéric Mistral, but it is in its way the most revealing of all Lorrain's ghost stories, in making the ghost a teller of tales of ambiguous antiquity. Within the story Fuldrade is so paradoxical a teller of tales that she never opens her mouth, but it was shortly after publishing this story that Lorrain became a teller of legendary tales himself, working a deeper darkness into the standardized fabric of the "art fairy tale" than anyone else had yet contrived.

Although the Decadent Movement's principal model as a writer of supernatural fiction was Edgar Poe, whose translation had provided Baudelaire with a regular income, Lorrain was fonder of the more surreal fantasies of the German writer E. T. A. Hoffmann. He often invoked Hoffmann's name in his tales of mysterious characters encountered at masked balls—of which there are at least a dozen in addition to "One of Them"—but with typical perversity he framed his most elaborate hommages as naturalistic tales like "Lanterne magique" (1891; tr. herein as "Magic Lantern") or tales whose supernatural intrusions are trivial timeslips, like "Nuit de Janvier" (tr. herein as "One January Night").

After completing the sequence of anecdotal *contes d'un buveur d'éther* and the "memoirs" associated with them Lorrain apparently lost interest in ether and in mock-nostalgic fake memoirs of frightful apparitions. The second story-collection he published hot on the heels of *Sensations et souvenirs* in 1895, Un démoniaque, does contain some similarly-framed stories, including two anecdotal tales that employ the Marquis de Sade as a name to conjure with, but the most notable sequence attempts to strike out in yet another new direction.

"La main d'ombre" (tr. here as "The Spectral Hand") was clearly intended as the first of a series of pot-boilers that would cash in on the fashionability of the Parisian occult underworld so successfully dramatized by Huysmans in *Là-Bas*. The second in the series, however, "Proie de ténèbres" (tr. here as "Prey to Darkness") demonstrates the difficulty Lorrain had in taking such notions seriously. The antics of the occultist who brings poor Tramsel out of his trance become rather tokenistic, the author having become far more interested in the quality of his visions. Those visions were to be much further elaborated in the novella "Un démoniaque" (tr. by Terry Hale as "One Possessed" in *The Dedalus Book of French Horror*, 1998). The ready expansion of "Un démoniaque" to novella length must have convinced Lorrain that this train of thought was best continued in longer works, and he re-used the entire text, in fragmented and revised form, in the mosaic novel *Monsieur de Phocas. Astarté*. After 1895, almost all of his short nightmare tales were cast in the form of *contes*.

There is no clear distinction in English between "tales" and "short stories", and by the time Lorrain was writing, the term *conte* was being used rather indiscriminately even in France, but there are useful distinctions to be made between different kinds of short fiction. Some modern fantasists have tried to reintroduce a narrower meaning of "tale", most notably Angela Carter, who explained in the afterword to her first collection, *Fireworks* (1974), that:

"Formally the tale differs from the short story in that it makes few pretences at the imitation of life. The tale does not log everyday experience, as the short story does; it interprets everyday experience through a system of imagery derived from subterranean areas behind everyday experience, and therefore . . . cannot betray its readers into a false knowledge of everyday experience."[1]

The same essay goes on to locate Carter's short work within what she calls "the Gothic tradition"—which, she admits, has strong links with such "subliterary forms" as pornography, ballads and dreams.

In French, the narrow definition of the term *conte* refers to a folktale or a modern fairy tale formed in the image of a folktale. Although the word was more often applied to all kinds of short fiction as the nineteenth and twentieth centuries progressed, some writers always preferred to refer to all short stories set in the present as *récits*, even though the narrow definition of that term referred specifically to anecdotes. Others were wont to refer to all third-person stories as *nouvelles*, irrespective of length. Lorrain's early stories, including the supernatural ones, are mostly *récits*

---

1. Angela Carter. *Fireworks*. London: Quartet, 1974. pp. 121-122.

even in the narrow sense, but those that were not anecdotal caused inevitable problems of classification—although one could certainly make out a case for all of them being associated with the Gothic Tradition, given their prolific use of dreams and ballads and their continual dabbling in pornography. After 1895, however, Lorrain seems to have taken the view that fantastic motifs could be far more comfortably and far more appropriately accommodated in the fairy-tale format with which he had begun to experiment in 1894, in "La princesse aux lys rouges" (tr. here as "The Princess of the Red Lilies"). Almost all the fantasies he produced after 1896 are cast in this mould, and his collections of *"contes"* were often separated thereafter in his bibliographical listings from his collections of *"récits et nouvelles"*. Almost all of his *contes*, however, belong to a particular subgenre; they are *contes cruels* in the purest possible sense of the term.

Because the phrase was used as the title of a highly influential collection published in 1883, the term *contes cruels* is irrevocably associated with the name of the Comte de Villiers de l'Isle Adam. A pedant might, however, argue that the vast majority of Villiers' *contes cruels* are actually *récits cruels*, and the same is true of the exemplary contributions to the new subgenre subsequently made by Octave Mirbeau and Maurice Level. The real popularizer of the *conte cruel*, in the narrower sense of the term, was Catulle Mendès—and his most enthusiastic literary disciple was Jean Lorrain. There is a certain irony in this; Lorrain felt obliged to loathe Mendès because Mendès had once been married to Judith Gautier—Lorrain had met her in 1873 shortly after their separation, when her resentment of his infidelities must have been at its most powerful—but there was no writer with whom he had more in common in purely literary terms. He was probably acutely aware of that confusion—but what was one more confusion to a man who already possessed so many?

Mendès had demonstrated what might be accomplished in the realm of the cynical mock-folktale in the brilliantly nasty-minded novella *Luscignole* (1892) but his shorter works in the same vein lacked the vitality of that masterpiece. Lorrain set out to repair that fault, rapidly moving on from the relatively conventional if mildly shocking moral fabulation of "The Princess of the Red Lilies" to a remarkable series of tales whose purpose was to visit horrible fates upon relatively innocent narcissists and lifestyle fantasists. Such tales as "La princesse aux sabbat" (1895; tr. here as "The Princess at the Sabbat" and "Narkiss" (1898; tr. here under the same title) are redolent with imagery carried over from Lorrain's earlier dream-fantasies, and all the usual symbols recur, to the extent the tales begin to repeat themselves: "La princesse aux miroirs" (1899; tr. here as "The Princess aux miroirs") is essentially the same story as "The Princess at the Sabbat", carefully exaggerated and recomplicated so as to make it even more nightmarish.

These stories provide clear proof that the images that haunted Lorrain while he was an ether-drinker continued to obsess him long after he had contrived the various attempted exorcisms collected in *Sensations et Souvenirs*. They demonstrate, too, that he found ways to remove himself to an even greater narrative distance while continuing to express them. He continued to produce tales of this kind, on occasion, after he abandoned Paris at the end of 1900, when he moved to Nice in search of a kinder climate, but he reduced the frequency of his contributions to newspapers quite considerably then, preferring to concentrate his efforts on books. It would not be too unreasonable to say that all his significant short fiction was produced in the thirteen years from 1887-1899 that virtually defined the *fin-de-siècle* period—the years covered by the stories collected in this volume.

※

From 1887 to 1900 Jean Lorrain had been the self-appointed chronicler of the *fin de siècle*. Once he reached his peak in 1896 he was probably the highest-paid journalist in Paris, but he won that status because he was the most outspokenly fascinated celebrant and most enthusiastic scourge of the folkways of the yellow nineties, and his tenure was always bound to be short-lived. The rhetoric of Decadence made much of the fact that the nineteenth century was winding down, approaching an end that was devoutly to be desired, and Lorrain was fully conscious of the extent to which his tirades would lose their force once the new century was born. His move to Nice anticipated the fact that his career was bound to enter into a rapid decline once the gestationial year of 1900 had been attained.

Once settled in Nice, Lorrain set out to write two novels that would provide a kind of retrospective summary of the Decadent Movement and the world that had given birth to it: *Monsieur de Phocas. Astarté* and *Le Vice errant* (1902). They were not greeted with any considerable critical or popular acclaim when they were published, and things began to go badly wrong for Lorrain immediately after the second appeared in print.

Although Sarah Bernhardt had spurned him, Lorrain had been drawn to a number of women of the kind who would nowadays be easily recognisable as "gay icons". Some of them, well aware of what he had done for Rachilde, took care to cultivate his acquaintance and to use it as fuel for their own calculatedly-scandalous reputations. They included the would-be courtesan Liane de Pougy and the would-be amazon Colette. Between 1892 and 1896 Lorrain had been courted in that manner by an artist named Jeanne Jacquemin, some of whose work (as noted in "Le visionnaire"; tr. herein as "The Visionary") he was proud to display in his "haunted house". Jacquemin, ambitious to acquire the same kind of reputation as Remy de Gourmont's sometime mistress Berthe de Courrière, who was widely credited with guiding Joris-Karl Huysmans around the occult Underworld of Paris while he was researching *Là-Bas*, attempted to do the same for Lorrain. Alas, the sceptical Lorrain could not take their expeditions very seriously—as evidenced by "Prey to Darkness"—and he eventually fell out with her. His perennial tendency to model the characters in his novels on his friends and acquaintances backfired spectacularly when Jacquemin, seemingly repentant of her colourful past, recognised herself in Madame de Charmaille, one of the characters in a *nouvelle* called "Les Pelléastres" that was serialised in *Le Journal* in 1902. Unable, as a mere woman, to send her seconds round to see him, she took him to court for defamation of character.

The case generated a great deal of bad publicity, and Lorrain was attacked from all sides by those who had once walked in fear of his sarcasm. The court—perhaps desirous of making an example of him, although it is unclear whose benefit the judges had in mind—required him to pay astonishingly high damages of 80,000 francs. The settlement of this suit left Lorrain financially ruined and conspicuously vulnerable to further attacks of a similar sort. He was soon to face a second, albeit more frivolous, lawsuit of the same kind and a formal charge of corrupting public morals by literary means, brought against *Monsieur de Phocas. Astarté.* A similar charge had once been the making of Baudelaire's reputation, but in Lorrain's case the accusation only served to illustrate how dramatically the tide had turned, and how ardently the people of twentieth century Paris desired to advertise that the nineteenth century was dead and gone. Lorrain was deeply disappointed that hardly anyone came forward to speak in his defence (the one notable exception was Colette) and particularly hurt by the fact that Huysmans chose to remain silent.

Lorrain had no alternative but to throw himself into his writing yet again in order to pay the debts he had accrued—but he was no longer the man he had been in 1887. He produced material at a furious pace, but it was pure hackwork. His health continued to deteriorate, and his fevers returned in full force. He took various "cures" in the spas of the Riviera, but they left him sicker than before. With grim irony he began signing his articles in *Le Journal* and *La Vie parisienne* "Le Cadavre". In June 1906 he returned to Paris to help organise an art exhibition and to assist in an adaptation for the opera of one of his *contes, La Princess sous verre* (1896), and it was there that he suffered his ignominious death.

※

Lorrain was far from being the most accomplished writer involved in the Decadent Movement, but he was the one whose life and art were bound together into the most seamless whole. He was the man who embodied, more intimately and more inescapably than any other, the absurdities, affectations, paradoxes and perversities of the Decadent style and the Decadent world-view. Baudelaire died without ever being fully conscious of what he had invented; Rimbaud gave up literary work as soon as he was old enough to know better; Verlaine came late to the celebration of Decadence and never could make up his mind whether he wanted to be a part of it or not; Huysmans graced the Movement with his brief presence and then went on about his private business; Rachilde wore a Decadent mask while retaining a secure hold on private respectability; Jean Lorrain, on the other hand, threw himself so completely into the Movement that it consumed his whole existence.

He always knew, of course, that it would end badly, although his nightmares never contrived to inform him how very badly it would end. Whatever advantage he hoped to win from the stimulant properties of ether he knew perfectly well that it would not lead him to enlightenment. He had certainly read Baudelaire's essay comparing and contrasting the effects of wine and hashish, "Du vin et du hashish" (1851), and must have taken due note of the way in which the essay swiftly passes on from the delights of alcoholic intoxication to a sarcastic description of the "supersublime" ignominies of drunkenness. He seems to have heeded that warning as best he could, resisting the temptation to overindulge in wine or in opiates—but he could no more resist the temptation of ether than he could resist the temptations that landed him with syphilis, and he paid in full for both concessions.

Monsieur de Phocas. Astarté is the most nightmarish of all Lorrain's reflections on the desires and habits that would kill him, but he probably could not have written that novel without putting in the practice that is constituted by the short stories in this collection—and it is at least arguable that they represent both the process and the ultimate achievement of the self-analytic insight that was all that the ether gave him in return for his premature death.

Brian Stableford

NIGHTMARES
OF AN ETHER-DRINKER

EARLY STORIES

The Egregore

In the grandiosely designed park
Where the Cydalises lost their way,
Among the unexpected fountains
In the marble of the clear pond,

Iris followed by a young flock,
Phillis, Églé, nymphs in love,
With their indecisive plumage
Scantily clad, showing their breasts,

Lycaste, Myrtil and Sylvandre
Come through the fresh undergrowth,
Towards the great dormant trees.

They wander in the white morning,
All dressed in satin, as charming
And as sad as Love itself.

THE young man sitting before the keyboard struck a plaintive and charming chord as the last verse was completed. The woman who had added words to the melody took up the fan of feathers that she had laid down on the piano and brought it to her face, touching it to the corners of her lips as if she were stifling a yawn.

The large room decked out in blue and gold, with screens of soft Japanese silk depicting peach-trees in flower and great zigzagging flights of storks, was suddenly filled with the creaky rustle of stiff fabrics and the discreetly honeyed whispers of enamoured women. Murmurs of "Ah! ah! delightful!" and "Bravo, brava" mingled with the patter of gloved palms: all the admiring and flattering chatter, sweetened by affectation, that was to be expected in well-mannered society.

Standing with the trains of their ball gowns gathered in straight-pleated tiers behind them, somewhat reminiscent of lovely serpents standing on their tails, bodices inclined to offer their breasts, women clustered around the performers, all of them conscious of being observed. Amid the incessant flapping of fans, the striking of pretty poses and the gracious movements of shoulders and bare arms, insignificant but exquisitely modulated questions were asked and answered.

"Adorable verses. Whose were they?"

"Monsieur de Banville's," the singer replied.

"Ah, Monsieur de Banville, my dear, author of *La Femme de Socrate*."[1]

"You remember, my dear, we went to see it three Tuesdays running, at the Française."

"Perfectly. Samary[2] wore a charming red dress."

"And the music?" chirped another voice. "By Messager, isn't it?"

"Messager, the author of *Deux pigeons!*"[3]

---

1. The Parnassian poet Théodore de Banville; the 1886 comedy in question is actually entitled *Socrate et sa femme*.
2. The actress Jeanne Samary (1857-1890).
3. The première of André Messager's ballet, knowing in English as *The Two Pigeons*, had also taken place in 1886.

"I beg your pardon," the accompanist intervened, while wiping the sweat from his unusually pale brow, "but the author is here—there, at the back of the room."

And all the heads turn, blonde and brunette alike. Necks crane . . . oh, what a delightful turning movement that assembly in the music room contrives!

"The author! But that's Hermann, dear Hermann."

And all the dresses take flight as the women move to the other end of the room; it is an abandonment, a complete desertion. Others of a riper vintage, and more "in the know"—all accompanied by bald men of solemn appearance—are already there, showering compliments on a tall, slim and beardless young man, who smiles and nods and tosses his head. His face is illuminated by two extraordinary black eyes. They are as lustrous and coldly black as his hair, which is thick with pomade, curled, combed and seemingly polished.

The singer is left behind, standing by the grand piano. The shrug of her shoulders is significant, as is the tight smile on her lightly-rouged lips. She whispers some secret impertinence to her companion, who raises his stool and smiles. His smile is as mysterious as hers. Then, taking up a sheaf of music from a scattered heap of scores, she opens it up and places it before her accompanist, pointing to a few bars at the bottom of a page. While he continues to mop the sweat from his brow with a cambric handkerchief, she sings the difficult passage in a undertone, while he accompanies her in muted fashion, barely touching the keys with the tips of his fingers. They are obviously rehearsing.

"Brother and sister," the physicist Forbster murmured in my ear. I had run into him again, purely by chance. "The

Comtesse de Mercoeur and the Marquis de Sarlys. They share a passion for difficult melodies, symphonies in C and the operas of Wagner, as practitioners as well as connoisseurs. The Comtesse possesses one of the most beautiful voices in Europe; ugly as she is, with her prominent jaw and her dead face, she can bring the audience at the Opéra to its feet, even at a premier. Ah! if she wished, she could earn two hundred thousand francs a year with Gailhard—yes, with Gailhard himself![1] But as you see, she doesn't want it! The brother's talents as a pianist are conspicuously ordinary, but it's a family matter, a pathological case."

"Another pathological case!"

"Or a fantastic one, as you prefer. The macabre is all around us here: we are undoubtedly—you, at least, would not doubt it—on the fringe of one of the blackest tales of Hoffmann. The Marquis de Sarlys, whom you see there rehearsing with his sister—Charles Bertrand de Vassenage, Marquis de Sarlys and Comte de Baudemont, a landed gentleman afflicted with an income of a hundred and forty thousand francs a year, a member of the Jockey Club, the Imperial and the Union, the proprietor until six months ago of a racing stable, all of which he has now given up—is well and truly on the way to utter exhaustion, entirely likely to become extinct at the age of twenty-eight, in the full bloom of youth, under the influence of an Egregore."[2]

---

1. The singer Pierre, or Pedro, Gailhard, was one of the administrators of the Paris Opéra from 1884 to 1903.
2. The term "égrégore," derived from the Greek, where it means "watcher" and is used in translations of various Old Testament and apocryphal writings, was employed rather enigmatically by Victor Hugo in *La Légende de siècle*, and elsewhere employed by the occultist who called himself Éliphas Lévi. Lorrain's adaptation of it to mean a

"What in God's name is an Egregore? I'm familiar with the reputation of the vampire, the lamia, the ghoul, the incubus and the succubus, but I have to admit, to my shame, that the Egregore has escaped me. It rhymes nicely with *mandragore*—is it also something that flourishes beneath the gallows?"[1]

"Not exactly. Its foliage belongs to the vegetable-mould of the cemetery and its root to the interior of a sturdy coffin, but as regards the flower, that can bloom anywhere, from the underworld to the finest milieu. In this very room, for example, we can count two."

"Two Egregores! I can't stay here a minute longer—I must run to the cloakroom to get my coat. Society is becoming too dangerous."

"You're not in any danger; I'll protect you. But look at poor Sarlys. See those hollow feverish eyes, all a-glimmer and ringed in blue; that moist pallor of a perpetual cold sweat; that tortured physiognomy, breathless and bruised—the dolorously ecstatic mask of a hysteric. Well, six months ago I knew that fellow as a strong and sanguine man, in good health: an accomplished game-player, a very good runner, joyful and vibrant, seen at all the fêtes and all the hunts. For six months, though, the fellow has had no mistress, has never touched a playing-card. He, who was once a veritable centaur, scarcely mounts a horse; he no longer hunts, no longer dines out, and no longer maintains his circle of acquaintances. Instead, to put it bluntly, he consumes himself, empties himself, exhausts himself

---

kind of psychic vampire is original to him.
1. Mandragore is the French term for the plant commonly known in English as the mandrake. Lorrain wrote one of his most colourful *contes* about it.

and murders himself in the scores of operas, symphonies and cantatas, riveted to a piano-stool between Hermann Barythine, the attractive young maestro, and the Marquise Annette de Mercoeur, née Sarlys, his sister."

"And the Egregore?"

"Is Barythine, that dear Hermann—the one those women are cooing over in their heady little voices. Look at him, now: slim, slender, svelte, with the supple form of a racing greyhound . . . or a fox. That rosy, almost adolescent beardless head perched on that elegant skeletal framework. Barythine is thirty years old. Who would believe it, eh? That youngster is older than the Marquis de Sarlys! I'll tell you the secret of that unnatural youth . . . . it was known in the Middle Ages. Oh, the head is fine, even feminine; the nose is delicate, the mouth finely chiselled but narrow and incisive: a mouth made for murder, red as blood . . . oh, that tell-tale red!

"Hermann Barythine has no mistress either, and keeps his distance from fencing-rooms and clubs. He is invisible by day, cloistered in his splendid hotel in the Rue Bassano, where he sits at the organ, the piano or the cello writing bizarre compositions. During the evening and by night, smiling politely, he goes forth to the salons to gather the applause and the swooning cheers of women. The whole world is crazy about him; he is the maestro of the moment. Tonight here, tomorrow evening there, he goes triumphantly into society, towing behind him poor Sarlys, who is no longer able to leave him, imprisoned as he is by the power of an authentic charm. Sarlys stubbornly exhausts himself every night in the interpretation, accompaniment and promotion of his works: Sarlys and the Marquise de Mercoeur, his sister. She is also an Egregore, after her own fashion, but is unconscious as yet of the fratricidal role that she is playing in this game of murder."

"A fascinating tale—but what proof do you have?"

"Proof . . . what more do you need? The sudden unreasoning passion that has derailed de Sarlys, the clubman, the muscular sportsman and rake, subjecting him to the alchemical talent of this Barythine, this unknown Pole of obscure nobility and fortune: this too young and too pretty Hermann Barythine; this enigmatic and no less disquieting creature of ambiguous sex and uncertain age."

"Then the Egregore . . ."

"Attaches itself only to its own sex, entirely in contrast to the ghoul, incubus or vampire. Their malevolent work is self-explanatory; it is with their kisses, with the accursed fire of their knowing caresses that they melt the flesh and the health of the living like wax. Their bedchamber is the Devil's crucible. The incubus drains and kills his mistress with sensuality; the succubus breathes in and drinks the wine of her lover. They are sent down here one after the other as accessories to the attraction of the sexes and the everpresence of lust. But the Egregore is another thing altogether. It is the unfeeling and deleterious influence of a creature of darkness, of a dead man or a dead woman that instals itself beside you in the guise of a living one, insinuating itself into your life, your habits and your admirations, meddling with your heart and taking odious root there, while its damnable mouth breathes a fatal passion into you: a commonplace madness; the folly of the artist or the amateur. And step by step, it increases the delusional and fascinating obsession, until you lie down one fine evening in the cold of the grave . . . the history of the Middle Ages is replete with the activities of Egregores. In

Madrid, at least eight or ten of them were burned every winter; but the Egregore country par excellence extends across Austria, Poland, Russia and Bohemia—the fatherland of Barythine. Do you want to see an example of its work, here and now? Go ask the Marquis de Sarlys, casually, what the Comtesse de Mercoeur will sing next. Go on, I'll explain afterwards."

I went to the piano to enquire, as courteously as I could, the title of the next ballad the Comtesse would sing.

"The *Adieu* of Barythine," was the reply.

"Always Barythine!" Forbster smiled. "Now I shall walk over to the young maestro and offer my compliments. I will ask if he will do me the favour of letting me hear a certain ballad of his entitled *Eros*. If, after these few words of conversation that I have outlined to you, the Marquis and the Comtesse—after having announced *Adieu* and without having had any communication with Barythine—proceed to play *Eros*, what would your incredulity say then, Monsieur?"

"In that case, I would have to agree with you. It would be useless to protest."

Forbster left me, and went to intercept the young composer as he wandered from group to group, always surrounded by a crowd. The physicist and the composer exchanged a few words. At exactly the same moment, Princess Narmof, our hostess, called for silence.

Sarlys picked out on his keyboard a series of strange and very poignant chords. To this accompaniment, as dull and rumbling as a distant storm, the Comtesse de Mercoeur, very straight and very pale, added a superbly calm and poised contralto voice:

> "*Standing in the fulgurant clarity of mountain peaks,*
> *The proud hunter Eros, the murderer of hearts,*
> *Shines, pure flame, above the abysses*
> *And hurls his sure and victorious darts.*"

"Now," said Forbster, "watch Barythine, Sarlys and his sister. Look very closely at their lips."

Her staring gaze locked with that of the composer, who was directly in front of her, the Comtesse resumed:

> "*A strike rings out across the sublime immensity,*
> *And under the glare of the implacable mocking sky*
> *A drop of blood, red produce of the crime,*
> *Falls at the naked feet of Eros, large as a flower.*"

"Oh!" I exclaimed, clutching Forbster's right arm hard enough to make him gasp. I was frightened by what I saw while the ballad of *Eros* was completed by the third and last verse.

> "*And the sun goes down and the immortal aurora*
> *Rises, Eros is there, in eternal glory*
> *Under the drops of blood, among the arrows of gold.*"

Applause rang out.

I let out a sigh of relief. The strange vision, the terrifying nightmare, had come to an end.

While the Comtesse sang, as if hypnotised by Barythine, I believed that I could distinctly see—and was still convinced that I had seen—their lips swell up and redden, becoming scarlet. Meanwhile, the lips of the poor Marquis had whitened, becoming ghastly, in a face that was suddenly afflicted with suffering. His lips had whitened as if they were being emptied of all the blood that inflated the lips of the others.

When the ballad ended, the phenomenon ceased . . . but I had drunk so much Chateau Margot at dinner with the princess that evening.

Funeral Oration

I HAVE just buried my friend Jacques. We were friends as children and as adults; we were still as close at thirty-four years of age as we had been in the little coastal village where we grew up together, scarcely touched by the somnolence and deadening calm of the province, with our eyes and our dreams eternally reaching out for the shifting horizons of the unquiet sea.

Even here, in Paris, I am still haunted by the vision of that interment in the country cemetery, its desolation increased by the calm white winter landscape; the memory pursues me like some obsessive nightmare.

Here, as down there, huge and heavy snowflakes fall from a blank leaden sky, continually impressing upon me the knowledge that there is nothing more tedious and oppressive than a graveyard clad in white, as though sheltering beneath a swansdown coverlet. . . .

※

In my vision, I am very much aware of the delicacy of the gates before each tomb, and the dark leaves of the evergreen bushes, each sharply emphasized by a fine edging of rime. The town is close by but there is no evident sign of its proximity, no noise of workshops or factory bells; all its various cries and murmurs are stifled by the thick snow, extinguished by its slow and gentle fall. It is like an autumnal fall of huge petals, immaculately white against the ink-black backcloth of the sea, which shows between the high cliffs, immaculately white against the profundity of the sad grey sky.

The funeral ceremony is already over; there is a confusion of winter overcoats, which are powdered with hoarfrost as their wearers hasten across the cemetery. At the entrance, the members of the family are arranged in their proper hierarchy, all dressed in black, bare-headed, shivering while they shake the proffered hands of all the guests, swamped by condolences and steeped in solemnity.

Jacques' brother has a sickly pallor, which becomes sicklier still beneath the sombre sky; some such pallor must have descended upon Napoleon's frozen troops as they suffered atrociously during the retreat from Moscow.

An expensive silk hat, gleaming among the shaggy head-dresses of the locals, attracts my attention; it signals the presence of a Parisian, who seems out of place at this pauper's funeral. I recognise de Saunis, a member at Jacques' club, whose path I have already crossed on arrival at the railway station

I go up to him, and we shake hands.

"Have you come from Paris for the sole purpose of attending the ceremony?" I ask.

"Yes, I have," he replied, lightly, from the depths of his furs. "I would never take the trouble for a wedding, but for a funeral, always." Then, after a pause, he continued, "Poor Armenjean was only thirty-three, wasn't he? Too soon for a man to be cashing in his chips. What did he die of—anemia, is that what they said? Worn out by life, more like—first by riotous living and then by ether . . . that dreadful ether! A nice habit he picked up from that Suzanne!"

So saying, the swaggering oaf takes a side path, slipping away, bowing his head beneath the falling snow, seemingly quite delighted to have spoiled the kindly impulse that brought him here by spreading a little stupid gossip; but there are others within earshot, and I suppose he must put on an exhibition for the provincials, sustaining his reputation as a Parisian of the *fin de siècle* by making an Entertainment out of speaking ill of the dead, pursuing his stupid trade as a commercial traveller even to the grave.

At the cemetery gateway, another surprise awaits. The door of a coupé is thrown back and Madame ***, a relative of Jacques'—a handsome woman in her thirties who has been, I believe, more or less his mistress—falls into my arms, stifling her sobs theatrically. No one could be better suited by the combination of healthy complexion, blonde hair and mourning-dress.

"What a tragedy this is, my friend!" (She calls me her friend, although she has only seen me twice in all her life, and conducts herself as if it were the end of the world!) "I knew he was ill, of course, but how could I foresee this? I have come from Rouen this very morning—I did not receive the telegram until yesterday and I had twenty-five people coming to dinner in the evening . . . impossible to put them all off—an official dinner! After the soirée I quite lost my head. . . . I felt like an actress who has just lost her mother."

I look into her eyes, which are dark blue and very beautiful, and all awash with pearly tears; she is more of an actress than she cares to admit, this handsome relative, for she did not allow her bereavement to cause her to miss one of the few balls of the winter. Rouen is thirty leagues away from this provincial hole, and her black dress fits her very well, as if it had come from a fashion-house.

But Madame has pulled me up into her coupé, and all the while she dabs at her eyelids with a fine lace handkerchief. "He loved the girl so much that he couldn't live without her, that he had to die for her, as she died." She clasps her arms nervously about me, saying meanwhile in the unmistakable fashion of a jealous woman: "Was she at least pretty, this Suzanne . . . brunette or blonde . . . because, you know, he has died as she died, an etheromaniac . . . poisoned. . . ."

※

While I gave her the information she requested, there emerged and was displayed before me a hidden drama of Jacques' last years, which I had somehow contrived not to notice. From the few words I had earlier exchanged with de Saunis and the conversation I was now having with Madame ****, a pattern emerged, clearly revealed to my eyes at last. I beheld the alarming silhouette of poor Suzanne Évrard, as I behold it now: as some kind of ghoul or vampire. That phantasmal and tragic being was once a pretty girl, perhaps a little too tall and a little too broad, but with such a supple figure that she seemed like a huge, heavy, weary flower; but I recall now as if in a sinister dream the flashing glimmer of her great black eyes—the feverish eyes of an etheromaniac, flaring amid the dull pallor of her complexion.

Two particular scenes emerge from the mists of memory to parade themselves before me, synthesizing for me the image—which I have until now refused to recognise—of a deadly evil spirit.

The first occasion was two years ago, on the night of the Opera Ball, when Jacques, Suzanne, myself and the rest of our motley crew of male and female merrymakers were stranded at the Maison d'Or, until three in the morning. . . .

I see it very clearly, like a memory recovered under hypnosis: the remains of the supper, half-consumed desserts still scattered about the stained tablecloth, the marquise's crystal champagne-glasses still half-full, the women standing before the mirrors in order to readjust their masks and to arrange the cowls of their dominoes upon their foreheads.

Jacques, having had his fill and then some, had crossed his arms before him on the table, rested his head upon them, and gone to sleep. He was very pale, poor chap, but nevertheless appeared very handsome by the light of the low-burning candles, which were on the point of splitting on the candlesticks: his pallor was like the pallor of a corpse, but his handsomeness was the handsomeness of one sunk in depravity, worn out by living to the utmost. His thin red moustache was curled up at the ends, and he had the impertinent profile of a swashbuckling pirate.

Suzanne rose from her seat and stood behind him, her great satin domino billowing around her and making her even larger than she was. She put her gloved hand on the shoulder of the sleeper in order to awaken him and tell him that it was time to go.

"He's as tight as a tick," sneered one of the others—and, indeed, Jacques was so stupefied by drink that he simply sank further forward on the table, and made no move to get up.

Suzanne took off her gloves then, and laid her bare fingers gently on the nape of his neck, at first stroking him teasingly and amorously, then scratching him with the tip of a fingernail while she imitated the purr of a cat. Jacques still did not stir. Evidently being of the opinion that serious illnesses require drastic remedies, the girl in the domino brought forth from the folds of her costume a gilded bottle, removed the stopper and tilted it over a champagne-glass. She brought the glass to the lips of the sleeper, and I saw Jacques start, suddenly awakened. Suzanne, smiling as ever, put the glass into his hand—and he, surprisingly sober all of a sudden—drained it. He got up, staggering more than a little, slipped on his fur-lined cloak, and begged our pardon. Then we left.

The restorative that Suzanne had poured into him was simply ether, that ether that never lets go, and which, six months later—by which time she fully deserved the name of etheromaniac—had put an end to her life. Now I can see her, standing there enfolded by her black domino, pouring poison into her lover, the act making a tragic and horrific mockery of the gesture that she made with the other hand, readjusting her mask of green satin. But at the time, I did not see her thus: Suzanne seemed then to be a fantasy of a different kind, the creation of that mask of pale green satin, which matched the delicate shade of her sleeves and the ribbons of her domino.

The second memory is more recent. Suzanne was already dead, and had been for at least ten months. I was with a party of night-prowling friends, run aground at Les Halles, at the Soulas or some similar all-night restaurant.

Clustered about the counter were market-gardeners in smocks, silken kerchiefs wrapped around their heads, drinking punch or hot toddy, conversing in rusty and raucous voices, harsh with catarrh. From a spiral staircase draped with green serge there came the sound of a waltz picked out by the finger of a drunken man.

In the next room, which was separated from the counter by a partition, an amusing scene was being enacted. A furious customer, assisted by a policeman and the proprietor of the establishment, had caught hold of the silken sleeves of a young woman.

This creature, a habitual haunter of the all-night restaurant, had approached the customer in the booth where he had eaten his meal. In order to get rid of the drink-cadger the man—a merchant from the provinces—had rummaged in his breast-pocket and given her twenty sous. Then, when the time came to pay his bill, the out-of-towner could not settle up; suddenly sobering up, he realised that twenty francs had gone missing, and jumped to the conclusion that instead of giving her a franc he must have given her a louis.

In a towering rage the man had immediately rushed down to the room below, where the girl was still to be found, stretched out on a bench, dead to the world. Now, while she loudly and stubbornly denied the charge brought against her, lashing out all the while at the proprietor and laughing at the policeman, she was gradually being stripped of her clothing as they rummaged about in search of the missing coin.

I can still see the great body of the woman lying on the bench, with her bare legs dangling out of her faded dress, her bonnet over her ear, and her happy, dazedly besotted smile, while careful inspection proved that there was nothing hidden in her black stockings. I can still see the drunken victim of the supposed theft, with his fixed stare and ruffled hair, strands of which hung limply down over his forehead. I remember his manner, despairing but determined, his murderous countenance. I remember the shrug of the shoulders with which the proprietor resigned the hope that he might collect what was due to him, and the way that the policeman, ambling back to his beat, paused at the corner to make the same gesture, tiredly and uncaringly.

But what I remember most clearly of all is the glimpse that I caught of a person ensconced in a corner of the dive. He wore an elegant black suit and a white cravat, and the buttonhole of his cape was decorated with a sprig of heather. He huddled over a flask of whisky, which he was mixing with ether.

He drank a large dose of the ether—a dose that would have scorched the stomach and entrails of someone like you or me. That etheromaniac—that exhausted nightprowler, that gallivanting party-goer, that neurotic who never went to his bed before eight o'clock in the morning and never got up until seven in the evening, when the city lights were burning again—that was him: Jacques, my childhood friend, the recently deceased! In the space of four years, one of the favoured sons of our fatherland had graduated from being a mere tippler of wine to become the victim of a terrible craving. What can one say? He sought to forget, and he forgot. . . .

I see again the prematurely aged face and the sickly complexion of that man who was twenty-nine-years old but looked as if he were fifty: dismal, mute and taciturn as he lurked in that shadowed corner of Les Halles. Ether had claimed him, in the same way that morphine had claimed so many others: Jacques, the lover of that poor Suzanne. Jacques—my friend Jacques—had become in the ten months following her death one of the oh-so-charming sots of the *fin de siècle*.

I saw that I had wrought a kind of legend out of Jacques' death, which I wanted to believe: that he had taken to the drug in order to poison the memory of an adored mistress, who had died while their affair was still in the full flush of its honeymoon, fervent with new-born love and sensual intoxication. But it was all a lie.

Now, I perceived the truth of the matter—the sinister and terrifying truth. Suzanne was an etheromaniac, and she had made an etheromaniac of him, too. The woman had been slain by her vice, but her influence extended beyond the tomb; she had left her lover a fatal bequest. Jacques had outlived her, but he had become an accessory to her crime, and in due course the dead had claimed the living.

They are together now, forever.

※

I have just buried my friend Jacques. We were friends as children and as adults; we were still as close at thirty-four years of age as we had been in the little coastal village where we grew up together, scarcely touched by the somnolence and deadening calm of the province, with our eyes and our dreams eternally reaching out for the shifting horizons of the unquiet sea.

The Locked Room

CERTAIN dwellings and provincial rooms are intrinsically hostile, with their close and mortuary atmosphere. I had never formed such a profound resentment than I did on that miserable and rainy October morning, when the door of the room where the farmhand had deposited my suitcase closed behind me, almost silently.

What autumnal malaise had brought me to that detached house lost in the wood? Me, the worst hunter in the world, in whom an instinctive indolence was wed to a near-physical horror of firearms. What had put into my head the insane impulse to come here to follow the Marquis de Hauthère's beaters through the forest—to leave the boulevards and newspapers of Paris in order to bury myself alive in these gloomy woods the day before the opening of *Cleopatra* and the long-awaited return of Réjane in a work by Meilhac.[1]

At the risk of seeming mad, I am convinced that when I stranded myself in that autumn-dilapidated and strangely solitary forest I was the near-helpless instrument of some

---

1. Victorien Sardou's *Cleopatra* opened at the Théâtre de la Porte-Saint-Martin in 1890, with Lorrain's idol Sarah Bernhardt in the lead. The actress Gabrielle Réjane had her first great success in Henri Meilhac's *Ma camarade* (1883); the reference must be to her subsequent appearance in his *Ma cousine* (1890).

unknown will, more powerful than my own. Although I was not conscious of it I was there to play a role in a drama of the Beyond!

Who had previously lived in that old Louis XIII house, with the high slate roof chequered with dormer windows, so miserably isolated on the bank of that pool clogged with dead leaves, in the profoundest depths of the great wood? It had belonged to de Hauthère's family for centuries, and the father of the present Marquis had transformed it into a guest-house where those people invited to hunting-parties for whom no place could be found in the chateau might be lodged. The guest-house of the Marquis de Hauthère stood beside that stagnant pool, in the midst of wild grasses, rotting in the rain. Its atmosphere was strange, unsettling and mysterious. The thick silence was undisturbed save for the weathervanes on the roof creaking in the October wind; all around was the conspiratorial silence of the voiceless and echoless woods, dormant beneath a blanket of fog.

Upon my arrival in the black and white tiled hallway, the impression that I had entered into a drama of the unknown was further emphasized. The room that had been assigned to me was on the first floor. The light of two huge windows, with faded curtains of antique silk, brightened the cavernous space despite the misery of the rain-drenched sky and the dreary forest. As I crossed the threshold, however, I had instinctively muffled my footsteps, as if I were entering a sickroom. A faint odour of ether was still perceptible in the air: ether gone rancid with age. There was dust everywhere: on the faded damask of the ancient curtains, on the cold and antiquatedly luxurious armchairs, on the canopy of the bed and the polished marble of the ancient console table. It was the black accumulation of years gone by, seemingly undisturbed for many long months.

> *Strange room: one would have said that it kept the secret*
> *Of some very sad event, and that it had grown weary*
> *Of having seen the mystery take flight within the glass. . . .*[1]

These exquisite lines by Rodenbach have always put me in mind of the peculiar effect that room had on me. It was certainly a room with a secret. There was a secret and a regret hidden in the past of its melancholy solitude and silence: the hostile and profound silence that still troubled the place in the woods to which I had been invited.

The impression was short-lived, because I had been invited to dinner at the chateau. After a day of beating the brushwood and a carefully-recorded bag of seventeen roe-deer, however—my spirit having been further enlivened by the happy diversion of a dinner set for twenty-two in the hunt ballroom and my blood was cheered by the best vintages of a famous cellar and my troubles seemed a long way off—the painful impression of the morning was swiftly reawakened at midnight, when I returned to my room in the guest-house.

Shivering, as if someone had walked over my grave, I sat up bolt upright in bed. My neck was moist with sweat and my heart was gripped by an inexpressible unease. I had neglected to close the curtains over the two windows that were positioned at the end of my bed, and in the room—which seemed to be enlarged by the silence—the moonlight shining through the panes fell softly upon the parquet

---
1. The lines are from Georges Rodenbach's "Du silence" (1888).

floor. A ship of cloud was chased eastwards by the wind across the ocean swell of the sky. Autumnal rain pattered monotonously against the window-glass.

All of a sudden, the ancient refrain of a gavotte sounded in the next room: a tune played on the harpsichord, so faint and doleful that it might have been played by invisible hands. Someone was there, in the room next door, behind the partition-wall; that much was certain. Tentative at first, within the silence and darkness of the deserted house, the music eventually began to flow more freely, its rhythms becoming more subtle and precise. It was an old *arietta* or a *chaconne*: the musical artifice of an earlier century, slowly exhumed, with tender and delicate grace: almost as if learned from the lips of portraits.

But I was not well-equipped, that night, to recall the words of poets: while my terror increased, I sat up straight and listened, with sweat on my back, clutching my pillow between my fingertips in the grip of an atrocious anxiety.

Someone had come in: some unknown being was prowling about the room next door, its ghostly hands lingering at that very moment upon the keys of a forgotten harpsichord.

I felt my heart rise within my breast and my eyes grew wide, as if hypnotised by fear. I was near to fainting when I felt the pressure of breath upon my face, rippling the silk curtains of that strangely cold bed. The mournful groan of a disembodied voice caused my hair to stand on end.

"Take me away. Take me away."

The voice pronounced the phrase twice. Mad with horror, I had jumped naked from my bed into the middle of the room. Then I heard—very distinctly—the noise of footsteps fleeing across the parquet, the click of a door closing, the creak of a key turning in a lock . . . .

And that was all.

The nearby harpsichord had fallen silent. The glossy pink curtains at the window of my moonlit room fell perfectly straight, without the slightest crease. Outside, the rain had ceased, and three huge beeches stood against the milky grey nocturnal sky, the foliage of their crowns pushed towards the guard-house by a freshening wind.

I recovered my composure. With my revolver clutched in my fist I went straight to the communicating door of the neighbouring room. I tried to open it, in vain. It was closed and locked, and resisted every effort.

Then I went to the door that let out into the corridor. The key that I had set therein—with my own hand—was no longer in the lock. That one too I tried in vain to open.

I was shut in; the room was locked.

Feverishly, I lit a candle. I put on my vest, underpants and slippers and set about barricading both doorways, dragging a commode across one and setting a large armchair with pink and green cushions before the other.

I installed myself in an armchair at the head of my bed, wrapped my feet in the coverlet, and opened a book—the most recent work of Anatole France[1]—having decided that I would stay on watch until dawn . . . .

※

And I woke up again in broad daylight, undressed and lying in my bed.

---

1. In 1890 Anatole France's latest novel was the historical fantasy *Thaïs*, in which an anchorite modelled on Saint Anthony is haunted by guilty memories and hallucinatory temptations after "saving" a famous courtesan from her life of sin.

Standing by the bedhead, quietly and respectfully awaiting my orders, was the farmhand who had been appointed to serve as my personal manservant while I was resident in that strange guard-house.

"What time is it?" was the first thing I said.

"Half past ten."

"Half past ten! Then the others must be hunting already."

"Oh yes, since seven. Monsieur can hear the sound of shots from here."

"What! And you have let me sleep!"

"Oh, Monsieur was sleeping so soundly. Monsieur seemed so very tired, so very pale, and was sleeping so contentedly that I did not dare to wake Monsieur. I let him sleep. Here is Monsieur's chocolate." And with a careless gesture, the lad drew my attention to the plate set on my bedside table.

Evidently, I had been dreaming. Nevertheless, a doubt remained, and as the servant went to leave my chamber when I had completed my toilet I said: "And the room next door . . ."

I tried to speak negligently but stopped suddenly, frightened by the abrupt alteration of my voice.

"The room next door?" the servant prompted.

"Yes, the room next door. Was someone sleeping there last night?"

"Next door, oh no, Monsieur. No one sleeps there any longer; the doors are blocked up. No, Monsieur, no one ever sleeps in Madame la Marquise's room."

"Madame la Marquise's room?"

"Yes, that's where the mother of Monsieur le Marquis died, a long time ago. Oh yes, it was at least thirty years ago."

I'd had all that I could stand of that fellow. I dismissed him. As soon as I was alone I made haste to put my eye to the keyhole. It was scarcely worthwhile; either the shutters had been closed over the neighbouring room's windows or a curtain had been hung in front of the door. It was impossible to make out anything. My curiosity was frustrated by a mute obscurity, as if of the tomb.

I found a means of belatedly joining the party, but I was accommodated at the chateau on the following night. At dinner the Marquis, informed of the manner in which I had passed the night in the isolated house in the forest, offered his apologies for having been forced to give me such terrible lodgings.

"But one of my guests is leaving in the morning," he exclaimed, with an equivocal smile. "His room was free. François will bring your baggage here this afternoon, and you shall sleep at the chateau tonight."

And that was all . . . .

I had undoubtedly been the victim of a hallucination; my over-imaginative nervous system, affected by the atmosphere of distress and forlorn gloom surrounding the lonely house, had worked on itself while I slept, and my nightmares had been the same as any other nightmare: the external extrapolation into a painful state of mind of an uncomfortable sensation.

And yet, I knew that my host's mother, the Marquise Saint-Henriette d'Hauthère, had died at twenty-eight years of age. She was a madwoman of sorts—or so, at least, the family had pretended. Some said that she had been sequestered because of the jealousy of a husband who belonged to a different era, in that ancient and bizarrely morose house in the woods. Given this, I had to ask myself whether, by some freak of chance, I had not been caught up, in spite of myself, in some awful mystery, and whether I might not have been thrown, for one single night, into some drama of the Beyond!

But then . . . in the confusion of my memories of yesterday, which are becoming ever more distant and remote . . . oh, already so far away . . . I have forgotten to tell you. . . .

That morning, after the night of my terrible vision, what should I find while moving about the room, upon the dusty marble of one of the console tables, but a rose.

It was a fresh white rose, its moist petals laden with raindrops, with a long supple stem from which the thorns had been stripped.

And in the dust on which it lay was the imprint of five fingertips. . . .

That flower, and that imprint: who could possible have put them there?

Magic Lantern

THE ORCHESTRA COLONNE completed, with muted strings teased by the tips of the bows, the most delightful movements of the *Sommeil de Faust*: the *Choir of Spirits* and the *Dance of the Sylphs*.[1] Entirely under the spell of that hallucinatory music—and perhaps brought down a little too abruptly from the height of my aesthetic reveries into the prosaic brouhaha of the interlude—I turned to the occupant of the next seat, the physicist Forbster, and took him to task, intending to relieve myself of the burden by means of this facile outburst:

"Admit, Monsieur, that it is as well that Berlioz was born in 1803. Had he been born yesterday, he would undoubtedly have included an electrophore in his symphony, or the submarine cable, or some other phonographic apparatus. Without that ridiculous and nauseating Romanticism, with which it is manifestly infected and impregnated, we would not be applauding the three hundred and eighty-somethingth performance of his *Damnation* today. Modern science has killed the Fantastic, and with the Fantastic, Poetry—which is also Fantasy. The last Fairy is well and truly buried—or dried, like a rare flower, between two pages

---

1. "Le Sommeil de Faust" is a dream-sequence in Hector Berlioz' opera *La Damnation de Faust*, first performed in 1846.

of Monsieur Balzac. Michelet has dissected the Witch and with the assistance of the novels of Monsieur Verne, not one of our descendants twenty years hence, on hearing the *Dance of the Sylphs*—not one!—will be capable of the least sensation of that legendary nostalgia that distracts me now."

"But it is a charming distraction, Monsieur, and a very amicable one."

"Oh, do you think so? I, Monsieur, am of the old school. I feel the shots fired in *Der Freischutz*. Yes, assuredly, the one will kill the other. Alas, the one will kill the other. We no longer have a trace of illusion in our heads, my dear Monsieur. We have an abstruse mathematical treatise in place of the heart, the appetites of a piglet in the belly, bridles and racing tips in the imagination, and a clockwork movement in the brain. Look at the man that we have all become, manufactured by the progress of science! If we still have some slight capacity for passion, it is because that old imbecile and simpleton, the Romantic troubadour—the "1830 article" derided by the moderns—clings hard to the saddle within us; but have patience, he is dying. Ten years hence, his whisper will no longer be audible. We shall all be built on the same model: utilitarians, sceptics and engineers. Ah yes, great Pan is dead, and you are numbered among those who have killed him—yes, you, Monsieur Physicist. You, with your horrid mania to explain everything, to put everything to the proof, are one of the Assassins of Fantasy. Compared with you, the savant Coppelius himself—the man with the wax doll—could almost be reckoned an honest man, at least in my humble opinion."[1]

---

1. Coppelius is the "mechanician" in Ernst Hoffmann's "Der Sand-

"But the aforesaid Coppelius, if I remember rightly, was guilty of conjuring away the reason of the Student Hoffmann. I feel obliged to point out that—so far, at least—I have not the slightest case of mental alienation on my conscience."

"I believe you! You suppress even Madness, the last citadel in which a man of spirit, at the limit of his patience, might retrench himself!"

"I suppress Madness? I'm glad to hear it—it's a rare and novel privilege. . . ."

"Yes and no. You suppress it in the end . . . after you have analysed it, explained it, determined it, localised it, you heal it as required—and by what means! By electricity and therapy! You have killed the Fantastic, Monsieur."

"Now then," said André Forbster, suddenly changing his tone as he half-turned towards me, "are you really serious in what you say? Where have you got hold of the notion that we have killed the Fantastic, and that the dear nobleman has disappeared from our mores? Never—never, in any era, not even the Middle Ages, when the mandrake shrieked in the middle of every night beneath the frightful dew dripping from the gallows—never has the Fantastic flourished, so sinister and so terrifying, as in modern life! We live in a world full of sorcery. The Fantastic surrounds us; worse than that, it invades us, chokes us and obsesses us—and one would have to be blind or very obstinate not to see that."

"Yes, I know. Hypnotism, magnetism, suggestion and hysteria. The experiments of Charcot at the Salpêtrière, the wild women who stretch themselves out on their

---

mann" (1816; tr. as "The Sandman") whose automaton is mistaken by the narrator for a real woman, with whom he becomes infatuated.

hands and merrily make hoops of themselves under the false pretext that the reflection of a spoon has manifested itself in their eye, the daily reproduction of the phenomena of somnambulism, and the table-turning of Mesdames Donatos.[1] For myself, I prefer the demon-possessed, the nuns of Loudun and the convulsants of Saint-Médard; at least the scenery was right."

"And you're in favour of appropriate scenery?"

"Absolutely. Tombs by moonlight, foggy winter skies, and—far above the writhings and whitenings of the damned—the eternal battle of the clouds, and the black cones of cypresses shaken by the wind . . . that, at least, grips the nerves and meets the expectations of the imagination. And what a *mise en scène* the most trivial exorcism makes! But what do we have in place of that now? A miserable little whitewashed hospital room, very clean and very cold, a window without curtains, and—thrown across a modern table—some unhappy woman of Saint-Lazare, stupefied in advance with morphine, naked to the waist. And clustered around that female meat, the decorated men—professors of the Faculty—and the undecorated men: interns and curiosity-seekers. Utterly lacking in dignity, the modern victims of possession lack any authority."

"Lacking, above all, the half-light of the church, the ambiguous light of stained-glass windows and the music of the organ. Admit that you miss all that Tony Johannot stuff!"[2]

---

1. The surname is taken from the stage hypnotist Donato (Alfred d'Hont), who became very popular in Paris and the provinces in the 1880s, providing a counterpoint to Jean Charcot's experiments; the "Mesdames" evidently refers to spiritist mediums, and that general appellation is evidently intended to imply the narrator's conviction that they are all frauds.
2. Tony Johannot (1803-1852) was a pioneer of French book

35

"Certainly I miss it."

"Very picturesque, to be sure, and sometimes moving—but how obstinate you are! If you would only take a little trouble, and set aside for the moment your gallows, undulous plants and cemetery crosses, you could very easily convince yourself that we live, even in the fullness of modernity, in the midst of the damned, surrounded by the spectres of human heads and other horrors; that every day we brush up against vampires and ghouls. I will lay you a bet if you like, that you number at least three or four witches among your acquaintances. I myself am acquainted with two egregores, and I shall easily be able, here in the Châtelet, to point out to you and to name more than fifteen people who are absolutely defunct, but whose cadavers have every appearance of life."

"You're joking, Monsieur."

"No more than you are, I think. Just take the trouble to look around you. We are in the full assembly of the Sabbat of Sabbats here, and I put it to you that every evening, every arena of Parisian society—including the Opéra and the gatherings of the great and the good of France—is a rendezvous of necromantic mages."

"Monsieur, this the joke to end all jokes."

"Then I shall put an end to it. Do me the favour of taking up those opera-glasses, and follow the directions that I will give to you. Look over there, at those three elegant women on the balcony dressed in plush with fashionable hats: three unmarried women, evidently. Look at those chalky complexions, those eyes blackened with kohl and

---

illustration, providing celebrated pictorial accompaniments to such texts as Cervantes' *Don Quixote* and *Le diable boiteux* by Alain René le Sage.

the scarlet stains of their pained lips, like bloody wounds gaping in the flesh of those dead face. Are they not veritable ghouls: damnable cadavers spewed from the tomb and escaped from the cemetery into the world of the living; flowers of the charnel-house sent forth to seduce, enchant and ruin young men? What is the magic that emanates from such creatures—for they are not even pretty, these marrow-crushers, but rather frightful, with their mortuary tint and their blood-tinged smiles? Well, do you see the thinnest? One of my friends killed himself for her. She has already devoured three racing stables and their proprietors, and is at this very moment consuming Bompard, the fat banker of the Rue des Petits-Champs. The others are of the same ilk. The Comte de Santiego, husband of a delightful young wife—perhaps the most beautiful in all the Spanish colonies—and, what's more, father of two adorable blonde Murillos, is in the process of ruining himself for Irma, the oldest of the three. By means of what horrible secret lust has that woman got her claws into him? Hold on, she has recognised me, and she is smiling at us: it is the smile of the ghoul, all moist with blood!

"Would you like to read a tale by Hoffmann now? Look down there, to the right of the fore-stage; see the beautiful Madame G***? Take note of those eyes, with their irises of crystal, and that gleaming tint of porcelain! Her hair is silken, her teeth authentically pearly, like those of dolls. She is enamelled, one presumes, to the navel, so that her ballgowns may be cut as low as fashion requires. Thanks to the articulated springs in her bodice she can say 'Papa', 'Mama', and 'Bonjour, Excellency'. Produced for export, she is bound for America. She knows how to handle a fan, to curtsey deeply, to flutter her eyelashes and to appear to breathe like a real person. Vaucanson is surpassed. Is that not the Olympia of Doctor Coppelius? And if a mechanism does not actually animate that mannequin on parade, what sort of vague and intermediary soul could possibly inhabit that breast? To hold between one's arms that rotating Sidonie, to run into those lips, as cold as lips of wax: does the idea not make you shudder?

"Use the opera-glasses to delve into the dim depths of the ground-floor boxes. See those flared nostrils, those linen pallors, those hypnotic eyes, those bloodless arms poking out of red crushed velvet, the nervous and febrile hands clutching bottles of salts or flapping fans? Those are the great melomaniac women of the world . . . the wives of Merchant Bankers and Sugar-Refiners, all of them morphinated, cauterised, dosed, drugged by psychotherapeutic novels and ether: medicated, anemiated androgynes, hysterics and consumptives. They are the possessed of the new aristocracy.

"Up there, in the second tier, I can see a young woman as honest and fresh as a rose, who never misses an execution. I know her and I recognise her: she was at Marchandon; she was at Gamahut; during the summer of the crime of the Rue Montaigne she was seen going to the Place de la Roquette on eight successive days so as not to miss the execution of Pranzini, a veritable fête.[1] She is an exquisite young woman, but she has adored assassins for twenty years, and shivers with profound sensuality every time she sees the fall of a severed head—eternally young, though, as if kept fresh by the sight of blood! The thirst for new sensations now extends to horrors! The witches

---

1. The execution of the triple murderer Henri Pranzini took place on 31 August, 1887.

of the Middle Ages were likewise excessively fond of the blood of executed criminals.

"Over there, three rows of seats behind us: that great hearty fellow with huge russet moustaches and the torso of a horseman is a specialist; he only loves consumptive women. All his mistresses die within the year. The lover of the condemned deserves a place in the finest comedy of Jules Lemaître; that kind of bizarre love should be classified under the heading of Demoniality.

"Finally, I see elsewhere a very pretty brunette—I shall not point her out to you because she is my friend—whom the Holy Inquisitions of the fifteen and sixteen hundreds would most certainly have put on the rack, pricked and burnt. In the year of grace 1891, however, she comes and she goes, operating in perfect liberty. That lovely woman is on her fourth experiment; three gallant husbands have already died in harness: a master of wolfhounds and two perfectly healthy captains of the army, one of them a cuirassier. Two years in the household: going, going, gone. Emptied, crushed to the marrow, breasts hollow, legs shaking: broken puppets. . . .

She, meanwhile, is always plump, pink and well-heeled: heir to their fortunes and, I suppose, their health. They melted like wax in the warmth of her bed. The fourth survives, for the moment, but he has already been deeply cut into. Have you read, in Balzac's *Contes drolatiques*, a fable called "The Succubus"? Under the Valois, nothing more would have been necessary for a wife to be dragged in a shift to the Place de Grève.

"But excuse me, Monsieur, the music is beginning. Much obliged."

The Glass of Blood

SHE stands at a window beside a lilac curtain patterned with silver thistle. She is supporting herself upon the sill while looking out over the courtyard of the hotel, at the avenue lined with chestnut-trees, resplendent in their green autumn foliage. Her pose is business-like, but just a little theatrical: her face uplifted, her right arm carelessly dangling.

Behind her, the high wall of the vast hallway curves away into the distance; beneath her feet the polished parquet floor carries the reflected gleam of the early morning sun. On the opposite wall is a mirror that reflects the sumptuous and glacially pure interior, which is devoid of furniture and ornament save for a large wooden table with curved legs. On top of the table is an immense vase of Venetian glass, moulded in the shape of a conch-shell lightly patterned with flecks of gold; and in the vase is a sheaf of delicate flowers.

All the flowers are white: white irises, white tulips, white narcissi. Only the textures are different, some as glossy as pearls, others sparkling like frost, others as smooth as drifting snow; the petals seem as delicate as translucent porcelain, glazed with a chimerical beauty. The only hint of colour is the pale gold at the heart of each narcissus.

The scent that the flowers exude is strangely equivocal: ethereal, but with a certain sharpness somehow suggestive of cruelty, whose hardness threatens to transform the irises into iron pikes, the tulips into jagged-edged cups, the narcissi into shooting-stars fallen from the winter sky.

And the woman, whose shadow extends from where she stands at the window to the foot of the table—she too has something of that same ambivalent coldness and apparent cruelty. She is dressed as if to resemble the floral spray, in a long dress of white velvet trimmed with fine-spun lace; her gold-filigreed belt has slipped down to rest upon her hips. Her pale-skinned arms protrude from loose satin sleeves and the white nape of her neck is visible beneath her ash-blonde hair. Her profile is clean-cut; her eyes are steel-grey; her pallid face seems bloodless save for the faint pinkness of her thin, half-smiling lips. The overall effect is that of a woman who fits her surroundings perfectly; she is clearly from the north—a typical woman of the fair-skinned kind, cold and refined but possessed of a controlled and meditative passion.

She is slightly nervous, occasionally glancing away from the window into the room; when she does so her eyes cannot help but encounter her image reflected in the mirror on the opposite wall. When that happens, she laughs; the sight reminds her of Juliet awaiting Romeo—the costume is almost right, and the pose is perfect.

> *Come, night! come Romeo! come, thou day in night!*
> *For thou wilt lie upon the wings of night*
> *Whiter than new snow upon a raven's back.*

As she looks into the mirror she sees herself once again

in the long white robe of the daughter of the Capulets; she strikes the remembered pose, and stands no longer in the plush corridor of the hotel but upon a balcony mounted above the wings of the stage in a great theatre, beneath the dazzling glare of the electric lights, before a Verona of painted cloth, tormenting herself with whispered words of love.

> *Wilt thou be gone? it is not yet near day:*
> *It was the nightingale, and not the lark,*
> *That pierced the fearful hollow of thine ear.*
> *Nightly she sings on yon pomegranate-tree:*
> *Believe me, love, it was the nightingale.*

And afterwards, how fervently she and her Romeo would be applauded, as they took their bows before the house!

After the triumph of Juliet, there had been the triumph of Marguerite, then the triumph of Ophelia—the Ophelia she had recreated for herself, her unforgettable performance now enshrined in legend: *That's rosemary, that's for remembrance; pray you, love, remember!* All dressed in white, garlanded with flowers in the birch-wood! Then she had played the Queen of the Night in *The Magic Flute*; and Flotow's *Martha*; the bride of *Tannhaüser*; Elsa in *Lohengrin*. She had played the parts of all the great heroines, personifying them as blondes, bringing them to life with the crystal clarity of her soprano voice and the perfection of her virginal profile, haloed by her golden hair.

She had made Juliet blonde, and Rosalind, and Desdemona, so that Paris, St. Petersburg, Vienna and London had not only accepted blondes in those roles but had applauded blondes—and had come, in the end, to expect and demand blondes. That was all her doing: the triumph of La Barnarina, who, as a little girl, had run bare-legged across the steppe, asking no more and no less than any other girl of her age, lying in wait for the sleighs and the troikas that passed through the tiny village—a poor hamlet of less than a hundred souls, with thirty muzjik peasants and a priest.

She was the daughter of peasants, but today she is a marquise—an authentic marquise, a millionaire four times over, the wedded wife of an ambassador whose name is inscribed in the golden book of the Venetian nobles, and entered upon the fortieth page of the *Almanach de Gotha*.

But this is still the same girl who once lived in the steppes, wild and indomitable. Even when she ceased to play in the falling snow, the snow continued to fall within her soul. She had never sought lovers among the wealthy men and the crowned princes who prostrated themselves before her; her heart, like her voice, remained flawless. The reputation, temperament and talent of the woman partook of exactly the same crystalline transparency and icy clarity.

She is married now, although it is a marriage that was not contracted out of love, nor in the cause of ambition. She has enriched her husband more than he has enriched her, and she cares nothing for the fact that he was once a celebrity of the Tuileries in the days of the Empire, nor that he became a star of the Biarritz season as soon as he returned to Paris from the Italian court, following the disaster of Sedan.

Why, then, did she marry that one rather than another? In fact, it was because she fell in love with his daughter.

The man was a widower, a widower with a very charming child, just fourteen years old. The daughter, Rosario, was an Italian from Madrid—her mother had been Spanish—with a face like a Murillo archangel: huge dark eyes, moist and radiant, and a wide, laughing mouth. She had all the childish, yet instinctively amorous, gaiety of the most favoured children of the sunny Mediterranean.

Badly brought up by the widower whom she adored, and spoiled by that overgenerous treatment that is reserved for the daughters of the nobility, this child had been seized by an adoring passion for the diva whom she had so often applauded in the theatre. Because she was endowed with a tolerably pleasant voice the child had come to cherish the dream of taking lessons from La Barnarina. That dream, as soon as it was once denied, had quickly become an overpowering desire: an obsession, an *idée fixe*; and the marquis had been forced to give way.

One day he had brought his daughter to the singer's home, secure in the knowledge that she would be politely received—La Barnarina was accepted as an equal by members of the finest aristocracies in Europe—but fully expecting her request to be refused. But the child, with all the gentleness of a little girl, with the half-grandiose manners of the young aristocrat, with the innocent warmth of the novice in matters of love, had amused, seduced and conquered the diva.

Rosario had become her pupil.

In time, she had come to regard her almost as a daughter.

Ten months after that first presentation, however, the marquis had been recalled by his government to Milan, where he expected to be asked to accept a position as envoy to some remote region—either Smyrna or Constantinople. He intended, of course, to take his daughter with him.

La Barnarina had not anticipated any such event, and had been unable to foresee what effect it would have on her.

When the time for the little girl's departure came, La Barnarina had felt a sudden coldness possessing her heart, and suddenly knew that the separation would be intolerable: this child had become part of her, her own soul and her own flesh. La Barnarina, the cold and the dispassionate, had found the rock upon which her wave must break; the claims of love that she had kept at bay for so long now exerted themselves with a vengeance.

La Barnarina was a mother who had never given birth, as immaculate as the divine mothers of the Eastern religions. In the flesh that had never yearned to produce fruit of its own there had been lit a very ardent passion for the child of another's loins.

Rosario had also been reduced to tears by the thought of the parting; and the marquis soon became annoyed by the way the two females persistently sobbed in one another's arms. He quickly lost patience with the business of trying to patch up the situation, but hesitated to suggest the only possible solution.

"Oh papa, what are we to do?" pleaded Rosario, in a choked whisper.

"Yes, marquis, tell us what to do," added the singer, as she stood before him embracing the young girl.

So the marquis, spreading his arms wide with the palms open, smiling as sadly as Cassandra, was left to point the way to the obvious conclusion.

"I believe, my dear children, there is one way...."

And with a grand salute, a truly courtly gesture, to the unhappy actress, he said:

"You must leave the stage and become my wife, so that you may take charge of the child!"

And so she married him, leaving behind the former life that she had loved so ardently, and which had made her so rich. At the height of her career, and with her talent still in full bloom, she had left behind the Opéra, her public, and all her triumphs. The star became a marquise—all for the love of Rosario.

It is that same Rosario for whom she is waiting at this very moment, slightly ruffled by impatience, as she stands before the high window in her white lace and her soft white velvet, in her pose that is just a little theatrical because she cannot help remembering Juliet awaiting the arrival of Romeo!

Romeo! As she silently stammers the name of Romeo, La Barnarina becomes even paler.

In Shakespeare's play, as she knows only too well, Romeo dies and Juliet cannot survive without his love; the two of them yield up their souls together, the one upon the corpse of the other: a dark wedding amid the shadows of the tomb. La Barnarina—who is, after all, the daughter of Russian peasants—is superstitious, and cannot help but regret her involuntary reverie.

Here, of all places, and now, of all times, she has dreamed of Romeo!

The reason for her distress is that Rosario, alas, has come to know suffering. Since the departure of her father she has changed, and changed considerably. The poor darling's features have been transfigured: the lips that were so red are now tinged with violet; dark shadowy circles like blurred splashes of kohl are visible beneath her eyes and they continue to deepen; she has lost that faint ambience, reminiscent of fresh raspberries, which testifies to the health of adolescents. She has never complained, never having been one to seek sympathy, but it did not take long for La Barnarina to become alarmed once she saw that the girl's complexion had taken on the pallor of wax, save for feverish periods when it would be inflamed by the colour of little red apples.

"It is nothing, my dear!" the child said, so lovingly—but La Barnarina hurried to seek advice.

The results of her consultations had been quite explicit, and La Barnarina felt that she had been touched by Death's cold hand. "You love that girl too much, madame," they had said, "and the child in her turn has learned to love you too much; you are killing her with your caresses."

Rosario did not understand, but her mother understood only too well; from that day on she had begun to cut the child off from her kisses and embraces; desperately, she had gone from doctor to doctor—seeking out the celebrated and the obscure, the empirically-inclined and the homeopathic—but at every turn she had been met with a sad shake of the head. Only one of them had taken it upon himself to indicate a possible remedy: Rosario must join the ranks of the consumptives who go at dawn to the abattoirs to drink lukewarm blood freshly taken from the calves that are bled to make veal.

On the first few occasions, the marquise had taken it upon herself to lead the child down into the abattoirs; but the horrid odour of the blood, the warm carcasses, the bellowing of the beasts as they came to be slaughtered, the carnage of the butchering . . . all that had caused her terrible anguish, and had sickened her heart. She could not stand it.

Rosario had been less intimidated. She had bravely swallowed the lukewarm blood, saying only: "This red milk is a little thick for my taste."

Now, it is a governess who has the task of conducting the girl into the depths; every morning they go down, at five or six o'clock, to that devils' kitchen beneath the Rue de Flandre, to an enclosure where the blood is drained from the living calves, to make the white and tender meat.

And while the young girl makes her descent into that place, where bright-burning fires warm the water in porcelain bathtubs to scald the flesh of the slaughtered beasts, La Barnarina stays here, by the window in the great hallway, perfectly tragic in her velvet and her lace, mirroring in her mode of dress the snow-whiteness of the narcissi, the frost-whiteness of the tulips, and the nacreous whiteness of the irises; here, striking a pose with just a hint of theatricality, she watches.

She keeps watch upon the courtyard of the hotel, and the empty avenue beyond the gate, and her anguish reaches into the uttermost depths of her soul while she anticipates the first kiss that the child will place upon her lips, as soon as she returns: a kiss that always carries an insipid trace of the taste of blood and a faint hint of that odour which perpetually defiles the Rue de Flandre, but which, strangely enough, she does not detest at all—quite the contrary—when it is upon the warm lips of her beloved Rosario.

Beyond

> "*Here among the oaks, the darkness is a strange mirror of dreams, and all the flowers are of kinds that have long and pensive lives; and when I look out beneath the branches at the rolling plains I imagine a funeral train of forgotten hours.*"[1]

I READ these verses—are they verses?—for the second time with pleasant but disquieting surprise. I was turning the pages while I sat beside a suburban footpath, but they redirected me towards some shadowy and profound solitude imported from a vast distance, hundreds of kilometres from the Porte d'Auteuil. Amid the frail and delicate decor of the pathways of the park, greyness splashed with green and gouached with violet by the emergence of new shoots, I seized upon the dream of a wild and calm forest-edge, steeped in shadow and silence; the corner of an obscure wood illumined here and there by blooming irises and periwinkles, like curious eyes.

Here *among the oaks, the darkness is a strange mirror of dreams, and all the flowers are of species that have long and pensive*

---

1. The quotation is from one of Francis Vielé-Griffin's experiments with *vers libre*. He cofounded the journal *Les Entretiens Politiques et Littéraires* with Bernard Lazare and Paul Adam in 1890.

lives: when I had, in fact, paused while taking a turn around a circular path dominated by the high battlements of the fortifications and fringed with spring undergrowth. The skinny frame of Saintis was but a few paces away, sharply silhouetted against the pale sky. That blue April morning had issued its invitation to him, too. Brisk and unselfconscious, he was returning from Passy by way of the Porte d'Auteuil and the park. His son—a child of four, ill-clad beneath his jersey—gambolled around his legs, all happy laughter and cries of "Papa" and "Talk to me, Daddy."

Saintis and I are in much the same business. He is a lively and intelligent man, resourceful, always busy, hurriedly churning out reportage and articles by the score for a host of newspapers and magazines: one of those indefatigable producers of copy paid by the line and published by the metre; a great follower of funerals, fêtes, literary banquets; a regular punter, frequently manifest at premières; one of those fellows that one sees everywhere. For ten years, without really knowing one another, we had exchanged hasty handshakes in theatre corridors and on editors' staircases: ten years of miming effusive gestures and muttering brief greetings from one end of the boulevard to the other. I have to admit, though, that I had never had a high opinion of him.

I knew that he was married to a delicate and sickly young woman, whom I had occasionally glimpsed in the half-light of a box during dress rehearsals. This unhappy creature had been confined by the medical profession to a succession of sickbeds, condemned for the last three years to lie on a chaise-longue, isolated and immobile. Saintis, meanwhile, had been shamelessly and cynically unfaithful, openly disporting himself in brothels and gambling-dens, conducting his one-night stands and monthly liaisons in the public places where we endeavour to cheat ennui. He gleaned his mistresses from the wings of petty theatres and music-halls, like the Folies or the Moulin-Rouge, but it seemed that his poor, lonely wife adored him. It was said that she worshipped him with a fervent amorous passion—a passion further exasperated by the chastity now imposed by circumstance on her young love. Beaten and bruised to the very core by marriage, crippled by maternity, she cherished the author of her suffering all the more: the clumsy and conscienceless husband whose defaults might prove to be the death of her.

To do him justice, though, Saintis made sure that his adoring dying wife enjoyed every comfort, and was surrounded by luxury. The frame within which Madame Saintis was slowly fading away comprised tasteful furniture, rare plants and bright silks.

It was also on doctor's orders that I had come from the centre of Paris to take refuge at Auteuil, and I had found the Saintis family installed in a smart little hotel in the Rue Michel-Ange, protected from the highway by a flower-laden embankment that was practically a park in itself. And on sunny afternoons, between one o'clock and two, it sometimes happened that I encountered Madame Saintis stretched out in a hired carriage, with her feet placed on the front seat, so very thin and pale within the blankets heaped upon her, her face drawn and so desperately tired.

The poor woman knew what kind of life her handsome Georges led. The work of a newspaperman is subject to so many demands that it can provide a wealth of excuses but he hardly bothered to keep up appearances. Perhaps it was too much trouble—he was away from home four or five nights a week. We had occasionally run into one another earlier that winter, waiting at the Gare Saint-Lazare for the six o'clock train—a train whose most wretched and miserable carriages are invariably full of the shirts and skirts of departing workers, while its first-class carriages are stuffed with the black coats and fur capes of returning revellers.

Anyhow, I had got the idea into my head that it was not so much her illness that was killing my pale neighbour of the Rue Michel-Ange as the infidelities of her husband, the rake. My increasing antipathy towards her husband— an antipathy born out of scorn for the careless hackwork he churned out, with no regard at all for literary artistry— was further aggravated by the sympathy I felt for his frail young wife, which moved me more every time I saw her. Sympathy, as Swinburne has written, is the most pitiless of all the sentiments,

And Saintis was now beside me.

After we had exchanged the usual banalities concerning the health of his wife, and the weather that was getting better at last, he sat down on the bench beside me, still stroking his son's curly hair. Mechanically, he reached out to the pile of magazines I had carried there, and took up the recent issue of a review that I had placed on top, open.

"Ah, *Les Entretiens*—a young writers' review," he said, sarcastically, as his eye fell on the very passage I had been reading. "It's this that pleased you, isn't it?" And in a serious and soothing voice that I had not suspected he possessed, he repeated Griffin's blank verse: "*Here among the oaks, the darkness is a strange mirror of dreams, and all the flowers are of kinds that have long and pensive lives; and when I look out beneath the branches at the rolling plains I imagine a funeral train of forgotten hours.* . . . Poetry—get away. . . ." And he interrupted himself in order to assume a different voice: ". . . *A funeral train of forgotten hours—or nearly . . . for now that I am old, they go towards the sunlit hills like girls and youths, singing, and I close my eyes . . . and I smiled, imagining that I was a different man, in a different time.* Ah, pre-existence—Baudelaire's anterior life: *I lived long ago beneath vast porticos.* Perhaps, after all, poets are only souls that remember, souls endowed with memory, those who can pass through and beyond present reality to evoke—and, above all, *consciously* evoke—all the ancient evils and vivid splendours of the Past."

As he closed the review, he concluded: "These young writers are part of a movement. Whether by cleverness or sincerity, they have sensed which way the wind blows. Naturalism is definitely on its last legs. We are tired of photographic renditions of low morals, and the public is sick to the stomach of the literature of the sink and the sewer. . . .

"The sublime flights of Romanticism declined into tawdry trinkets and gewgaws, and yet there is certainly something else . . . perhaps the study of mystery, of the imperceptible and the foreshadowed, which surrounds us and yet always escapes us! But the quivering sensations of the soul as it is brushed by the invisible world, which literature makes tangible . . . oh, to know that they are before us, that there is something beyond. . . .

"Does it astonish you, that I should say this to you? Yes it does, because I'm the kind of man who is always out on the town every night, a frequenter of the brothels of Les Halles, so you imagine. . . . Listen, I know that you don't like me much"—he ignored my gesture of protest—"and that's entirely understandable. Given the literary work that you have produced, and the temperament that I believe you to have, you can't help finding the person you see in me—the copy-merchant, the restaurant idler—quite odious . . . and I flaunt my infidelities in public, with all manner of strumpets, do I not? And I have a lovely little wife, heart-broken and ill, who adores me and whom you must like very much—for Madame Saintis is the very model of the kind of woman who is most attractive to men like you, sensitive and cold at the same time. . . .

"But I, too, adore my wife. I adore her, I tell you—and the proof of it is that I married her for love, without a sou of dowry, despite the opposition of my family, and that I grind out three or four articles a day in order to provide the welfare that she has. But as chance would have it, I—who was married by full-blooded passion and sensuality—have a wife who is no longer a wife. . . .

"Do you understand? Since her first confinement, four years ago, and the subsequent birth of this boy"—he gently pushed away the infant that he had been grasping a trifle brutally, instructing him to go and play—"since the birth of that child, she is but a sister to me, so to speak: a friend, a comrade . . . and what a comrade! An unhappy and miserable creature condemned to death: what a ball and chain!" The phrase was followed by a cruel laugh. "And nothing more between us . . . nothing for her but death, and not long delayed . . . but my wife still loves me, and still wants me, poor thing. . . . Oh yes, she loves me. She maintains her silence, but I feel it. I'm thirty-two years old, and I'm not a dreamer and a neurotic like you. I'm healthy, I hunt and I ride . . . and there is such sadness at home, with that unhappy young woman who suffers and dares not complain, always lying still upon her bed, a silent martyr racking and rending her incurable wound. . . and it's all so unjust. So I take my hat and I go out. I go to Paris, anywhere—and in the first evil place I come to, I forget. . . .

"I forget . . . or I try to forget.

"Those whores are no more than comfortable mattresses of flesh. Whenever one can sleep with one of them, it is a small victory over old age and the dreary daily grind. Nowadays, while I have a thin and emaciated invalid at home, I've acquired a preference for girls who are robust and nicely rounded, with solid rumps and firm and ample breasts. A month ago I was with one such, Lucy Margat—you may know her in another context. At about two o'clock in the morning, with my duty done and my feelings finally calmed, I found myself suddenly sitting bolt upright, my heart in my mouth, seized by an abrupt disgust, for the girl and for myself. It was as if the stink of human corruption was rising from the tritely sumptuous bed of that hundred-franc whore.

"Leaning over her, I watched her sleep. She was spread-eagled face down across the bed with her thighs apart. Her face was hidden in the pillow, as if it had been squashed by the weight of her disordered hair. She was snoring. The round swell of her enormous rump was shamelessly exposed by the disordered bedclothes.

"I swear to you that the flesh that I had used, bestially, two or three times since midnight, now filled me with horror. Its wallowing had released into the rarefied atmosphere of the room such a terrible stink of human animality, such a gross exaggeration of the sum of female odours, that I leapt to the end of the bed. Faint with awful distress, with my heart fluttering in my breast and the taste of dead meat in my mouth, I quickly slipped into my clothes, emptied one of my pockets on to the mantelpiece, and left.

"By the time I was breathing in the fresh outdoor air it was half past two. There were no cabs, but I was so desperate to get away from Les Halles, on that frightful night, to try to drown the disgusting taste in my mouth in the salt water of a dozen oysters and the effervescence of soda . . . the animal odour of that girl seemed to have seeped into my skin and my clothes. Oh, that stink! So I set out to come back: back to my invalid, to the sweet and plaintive wife I had abandoned.

"The market stallholders had begun to arrive. The florists were setting out their wares in the murmurous dawn, between the bays containing butter and fruit. Reflexively, I bought bouquets, one of narcissi and one of white gillyflowers perfumed with vanilla and pepper. At a quarter to six I was at the Gare Saint-Lazare, on the workingmen's train, my arms full of flowers.

"I arrived home at Auteuil at half past six. Marthe was asleep. She didn't hear me come in and I was able to undress myself carefully and go to bed in my own room—which is next to hers—without disturbing her sleep: that precious morning sleep, which restores the blood and the strength sapped by sickness . . . and it was at about ten o'clock that I woke up to hear her voice, addressing me from her own room, asking: 'Did you sleep badly? You were dreaming all night. You called out my name two or three times.'

"'Not I,' I told her. 'It's you who was dreaming, my love.'

"'Not at all. I couldn't sleep. I got up to pour myself a spoonful of chloral, and you called my name twice, quite distinctly. *Marthe, Marthe* . . . I asked what you wanted, but you didn't reply . . . so I thought that you were dreaming, and that I should let you sleep.

"'I looked at my watch and at the clock on the wall of my room. My watch showed two o'clock, the wall-clock ten past two. I wasn't asleep, you see.'

"'Then it must have been me who was dreaming,' I confirmed, not wishing her to know that I had not even been at home that night, for fear of alarming her.

"Two o'clock in the morning! You must admit, at least, that it is a strange coincidence. At the very moment when I had been seized by an abominable anguish, in a whore's room in the centre of Paris, my wife, in bed at Auteuil, distinctly heard my voice call out her name twice. *Marthe, Marthe*. Are there, then, occult affinities that extend across considerable distances, uniting our souls?

"Yes, I tell you," he concluded, placing his index finger on the review as he got up, "these young writers have lifted their noses and scented something in the wind . . . there is certainly an unexplored thread in the unknown, in the thrill of the Beyond."

Glaucous Eyes

Pale mask, set with neither stone
Nor funeral laurel, beyond death's reach,
I have seen the life in your gemlike eyes
And I know the past contained in their mute speech.
          Henri de Régnier, *Poèmes anciens et romanesques*

"NOW, do you think there's anything extraordinary about that woman? To me she seems old, overpainted and false—she cut a fine figure once, perhaps, but what a figure she cuts now! She certainly puts on airs, though, the lovely Nelly Forah." The young Marquis de Nor-Saluces was sprawled in his rocking-chair, smoke climbing high above his cigarette in a long bluish spiral. Its delicate incense formed a floating haze against the cloudy sky.

"Couldn't agree more, Stani. I've never understood what sort of spice one could find in that woman! I've always found her angular and insipid. There's something morbid about her, and she has no more hips than the back of my hand! Even when she was young I'd as soon have made love to an eel as had a mistress like that."

"Now, Fontenay, don't insult eels—they're wonderfully flexible."

"So are your vices, Chauchat, we all know that—but

for honest men whose tastes are admissible and allowed by the law, the merit of a woman lies in her being a true woman, not in giving one the impression of making love to a fish."

"That's right. But poor devils of our sort still provide patrimonial grist to be crushed in Nelly Forah's mill. At this very moment, if you need proof, the junior attaché of the Russian ambassador accompanies her everywhere, oblivious to the fact that his idol is long past the age of adoration."

Fontenay made a rude noise. "What does that prove? The whole nation is mad. Anyway, as for women and love, I'm content to take the advice of the poet:

> *"Begone, you are no more, even on the best of days,*
> *Than a banal instrument beneath my all-conquering bow,*
> *Or a tune that echoes in the wooden hollows of guitars*
> *That I have made to sound my ideal in the void of your heart.*[1]

"Ah, the ideal and the all-conquering bow of Fontenay! That's very good!" chortled fat Chauchat, stroking his silky beard. "Since you quote verse, I will favour you with some Chamfort—you have read Chamfort, of course?[2]

1. The lines are slightly misquoted from Louis Bouilhet's poem "À une femme." (1859).
2. Sébastien-Roch Nicolas Chamfort (1740-94) was a successful pre-Revolutionary journalist and litterateur who was elected to the Académie Française in 1781. The compromises involved in his exploitation of the extant system of patronage pricked his conscience to the extent of inspiring him to plan a furiously bitter demolition of the mores of the *ancien régime* which he intended to call *Produits de la civilization perfectionée*. Having joined the Jacobins and committed suicide during the Terror he never completed it, but his notes were published posthumously as *Maximes, pensées, caractères et anecdotes*, including

Take heed of this: *One must choose either to love women or to know them; there is no middle course."*

This was the animated and sarcastic conversation of a group of smokers loitering on the terrace of the casino at Dieppe, which looked out over the mirror-bright sea. None of them appeared to be much concerned by the dinner bells sounding their summons in all the hotels ranged along the length of the boulevard. One tall fellow of some thirty years, with a handsome face bisected by a long brown moustache, who had not yet breathed a word, seemed absorbed in contemplation of the distant horizon—but he had been paying attention.

Michel Stourdof—for that was his name—turned his square face slowly towards Nelly Forah's two most outspoken detractors and allowed a few words to fall from his lips, in a soft and musical voice that seemed ill-fitted to such a large body. "Poor Nelly—I know her well. Have you noticed her eyes?"

The sentence sounded so strange in the mouth of that colossus, who was generally indifferent to everything, that all the chairs suddenly turned in his direction—for the Parisians, of course, mostly had their backs to the ocean and the twenty kilometres of cliffs receding to the horizon.

"Isn't Narisnaskine, the one who is presently ruining himself for her, one of your compatriots, Michel?" ventured young de Nor-Saluces, teasingly.

"Yes, he's from Moscow, and he's also my friend," the Slav intoned slowly, "but that makes no difference. I'm talking about Nelly. I'll wager that you've never seen—or

the item cited. His cynical pessimism was admired not only by writers involved in the Decadent Movement but also by Arthur Schopenhauer, Friedrich Nietzsche and the Existentialists.

60

at least, never looked closely at—her eyes. Isn't that so, Marquis?"

"Her eyes?" Saluces said, quite nonplussed. "How could I have seen her eyes? She walks about wrapped in a mosquito net—bundled up like a snowman in a kilometre of net and gauze. You've seen them, have you—her eyes? You've had the opportunity—I suppose it was a long time ago."

"I dined with her the day before yesterday."

"At the Villa des Lierres? You're a lucky devil." And Nor-Saluces turned towards the other members of the group. "Rumour has it that she lives in rare luxury. Cordons of orchids are draped like snakes across the tablecloths, and the cutlery is antique, and there's engraved crystal instead of crockery."

To which the imperturbable Stourdof replied: "I'll take you there, Monsieur de Nor-Saluces, if you wish. I can arrange it. Within three days, you'll have dined there yourself."

"And I'll have seen those eyes? Those invisible and miraculous eyes?" the marquis riposted. "All right—I accept. Perhaps she has a little colour after all. Who knows what might be found behind her veil, given that she has eyes."

"She has a very good complexion," Stourdof declared, his voice as soft as a caress, but implacable nevertheless.

"And her hair is natural?" the Marquis asked, sarcastically.

"It's other people's hair that requires colouring," the Slav replied, slowly. "In the fifteen years that I've known Nelly, hers was never more luxurious, or more luminous, than it is today. When Nelly combs her hair in the morning, she unravels the dawn."

"You must be in love with her, to say that!" exclaimed Saluces.

"Not me, but another . . . a friend of mine, dead now—for love of those eyes."

"But that's an old story," Fontenay interrupted. "I think it's time for dinner." He got up, indicating his intention to leave and calling for the court to adjourn. The others followed his example, but their curiosity had been piqued by Michel Stourdof's "old story"—although Stourdof no longer seemed to have any desire to relate it.

When they had all returned to their hotel, still grouped together, fat Chauchat—who was evidently intrigued—took the Slav's arm firmly in his own in a friendly manner. "For my own part, you know," he said, "I've always found her charming, no matter what spiteful gossip these fellows may hurl at her. Perhaps she's a little too dear for them." He added a wink of the eye for emphasis. "She only goes for the big prizes, your lovely friend, and she prefers international events. Her score takes some adding up."

"So does her age," Saluces put in.

"Vintage wines are too good for farmhands," Chauchat countered, leaning on the Slav's arm in a familiar way. "Go on, sing us your ballad. Tell us, you who have seen them, what these eyes are like."

"Her eyes are not quite blue, but a pale blue-green. When the sea is calm, save for the breaking waves, it has a similar greenish-blue tint. Your great painter Baudry gave exactly that tint to shallows combed by waves—foam-flecked waves in which he set female bodies, so deliciously white.[1] We admire his paintings in Russia. That's the kind of eyes that Nelly has."

---

1. Paul Baudry (1828-1886) was famous for his large murals and his use of colour.

"Glaucous eyes," Fontenay suggested.

"The eyes of a Nereid," Saluces added.

"The eyes of the Lorelei," the Slav said, continuing the sequence. "Do you know Schiller's ballads in France?"

Chauchat, ever modest and good-humoured, said: "Goethe too, a little."

"But such eyes, you see, are more than just eyes. They possess a charm, a power that you Frenchmen are probably able to resist, but to which my countrymen always fall prey. Nelly Forah is no longer young, but she is immune to old age. While she has those eyes, the men of the all northern nations, who are creatures of passion and vision, Slavs and Danes and Swedes and Russians, will all adore her. . . ."

And when they cried out for more, Michel Stourdof obliged them.

"Nelly's eyes are the supreme love-philtre, the incarnation of the death-wish, the fatal attraction of the Void. It is the promise of forgetfulness that dwells in her eyes and, as the mistress of forgetfulness, she is the mistress to be coveted and adored above all others. She is a sorceress, and not merely because her eyes are blue, the colour of the sky, of the ocean and of dreams. That is part of it, certainly, and without that primordial and celestial colouration Nelly's eyes could not possess that which now lives and dreams in them, but there is more. There remains within them the reflection of the fond farewell of a dying man. They retain within their tears the eternal youth of a worshipful lover who died while looking into them."

His listeners exchanged mute glances, thinking that this was nothing but madness and mystification, but Michel Stourdof continued stubbornly. "A legend of my country holds that the soul of a lover who dies while looking into the eyes of his mistress will live on in those eyes, and gift them with an eternal youth in the estimation of other men, so that she will always be desired and will never be withered by age.

"My friend Serge Streganof was once Nelly's lover. He told her that peasant tale—and how could Nelly, who was always a devotee of the fantastic and the enigmatic, resist the temptation to put the veracity of the legend to the proof, with Serge as her experimental subject? So, one night while they were staying in Naples—where they habitually took a boat out into the Bay of Capri, by themselves—Nelly returned in terrible distress to the hotel in the early hours, without her lover. There, lividly pale, her teeth chattering with anguish, she told the people who ran to her aid that during their expedition Serge, prompted by the heat, had decided that he absolutely had to take a dip. He had given the oars to her, undressed himself, and had swum for some time behind the boat, frolicking delightedly in the moonlight. Then, to her great consternation, he had suddenly sunk beneath the waves and had never resurfaced. The following evening, fishermen found the corpse washed up on the beach at Torre del Greco."

"And you assumed. . . ?" Chauchat put in.

"I assume nothing—but I can easily see Nelly, sitting in the bow of the boat, rowing steadily and steering it, while my poor friend Serge swims with slow and graceful strokes. The moon, like a great gas-lamp, bathes both of them in light, silvering Serge's naked torso as it rises above the water and Nelly's white bodice as she sits in the boat. They are a beautiful couple, and so there comes a time when they come together to gaze into one another's eyes, smiling at one another. Serge is tired now; he is gradually getting out of breath. He wants to get back aboard, and he tells Nelly to stop—but Nelly takes no notice. With smiling lips, her gaze fixed upon his, she continues to row, steadily, and the boat moves ever on. Serge, at first, thinks that she is teasing him. . . .

"As the boat recedes by slow degrees. Serge flounders in its wake and sinks. All around him the night is bright; the sea is drenched with the transparent light of the full moon; the purple hills of Capri are upon the horizon. What a beautiful night to die! Serge understands what is happening; he thrashes back to the surface; he is at his last gasp, his mouth already full of water, but his eyes are fixed on Nelly's. The boat bobs up and down in front of him; she is still smiling, leaning on the oars—and the water roars in the ears of the desperate Serge, who is clutching in vain at the froth on the waves, descending into the green moon-shadow beneath the surface. . . .

"And the boat makes its leisurely way back to Naples, skirting Capri."

"But on what do you base this supposition?"

"On Serge's expression, which I always rediscover in Nelly's eyes."

"Has he at least left a will, which assures her of his fortune?" demanded the young Marquis.

At which the Slav, with the disdainful shrug of a little mistress, said: "Oh, you're just being vulgar now! You're insulting Nelly—and there's no need to make a lie out of a legend."

SENSATIONS

One of Them
or
The Spirit of the Masque

THE imperishable mystery of the masque, attractive and repulsive at the same time, demonstrates the techniques and the key images—and, above all, the imperious need—according to which certain individuals, on appointed days, contrive to make themselves up, to disguise themselves, to change their identity and to cease to be that which they are: in a word, to escape themselves.

What instincts, what appetites, what hopes, what lusts, what maladies of the soul underlie the gaudily coloured cardboard of false chins and false noses, the horsehair of false beards, the shimmering satin of black masks, the white cloth of hooded cloaks? What intoxication of hashish or morphine, what loss of self, what equivocal and evil adventure, precipitates that lamentable and grotesque procession of dominos and penitents on the days when masked balls are held?

They are noisy affairs, these masques, overflowing with movement and florid gestures, and yet their gaiety is sad; their celebrants are more like spectres than living beings. They walk abroad like phantoms, the majority enveloped in long folds of material—and like phantoms, their faces are never seen. Why should there not be witches under those long cloaks, framing clotted faces with velvet and silk? Why should they not be empty, with nothing at all within those vast Pierrot blouses draped like shrouds upon the sharp angles of tibia and humerus? Is not the humanity that hides itself in order to mingle with the crowd already outside nature, and the law? It is evidently maleficent, since it wishes to remain incognito, and must intend culpable evil, since it seeks to betray both assumption and instinct. Sardonic and macabre, it fills the hesitant stupor of the streets with scrimmages, jeers and hoots, makes women tremble delightedly and children fall down in fits, suddenly disquieted by the ambiguous sex of fancy dress.

The masque is the disturbed and disturbing face of the unknown. It is the smile of mendacity. It is the very soul of that terrifying perversity which understands depravity. It is lust spiced with fear, the alarming and delicious risk of throwing down a challenge to the curiosity of the senses: "Is she ugly? Is she beautiful? Is she young? Is she old?" It is politeness seasoned by the macabre and heightened, perhaps, by a dash of baseness and a taste of blood—for where will the adventure end? In a cheap hotel or the residence of some great demi-mondaine? Or perhaps the police station, for thieves also conceal themselves in order to commit their crimes. With their solicitous and terrible false faces, masques may serve cut-throats as well as the cemetery does; there are bag-snatchers there, and whores ... and revenants.

For my own part, the impression with which masques leave me is a trifle oppressive, and also depressing—but that is an entirely personal matter. Would it not, however, be interesting to understand the spirit of one such masque, past or present? To isolate one of those mysterious beings of silk and cardboard that can be seen everywhere on the nights of masked balls, wandering from one pavement to another, shivering piteously beneath the gibes of passers-by? To know the reason for the costume and the disguise of one of those disquieting derelicts run aground on some popular pleasure-beach in the big city on a frosty night: a nocturnal marionette born, perhaps, in the livid light of a gas-burner or an electric lamp, only to vanish again at daybreak?

Twelve years ago, on the night of a masked ball, I happened to encounter one of these mysteriously anonymous masked figures in circumstances which, I have thought ever since, conferred upon the figure of the being with whom I rubbed shoulders a certain tragic grandeur. That disguised individual remains, for me, the very archetype of the masque, the living symbol of a nameless mystery and a portentous puzzle.

I was based, that winter, in the outskirts of Paris. I had a long and detailed work to complete, and for reasons of health—and economy too—had decided to move away for a while. Because business matters often summoned me to the Rue de Richelieu or the Rue Saint-Lazare I had found a niche in the suburbs, on the westward railway line, and was hibernating rather miserably in a little village between Triel and Poissy.

The Sunday before Mardi Gras fell, that year, on the twenty-fifth of February. The coincidence of the need to close a deal with the editor of a journal and an invitation to dinner had brought me to Paris. There was a ball at the Opera, and I lingered in spite of the falling snow to look at the masked and caped figures ranged along the steps of the Garnier Monument. Cabs and private carriages were unloading more of them every minute under the peristyle of the theatre or in front of the cafes and the brasseries. Groups of pierrots and monks were drawn towards the Place, capering about and forming rounds in the open spaces reserved for the circulating carriages in spite of the mounted police who stood guard there. It was as if a crazy wind were blowing over the city that night—to the extent that I was so well amused, and interested in spite of myself, that I forgot the time of the last train. At half past midnight I was still sitting there, at a cafe table. There was now no train before two a.m. but I was quite happy to stay because the Boulevard was still thronged with curiosity-seekers, shouting and hooting, and the brasseries were crammed with costumes.

As one o'clock approached, however, the streets and their various establishments emptied; the disguised figures went back to the ball and the idlers to their lodgings. Life and movement would not return until breakfast-time. Everything was closing and as the snow began to fall more thickly I got up rather sadly and headed for the station.

There was also a ball at the Eden that night, and the muffled rumble of a monstrous bacchanal rose from behind the illuminated facade of the Rue Boudreau. In the distance, like an echo, the sound of dance-music was still coming from the Opéra. In the Rue Auber, which was already dark, a masked figure was walking in front of me, enveloped in a capacious Arab burnoose with a dark monk's hood. He was obviously going to the Eden.

He had not gone to any expense, for the burnoose, the monk's hood and the general incoherence of the makeshift costume spoke of a hastily improvised disguise, manufactured at the last moment with whatever happened to be in the drawer. My eyes followed him anyway, reflexively. Once he was under the lights of the Eden, however, the masked figure stopped. After hesitating at the entrance, treading down the soft snow and surveying the pavement he finally set off again along the Rue Auber in the direction of the Opéra.

But I had seen him more clearly now. What I had taken for a black monk's hood was in fact the hood of a green velvet cape, and the oval aperture of that hood revealed the gleaming metallic material, pierced where the eyes were: a penitent's hood of silver cloth that shone in a bizarre fashion.

A chap who can't make up his mind, I thought to myself. And I went on my way.

I arrived in the Cour de Rome in time to have a last drink in one of the neighbouring brasseries. I climbed the steps, went into the waiting room and started in surprise: that huge silky mantle, that chalky face in the green velvet hood! My masked man was there! There were only the two of us in the banal and desolate setting of the big room, where the gas burned brightly between the oak-panelled walls. The strange traveller was slumped in one of the green velour armchairs, one hand supporting his chin, obviously waiting for the train that I had come to catch.

I thought he was at the ball, and the inexplicability of his presence gave me a bit of a fright. Could he have followed me? No, since I had found him already here. He did not budge, and following the direction of his eyes I saw that he was absorbed in the contemplation of his legs.

The burnoose was slightly open, revealing thighs encased, as if moulded, by black silk tights. A bizarre thing, though: whereas the lower part of the right leg was clad in a woman's stocking—a sea-green stocking secured above the knee by a silk garter—the other foot bore a man's sock, albeit a fancy one patterned with little flowers. The figure seemed, in consequence, doubly masked, by the combination of the terrifying charm of that ghoulish face and the disturbing ambiguity of a sex of which I could no longer be certain.

The costume, as I examined it more closely, revealed further affectations: an enormous frog was displayed at the position of the heart, embroidered in silk. I had not noticed at first that there was a braided crown around the green velvet hood, composed of frogs and lizards. The Arab burnoose enveloped the figure like a shroud, and the inner hood of silver cloth brought to mind the pestilential curses of the Middle Ages: leprosy and plague. The grimace behind the mask was surely that of a damned soul; it was simultaneously oriental, monastic and demonic, redolent of the lazaret, the swamp and the cemetery. The lineaments of the firm and supple flesh were given aphrodisiac emphasis by the black tights. Was it man or woman, monk or witch?

When he got up, in response to an employee's call for passenger's to board the train, I thought I saw, standing before me, the spectre of Eternal Lust: the Lust of the Orient and of cloisters; the lust of a face devoured by syphilitic sores; the Lust of a heart as cold and flaccid as a reptile's body; androgynous Lust, neither male nor female; impotent Lust—because, perhaps the most telling detail of all, the masked figure clutched within its hand the large flower of a water-lily.

The creature in the burnoose climbed into the first-class carriage. I waited until he was seated before climbing in turn into my own compartment. I would sooner have stayed in a sleeper than travel face-to-face with that face of shadow; but I was obsessed by curiosity, and also by distress, and I hardly drew breath until the train began to move.

The first quarter of an hour was dire. If the masked figure were to come into my compartment, from which side would he appear? I watched the two doors, ready for either eventuality, but my neighbour never budged, or made the slightest noise. In the end, the temptation was too strong; I got up and approached the little window in the communicating door.

Under the diffuse light of the lamp, the masked figure was leaning over, almost lying down, in the voluminous folds of the burnoose, its two astonishingly slender legs stretched out on the seat. It held a little pocket mirror in one hand, into which it was looking steadily. It studied itself carefully, with its face still concealed by the silvery hood.

Strange traveller!

I could not tear myself away from my observation-post.

The interminably slow night-train rolled through the snow covered suburbs.

The masked figure got off at the fourth station. It was nearly three o'clock in the morning. There was neither cab nor coach at the station, no one at all. The figure gave his ticket to the attendant, passed through the barrier and vanished into open country: into the night, into the cold, into the unknown.

An Undesirable Residence

IT was, to tell the truth, a rather bizarre apartment. The suite of rooms set in the corner of a very old building was in good order, but a slightly unpleasant sensation caused me to hesitate on the threshold the first time I went to visit Allitof there. How, I wondered, could a man of such refined artistic tastes have reconciled himself to the dubious presence of the innkeeper who lived on the ground floor, or the sordid squalor of the narrow hallway, or—most of all—the perennially dark staircase with the broken steps, whose leaden fittings exuded an evil smell on every floor?

True, Allitof had picked it up for next to nothing, in a very nice neighbourhood within walking distance of the Place de la Concorde: three big rooms, astonishingly airy, all of which looked out, across a quiet little square blessed with an almost provincial serenity, upon the enclosed lawns and gardens of an old Louis XVI hotel. The advantages of the sunlight and the neighbourhood, and especially the view over the greens and hedges, went a long way to compensate for the horrible ground-floor facade, which was decorated with cues and billiard-balls painted on a wine-coloured background—but that staircase and that hallway! What a dump!

Speaking for myself, I must say that I could never have reconciled myself to the place—but once one was inside, the surprise was all the more pleasant. The light-flooded apartment had been fitted out, furnished and ornamented with an unexpected wisdom—one might even say with sensuality—that clashed with the old workhouse that contained it like silk and lace suddenly discovered in a pile of rags. Was that, I wondered, the effect that Allitof wanted?

Once the door was opened, it was as if one had been deceived—and one had to give due credit for the ingenuity of the deception. Contrary to expectations, the ugliness of the frame improved the portrait lodged within it. To find a bachelor flat fit for an artist hidden in the core of that dubious lodging-house was rather charming—as if it were some exquisite fruit concealed by a rough and ugly rind. It posed, in sum, a defiant challenge to the assumptions of contemporary snobbery, and confounded them.

Allitof had not seen it in that light, or so he claimed. He had been attracted by the low cost of the lease—nine hundred francs—and the unexpected opportunity to take it fully furnished. The apartment had previously been occupied by one of Serge's friends, a footloose provincial who had used it as a well-upholstered love-nest for smart whores and birds of passage. It had been offered to him cheap, complete with all its excellent amenities: leaded windows, tapestries, carpets and a dressing-room. It's true that the rugs from Persia and Smyrna were patterned in ordinary checks and that the tapestries—rose-pink in the drawing-room and blue shading to green in the bedroom—were hiding poorly whitewashed walls . . . but all for nine hundred francs!

Into this voluptuous setting, whose subtle shades and uncertain tints had accommodated lovely visitors, Serge had only needed to import those movable effects of a nomadic literary artist—a way of life to which he had been committed since the age of fifteen—that he had bought second-hand and in sales. So, on the pleasant April morning when I first entered that bright suite of rooms with its iridescent fabrics and water-colours on the walls, interrupted here and there by the portly profile of handsome pieces of copper-trimmed furniture and slender statuettes standing among pallid vases of old Venetian glass, I could not help admiring his discovery and complimenting him upon it. All the cheerfulness of the gardens that it overlooked flowed in through the five high windows, which all stood open, filling the three rooms. In the midst of the bibelots a bouquet of blue irises had been set upon the table, and their foliage provided a scent of spring, reminiscent of vanilla.

I could not help telling him how much I envied him his find—at which Serge, tapping me amiably upon the shoulder, said: "And all the joys! No domestic—an orderly! What luck!" He pointed through the half-open door of his room at a closely-shaven cranium and two arms with ruddy hands that were busy with an embroidered bedcover: "By courtesy of General de C***, my neighbour on the other side of the street, who was determined to lend him to me. Comes to me at nine in the morning and goes at noon, and I don't see him again all day. At five my bed is made and my clothes laid out upon it, as if by magic. Invisible service—I've solved the age-old problem! All very well in April, you may say, but what about the fires in winter? Of the five winter months, I shall spend two in Nice, and then the general will lend him to me again. At thirty francs a month, I can easily afford it—but let's go to dinner."

That spring, Serge and I spent a great many evenings together, at the circus, in society—the Paris season makes surprisingly close connections between the avenues of Saint-Germain and the by-ways of the Champs-Élysées. We met up, on average, three times a week, until summer arrived, when I left for Aix and Allitof for London and we lost sight of one another.

Six months slipped by without any furtherance of our old friendship, even by letter—but that's life in Paris for you!

※

One day in the following February, as I came down some editor's stairway at about six o'clock, my elbow carelessly jogged a tall hat, which, along with the lifted collar of a long fur cloak, was hiding the face of someone who was climbing up in the opposite direction—but so slowly, so painfully! I was offering my excuses when a voice suddenly addressed me by name.

I was astonished to find that it was Allitof.

"So you didn't recognise me, old man."

"But of course!" I stumbled over the lie.

"I've changed, haven't I?" he said, with an equivocal smile, ironic and yet heart-rending. "Admit that you would never have recognised me had I not spoken. To tell the truth, I've been quite ill. You're lucky to run into me—I no longer go out much in the evenings. The quarter is so miserable—it only comes to life in the spring, people return so late to Paris nowadays."

"So you're still living in your frightful house?"

"Yes, my frightful house." His voice altered so strangely

as it pronounced the word *frightful* that I could not help shivering slightly.

"You didn't go to Nice this winter?"

"No, not any more. I'm working. Come to see me one evening when you have nothing else to do. Come for dinner—about six, because that's when I eat nowadays, in my frightful house."

Nearly a month passed, though, before I went to see him in his bizarre bachelor flat. To tell the truth, I was scarcely looking forward to shutting myself in for an entire evening with the singularly consumptive appearance and hoarse voice that poor Sergeon (as he had been called when he was a little boy) now manifested. Selfishness caused me to forget my promise. Once Lent had begun, though, I was seized by remorse, and also by curiosity, following a conversation I overheard into which someone—young de Royaumont, I think—had carelessly dropped Serge's nickname.

"You know that he's very ill," he had said to his companion. "He's hallucinating now. It seems that he can be heard from the other side of the street, howling in the night—and what's worse, he can't stand anyone near him. He sleeps alone in that den of his—and God only knows what must be going on there, if it's true that the spirits that corrupt its atmosphere are the produce of evil actions. Who knows what fat Lestorg used to get up to in Allitof's sea-green bedroom? What possessed him to take up residence in a dingy place like that, no one any longer has the least idea. Have you ever noticed the wine merchant's shopfront below, with the blood red bars across his windows? The other evening, after dining at General C***'s, we were looking at that astounding facade. There's only one street-light on the corner and it was raining. In that little deserted square, with the wall of the garden in the background and that wan light—why, it was positively sinister!—that house seemed to be spattered with blood: a slaughterhouse or some cut-throat's den. Directly above the red stripes, Sergeon's five windows, curtained but unshuttered, were all ablaze. The lights were extinguished, one by one, between half past ten and an hour after midnight—we saw it for ourselves, from the general's house—and I tell you, honestly, it was like being in one of Edgar Poe's tales. When we left, the house was lit up again! What can he be doing, every evening in winter, in those three great rooms? It seems that he talks and talks to himself, and stays up at all hours. Anyone would have nightmares! Who would ever have believed it of such a gentle fellow?"

In the gossiping mouth of young de Royaumont, the story sounded so terribly like a funeral oration that I felt like a criminal for my treatment of poor Sergeon. My awareness of my sin of omission was echoed and exaggerated by that tale of de Royaumont's. Surely I, poor Allitof's friend, could devote an evening or two to cheering up his morbid solitude. It was not too late.

On the evening of the day after next, having dined in the quarter, I went up to the poor fellow's home. It had rained all day, and as eight o'clock approached a gusty wind had sprung up. A squally shower had broken out, a veritable deluge pattering on the pavements and flooding the gutters and kerbside drains. Although it was no later than half past nine, no one was out and about in that part of Saint-Germain on that particular night. It was so dismally deserted that as I arrived at the sinister little square, with the wind rustling the leafless branches in the park and the high black houses all around, I couldn't resist a certain feeling of malaise. As I entered the damp corridor and ascended the stairway of that dreadful house my heart was oppressed by some inexpressible presentiment.

Scarcely illuminated by a wretched oil-lamp hanging on the wall, that stairway suggested the site of an ambush. The noise of loud voices from the wine-merchant's was audible through the partition-wall and a mouldy odour fermenting in the stairwell further exaggerated the horrible impression. Outside, the rain beat down, causing vile streams brought up from the depths of the drains to flood the pavement from the gutters, accompanied by disgusting gurgling sounds. The walls oozed an insipid kind of humidity . . . it was most certainly a frightful house!

Allitof opened the door to me himself—but that is not to say that the operation was accomplished without difficulty. It had been bolted and padlocked, sealed like a fortress. The door itself, made from stout heart of oak, had a spy-hole with a grille set at head height, and it was only after a prudent "Who's there?" and the removal from within of the chains and bolts that it was drawn ajar. Given the appearance of the abode and the dubious impression of the staircase, however, these excessive precautions did not seem so very surprising. Besides, I found Serge much less strange and much less changed than I had been led to expect and dread.

My visit put him in a good mood, and revived him somewhat. Although he was still extraordinarily pale, he did not seem to me to be as thin as before. He was wearing a loose homespun costume whose folds hung down from a foxfur cape. I had surprised him just as he had had his fill of work and was quite happy to be interrupted.

He seated himself across the hearth from me, in a large chair embroidered in petit-point, and threw himself into conversation cheerfully, if perhaps a trifle feverishly. A beech-log fire was burning, making huge shadows dance madly on the taut fabric of the ceiling, while two tall standard lamps set haphazardly among the furniture put out a steadier light. That created a sense of intimacy and of well-being within the large, warm and peaceful room, hermetically sealed by the curtains closed over the windows. Flowers from Nice were fanned out in a vase. The entire apartment was redolent with the faint but persistent odour of ether, but there did not seem to be anything hallucinatory about it.

Serge had brought me into his bedroom because it was warmer than his drawing-room. On the silk-embroidered counterpane, a confused heap of books that had been there when I came in testified that he had been pursuing his studies in bed.

"I'm making a study of witchcraft in the Middle Ages, particularly of sympathetic magic—because Michelet couldn't cover everything, even in such a masterpiece as this," he said, taking a copy of *La Sorcière* from his desk. "If you knew how many volumes I have deciphered during these last three months: authentic grimoires, Latin texts by alchemists and monks, others in Gothic, semi-barbarous Greek, even some in Hebrew!"

"You know Hebrew now!"

"No, not at all well—but I have a friend who is a rabbi." When I made a face, he continued. "Well, as you know, science has neither religion nor homeland. Like Huysmans, I shall consort with sorcerers if I must. Because, you see, the art of necromancy that has attracted such calumny throughout the centuries and has fallen so low today is the science of sciences: the supreme wisdom, and the supreme power also.

"And it'll make you a lot of money?"

"A lot—well, yes and no. About twelve thousand. But this is only a critical study. I swear to you that if I'd known what I know now I'd have taken the book on for nothing, purely for pleasure. That's how passionate I am."

And with the excitement of an obsessive rising to flattery, he embarked on a series of intoxicated accounts of witcheries and demonic possessions. He had set a silver kettle before the fire, in which a punch he had mixed himself was simmering—made to a fifteenth-century recipe, he informed me blithely, which he had found in one of his old books.

While the rain fell in torrents outside, the kettle at our feet began to sing. Flushed with well-being, I felt as if I were in a dream-world as I listened to Allitof's mock-Medieval ramblings.

We were, I think, in the middle of an account of the mandrake, as pleasantly ingenious as any authentic folktale, when Serge suddenly stopped talking and became as pale as linen. He leapt up from his chair as if he had been launched by a spring.

"Do you hear that?" His voice, horribly changed, was not his own. "Footsteps. There are footsteps, pacing within the walls!"

I listened. There was indeed a noise of pacing feet, just perceptible with the apartment—but it came from outside. Someone was walking under the windows.

Allitof was still upright, his neck taut, prey to some fearful anxiety. "You hear it?" It was more a tremor of the lips than a stammered sentence.

"Of course I hear it. But that's a fine state to get into because some passer-by goes along the street. These walls are oddly resonant, that's all."

I had risen to my feet too. The footsteps were fading away into the distance; then they were lost in the night.

"A passer-by in the street, eh? That's what you think, is it?" Serge wore an equivocal smile.

I went over to one of the windows, parted the curtains and looked down into the little square. The rain had relented and two guardians of the peace, with their caps drawn low over their brows, were walking along the pavement.

"There. Come and see. Look, there's your footsteps!"

When Serge had seen what I had seen, his expression changed again, although the same strange smile lingered upon his lips. "Ah! You think that it was them. You can see them well enough, but they cannot be heard." And, indeed, the two men were walking so quietly that they made scarcely any sound. They could no longer be heard.

We came back to the fire, but the conversation could not be resumed. There was a suspicious tension between us, an unease in the face of the unexplained that had made us wary of one another. After a few minutes of silence, I got up to go. "It's becoming late, and I'm staying the devil of a way off, in Passy. Where did you put my overcoat?"

"You're going?" Allitof pronounced these words with such anguish that I stopped in my tracks, dumbstruck.

"Of course. You didn't think that I intended to stay the night, did you?"

He lowered his head. "It's such a long return journey, in this weather. Wouldn't it be safer to stay here?"

"I'll take a cab. I won't get soaked."

"A cab, at this hour! This place is so far out of the

way that you'll probably have to wait the best part of an hour."

I consulted my watch. It was half past midnight. "Oh well—I'll go across the bridge to the Place de la Concorde. One can always be sure of finding one there. Besides, it's not raining any more."

His tone became resigned then. "Yes, the rain's stopped—but you must have another glass of punch before you go. Definitely."

He poured fiery liquid into two Kirby goblets. Neither of us said anything, and the uncomfortable silence made it easier for me to hear the wheeze of Allitof's chest. His breath was coming in gasps, and I felt a dull oppression weighing down on me.

"The rain's stopped, has it? Listen!" Serge said, suddenly. The wind was hurling raindrops at the windowpanes again. They came in waves, as if by the bucketful. "You can't possibly go out in this weather." As I made a gesture of impatience, he went on. "Listen, I'm not well this evening. You'd be doing me a great favour—much greater than you can possibly know—if you'd stay here."

"In the armchair, I suppose?" I said, laughing sardonically.

"No, I have three mattresses on my bed. I'll take two off and make up a bed for you on the floor, in front of the fire. You'll be perfectly all right. I beg you not to leave me alone here tonight. I shan't be able to close my eyes. You know what it's like outside in that rain! But that's by the by. Such extraordinary things happen in this house, but I think that with you close by I'll finally be able to get some sleep—and it's such a long time since I slept!"

He had put his hands together reflexively, in a prayerful attitude, and his voice was that of a child. Where was the robust and upstanding fellow that I had known six months before, so cheerful and full of life? I was moved to pity. I felt, too, that I had stumbled upon a mystery, something incomprehensible. I was intrigued, and I wanted to get to the bottom of it. I agreed to stay.

The night was, indeed, rather bizarre, and the house was, in truth, unusual. At half past three or thereabouts Serge, who had allowed me to go to sleep, woke me up with a jolt with his inevitable: "Do you hear that? Knocking! They're at the door!"

Is fear contagious? Do hallucinations develop naturally in certain situations? There was an actual rapping at the door of the antechamber. I heard the sound quite clearly from my improvised bed.

"Wait here," I said. "I'll go."

But Allitof, in a strangled tone, said: "Don't go! Don't answer! Don't switch on the light! They'll go away eventually."

In the depths of the apartment the door was still making a muffled groaning noise, as if it were being shaken. "But why don't they ring?" I asked Serge, as I slid to the foot of his bed in my nightshirt. The noise had finally ceased. Footsteps faded into the distance, descending the staircase, and I heard the main door of the building close down below.

"They come, and they go," Serge murmured, with a sigh. He had sunk back upon his pillow, drowsily.

Towards five o'clock, when the night was darkest, I was woken up again by a flare of light. Allitof was on watch again, sitting bolt upright in his armchair, listening intently. He had lit three candles in a single holder. His face was distressed by terror, his eyes fixed in an extraordinary stare.

He seemed to be on the look-out for some dreadful visitor. His right hand was fiddling with a revolver while the left was crumpling the loose collar of his nightshirt, which was spattered with blood where his fingernails had dug into his neck.

Suddenly, he met my eye and he blew out the candles abruptly, and I heard him muttering under his sheets.

※

"Your house really is too bad," I said to him the following morning, when I left at about nine o'clock. "There are comings and goings all night long, and one is afraid to go to sleep. Who are these tenants who troop up and down the stairs at three in the morning? You shouldn't stay here." Serge shook my hand silently, without even thanking me.

Some time afterwards, when I met him in the boulevard, his eyes were not so shiny and his cheeks not so pale. "I've left that awful apartment, you know, where one can't sleep," he said. "I'm letting it out, and staying here in the meantime." He pointed to the Grand Hôtel.

"Oh, congratulations. So much the better. And the book on witchcraft, are you still working on it?"

"Harder than ever," he said, his expression suddenly animated. "It's my only passion."

"And you're sleeping well?"

"Oh yes, oh yes! Quite well, now."

Three days later, however, Serge came to my home. This time, his hands were restless, his hair was disordered and his complexion was slightly green. "I had to leave, you know. It's impossible to sleep in that diabolical hotel.

There's a reek of decay in the rooms that makes one throw up; someone has certainly been murdered in mine."

"What? You're no longer there?"

"No, I checked out this morning. I'm leaving."

"You're leaving?"

"This very evening, for Marseilles—and from there to Tunis, where I hope to find the vital information I need in order to complete my book."

"That famous book has made you go off your head. You'll never make me believe that the hotel you've just left is so bad."

"Oh, you think not! Only yesterday a foetus was found in the slop-bucket of a woman who had left the evening before—a foetus delivered prematurely, like those that the witches of Arras used to go to the Sabbat. Everywhere—under every bed and in every wardrobe, I tell you—there are corpses. I wanted to say goodbye, but I'm going. Goodbye. If I stayed, I'd go mad."

The poor fellow was already mad. Three months passed without any news. It was General de C***, his old neighbour, who had to bring me up to date.

"Oh yes, poor Allitof, the man with the magic books. His uncle had to intervene, to make him leave Paris. He's living in Algeria now, permanently, I think, and he's as well as you or I."

"And his apartment?"

"The famous apartment where there are footsteps within the walls? It was let fifteen days ago, with all its fixtures and fittings. That's an apartment that has seen some funny things, from fat Lestorg's girls to your friend's nightmares. It was his books that drove him mad, you know."

"Yes, perhaps, but I wouldn't have liked to live there myself."

"Indeed. It had a good view, but what a frightful house!"

A frightful house indeed—on which subject Allitof himself had to give me the final word. Serge returned from Algeria fattened up and sunburned, a smile upon his lips, his eyes calm and almost child-like: a Serge hardly recognisable, who tapped me on the shoulder at the exit from the Nouveau Cirque and led me away to supper at Durand's.

"Changed, eh, your old friend Serge? I'm cured, and I'll stay cured. Bewitched no longer, I no longer hear anything within walls. That evil apartment cast a spell on me, I tell you. It was time to leave. The sun down south is such good medicine. By the way, did you know that the famous apartment where I could never sleep carried on its unhappy tradition? My successor committed suicide less than a month ago—an honest bureaucrat in the Ministry of the Interior, after spending six weeks in the place, was driven to howling in the night, having heard and seen that which tormented me. In short, he killed himself. I've come back in order to sell the furniture, because I don't want to keep anything that was in the place, and then I'll be off again."

"Back to Algeria?"

"Of course. Do you want me to have another spell here? You were quite right, old friend, when you said that it was a frightful house!"

A Troubled Night

"ALL the mystery and terror that is adrift in the impalpable and the invisible; the affinities of certain phantasmal elements—like the wind for example—with certain animal forms that inhabit dreams and nightmares; the supernatural quality of certain landscapes glimpsed at times of disturbance; and the equivocal character of some creatures, including birds; actual outlines of gnomes and monsters escaped from a Temptation by Callot or some bohemian scene by Goya; no one has given better expression to quivering dread and morbid anguish than this sly peasant poet in his book called *Nature*."

De Jacquels, with a gesture of calculated indifference, placed Maurice Rollinat's most recent volume upon the table, wide open.[1]

"Have you read his account of a stormy night, passed in the heavy and poisonous atmosphere of a room in a country-house, haunted by old portraits? Malign portraits

---

1. Maurice Rollinat (1846-1903) was a Parnassian poet and a leading member of the Hydropathes, who used to play the paino in Le Chat Noir when Lorrain began to hang out there, accompanying his own songs or Jean Richepin's. *La Nature*, the fourth of his five collections, was published in 1892. The verses quoted are from "La nuit d'orage" (A Stormy Night).

with fixed stares, frigid narrow smiles; morbid and miserable, replete with darkly reasoned obsessions reanimated by the supernatural:

> *"There before your shadowed deluded eyes*
> *In the window, where the wind whispers,*
> *A form is outlined, inert and yet moving.*

> *"'Having surely borne witness to monstrous drama,*
> *To many a last breath and many a burial*
> *Do the walls not seem to you to be alive just now,*
> *With a swarm of spectres and stirrings of the soul.'*

"With a swarm of spectres and stirrings of the soul! Well, there was a feverish and fearful night when even I, who am neither superstitious nor of a nervous disposition, lived through an experience so strange that I feel compelled to tell you about it. The verses of that devil Rollinat have brought it all back to me—and given that you're all scribblers, to a greater or lesser extent, you ought to reckon a story of this kind a godsend.

"It happened four years ago, at this time of the year. I had received an invitation from a friend in the provinces, who was soon to be married and intended to hold a grand costumed ball for the whole town in honour of his bride to be. I had gone down to his place, having agreed to illuminate the fête with my presence. I arrived the evening before the great day, in all the confusion of the final preparations, at a house from which they were on the point of moving out of. I was consigned to the farthest extremity of the house, lodged in a wing that was not normally used. My friend and his young bride offered profuse apologies for placing me so far away, but the other rooms had been cleared of their furniture. They assured me, however, that the three nights of my stay would pass quickly enough—and besides, I would have the most beautiful view of the surrounding countryside and the nearby wood.

"My friend lived on the edge of the town, near the gate, and the building where I had been confined looked outwards over the wall and across roads to the greatest expanse of valleys and forests that one could ever have desired—but it seemed lonely and redolent with sadness and solitude beneath the sullen and yellow winter sky!

"It was certainly superb, that landscape, but so depressing as to drown one's soul in spleen. My first impulse, on seeing it through the clear panes of the two white-curtained windows, was to pack my suitcase and take the Paris train that same evening. With its tiled floor, narrow fireplace and its Empire furniture, the room was, in any case, as cold and dry as a convent parlour. Every corner seemed to exhale an indefinable odour of old amber and ripe pears. My God, what was I doing there? It would have needed whole tree-trunks to heat a room like that—and in all the confusion, my hosts had completely forgotten to set and light the fire.

"They did think of it eventually, but rather belatedly. It wasn't until we had finished eating, when one of the servants announced that it was snowing heavily and that everything outside was already blanketed by snow.

"'Oh, dear Lord, my ball!' the young lady sighed. 'No one will come in this weather!'

"'And Edward's room!' my friend suddenly cried out. 'You'll freeze, poor fellow. No one thought to make up the fire in your room. It's absurd, isn't it? All this fuss. We'll forget our heads next. Light a fire at once in Monsieur's room.'

"The domestic thus called upon then observed, very reasonably, that no wood fire lit at such an hour could possible make such a room seem warm. It would be much simpler, he suggested, to instal one of the *chouberskis* there. A number of those huge oil-burners—five or six at least—had been placed in the ground-floor rooms and in the main hall in anticipation of the forthcoming celebrations. So one of the *chouberskis* was taken to my room, on the strict understanding that it must be removed, for safety's sake, as soon as I went to bed.

"At ten o'clock I took leave of my hosts and was guided by a servant, candle in hand, through the interminable corridors of the deserted house, I was securely locked up in my glacier . . . no, glacier is an exaggeration; thanks to the *chouberski*, which was now removed, the temperature was actually quite tolerable. Outside, however, the snowstorm raged unchecked. A mad whirl of confused noises and groanings was hurled upon my lodgings from the ghastly darkness of the surrounding countryside. At least, I supposed it was ghastly, for I had no wish to depress myself with the dismal appearance of the landscape. Undressing in the blink of an eye, I quickly put myself to bed, sighing: 'If I could only go to sleep!'

"And, indeed, I was sleeping the sleep of the just when, at about two in the morning, an unusual noise woke me up.

"Outside, the wind had calmed; weary of whistling and groaning around the silent house, it had finally gone to sleep. In the uneasy quiet of my room the sound that had woken me could still be heard, jerky and feeble, like that of a body knocking against the inside of a wardrobe.

"Strangely excited, I pricked up my ears. The noise, which had died away momentarily, resumed. It was coming from the fireplace, where the metal screen was lowered. There was a sound like the fluttering of alarmed wings, mingled with muffled yelps. Some bird of passage swept up by the storm had obviously fallen into the chimney, where it was beating its wings miserably,

"One swift movement brought me to my feet; another brought me to my knees before the fireplace, a lighted candle in my hand. I lifted up the screen.

"With an abrupt flurry of wings, a creature crouching in the shadows suddenly reared up and moved back, opening an immoderately large and hideous goitred beak—the membranous beak of a monstrous cormorant. I moved back in my turn. What was this creature? To what species did it belong? Hideous and phantasmal, with its enormous paunch—as if bloated with fat—it leapt on to the hearth now. It hopped up and down on its long legs, pock-marked and granular, and its splayed feet, like those of a duck. Then, mewling like a fearful infant, it retreated into a corner, where its huge batlike wings clashed together with a strange flaccid sound.

"Awful and menacing, it fixed me with its round vulturine eye and—while drawing back the rest of its body—extended its sword-like beak towards me. It was tapered like a poniard and sharp-edged.

"The hideous creature seemed to me to be part-gnome and part-witch, part-nightjar and part-dwarf. It seemed disgustingly obscene as it puffed out its paunch and displayed its long naked legs, suggestive of swamps and ruins, dead leaves and the Sabbat. I stared at it, quite terrified.

"Then I was seized by a sudden rage, and I took hold of the fire tongs. I fell upon the monster, stabbing its sides and belly, trying to break its long vulture's neck or to perforate its ghastly skin. I was annoyed, intoxicated and insane—and the phantom bird creature leapt up at me, uttering wild cries like those of a corncrake, trying to defend itself with its sword-like beak and the extended talons of its splayed feet. It was not so haughty now, in spite of its widespread wings.

"It finished up by collapsing upon itself, in a confused heap of flesh and vertebrae, weakened by the blows of the tongs. My heart lurched with each blow that I struck into its sides. Finally, when I had caused it to crouch in the fireplace, clicking its beak miserably, the hideous membranes that served as eyelids having fallen over its leaden eyes, I was exhausted too. Quickly closing the firescreen over the inert creature, I let the bloody tongs fall, and only just had time to run to my dressing-case to get my flask of ether.

"One drop, two drops . . . and with my lungs reinvigorated and my heart set free, I put myself back to bed and went to sleep like a baby.

"How many minutes later was it when I woke up again? Was it the clatter of a beak or the gossipy chatter of an old woman that woke me?

"The hallucination had resumed, but the chimney was mute now—no, the noise came from the casement window.

"I sat up in bed, and in the frame of one of the windows—how had the servant neglected to close the curtains and the shutters?—what did I see?

"Silhouetted in black against the misty winter sky and the landscape blanched by snow and moonlight . . . were two monstrous birds with beaks like cormorants and the flaccid and swollen paunches of vampires: two nightmarish beings like the creature lying dead in the fireplace, perched on the outer sill of the window, clicking their long beaks and puffing up their goitres. They studied me craftily.

"Striking an attitude that was both priestly and comic, like sculpted gargoyles keeping their eternal vigil upon the balustrade of a cathedral, the two winged monsters were obviously talking about me. They were hatching some plot to take their revenge while sharpening their beaks in the angles of the stone window-surround, mocking me with bizarre laughter and sly winks of their menacing eyes.

"Enfeebled by the thought of that conference, and wishing to put an end to the vision, I got up again. I ran to the window and thumped on the panes to frighten the strange visitors and make them fly away. Scarcely discomfited, the two monsters fixed their membranously-lidded eyes upon me, and continued their banter. Without moving their bodies they stretched out their necks, pecking the window-panes with their beaks.

"The nightmare had definitely been too far prolonged. A cold sweat broke out on my face. I felt quite overwhelmed by cold and faintness. I was ready for the end. I threw myself back towards the bed again and got down on my hands and knees to gather up the tongs. While groping about on the boards, though, my hand collided with something soft and damp—something that was alive, but as light to the touch as a vampire.

"The crawling spectre dealt me a formidable peck with the horny edge of its beak, and nearly severed my thumb from my hand.

"The creature that I had left for dead in the bottom of the fireplace had obviously only been stunned. But how had it lifted up the metal firescreen? While dragging itself, half-dead, across the room towards the two companions it had glimpsed, it had found me within its reach and had taken the opportunity to avenge itself by mutilating me.

"And what of the two others, outside in the cold and the snow, whose sinister laughter I had heard? At that moment, I swear, the pain and dread that I experienced within my flesh gave me such a powerful extra twist that I sprawled on the floor-tiles and fainted."

"And the next day?" the members of de Jacquels' audience demanded, raptly.

"The next day," he said, "I awoke in bed with a raging fever and my friends at my bedside. The curtains were drawn and the shutters were closed. In the fireplace, whose hearth I was quick to inspect, there was no trace of the bird . . . except for that on my hand. On my hand, between the thumb and the index finger, there was a long gash—and in the very centre of the room, surrounded by a disordered mess of overturned furniture, lay a pair of tongs, whose two prongs were red with clotted blood. And my flesh was boiling, and I was panting madly. . . .

"It had been a dream—and yet, not entirely a dream. I left my young friends that same day, vowing that I would never return to that house. I did not care to stay a moment longer in a town haunted by the likes of those nightbirds.

"The wound on my hand took a long time to heal, in which time I had occasion to consult more than one doctor . . . and a mystery still hovers over that dreadful night, whose enigma is yet to be fully deciphered. At any rate, you will not find the final solution in this letter . . . a letter from my friend, which arrived the day before yesterday."

De Jacquels read aloud:

> "*We have had a good laugh, my wife and I, at a strange discovery made this morning by the chimney-sweep. When he came to clean the chimney of that famous nightmare room where you stayed one night, what should he find in the flue, two metres above the mantelpiece, but the skeletons of three baby owls? They were huddled together: three tiny skeletons as white as ivory, which we shall place at your disposal, since it was you that killed them. They must have been asphyxiated by the fumes from the* chouberski *that we put in the room, on the night when you slept there.*

"And what," de Jacquels concluded, "would the souls of owls look like?"

A Posthumous Protest

Suspended above the bed, the head with painted lips,
Calmly and palely yields its thickened blood
To the care of a brightly-burnished copper bowl
Filled up to the rim with lilies and hyacinths.

The pupils of the eye are drowned in deep sea-green,
The red-blonde tresses, like a halo of flavescent gold,
Enfold the harsh purplish gouts of blood which spatter
The martyred neck, choked with muffled accusations.

The one who painted them, while drunk with wild hope,
When the fire in his hearth had died away to ashes,
Languorously kissed that rouged mouth,

Hung the head on the wall, dressed in mourning,
And made of his human sentiment a dismal flattery:
An artist in love with the plaster which he brought to life.

"AND what is that head which you have up there? Is it made of plaster or of painted wax? The expression of horror is very well-done—it displays a nicely-perverted taste, the chopped-off head above a copper bowl brimming with lilies-of-the-valley and hyacinths! It is surely an

Old Master . . . perhaps a depiction of St. Cecilia . . . is it very old?"

So saying, de Romer lifted himself up on tip-toe, elevating his myopic eye from the tapestry he had been inspecting, his curiosity prodigiously excited by the painted plaster head hanging on the wall of my studio.

I confessed that the Old Master that he admired so frankly was actually a copy made from a cast taken from an original in the Louvre—from the famous *Unknown Woman* of Donatello, in fact—which I had decapitated in accordance with a whim. I had been possessed by a fancy that had led me to represent her head as the head of a martyr, covered in blood; the disengagement of the bust had been my own idea, and I had commissioned the moulder to add on the clots of blood.

I felt slightly embarrassed, as if I were a child caught in some petty fault, when I explained that the barbaric colouring of the plaster—the greyish-green of the dead eyes, the faded pinkness of the lips, the touches of gold in the hair and the lurid crimson of the blood-clots—were my own paintwork: the result of an idle day wasted in maladroit fumbling.

"This isn't so very maladroit," mumbled de Romer, reaching out to touch the plaster moulding that had taken him in, feeling the clots of blood. "Not so maladroit at all. On the contrary, although the execution is naive you have captured some essential truth of sentiment and sensation . . . guided, I suppose, by intuition, for I take it for granted that you have never actually seen the head of a guillotined woman!"

"Certainly not!" I replied, stammering slightly with embarrassment.

Then de Romer turned to face me, having suddenly become very serious, and captured my gaze with his own penetrating eyes. "So the perversion and the audacity is all your own, then? You have taken to mutilating masterpieces now!"

Stunned by the aggression in his tone, I shook my head.

He was not to be fobbed off so easily. "You are guilty of a crime against Donatello—a crime against his artistry, a profanation. You have decapitated his dream, and martyred his creation. That unknown woman whose head you have taken off and remade has a life of her own, if not in reality then at least in the mind of the artist—a life infinitely superior to your miserable human existence. Since she was first evoked by those visionary eyes, which were extinguished long ago, she has crossed the centuries, outlasting revolutions; even in the tedium of our dismal museums she continues to haunt us—we moderns who have all but lost the gifts of vision and faith—with her beautiful smile and her imperishable beauty."

"Do you really believe that?" I murmured, moved in spite of myself by the passionate seriousness of his tone.

"For myself, I believe nothing," said de Romer, "other than that you are an executioner. What kind of Satanic impulse can have taken hold of you, to make you mutilate that bust? Your fancy must have been diabolical in origin, have no doubt of it. Not that you have lost any sleep over it, I suppose? Oh, you are a great criminal, quite unconscious of your crime—and that is the most dangerous kind. Have you slept in this room—or, if you have not actually slept, have you worked late into the evening, alone here by night? And you have never had nightmares, or experienced any disturbance? Oh well, you evidently have a good constitution. I am sure that I could not have given such a good account of myself."

I did not know what he meant, and tried to draw him out further, but he would not be drawn.

"I have nothing more to say to you," he said, putting an end to the conversation, "except that the mutilation of a masterpiece is a veritable act of murder, and that it can be a dangerous game to play." And without further ado he shook me by the hand and took himself off.

I concluded that de Romer was a little touched—that he had been unbalanced by the power of his own imagination. His common sense had foundered in a sea of occult ideas and obsessions, which had been whipped up into a storm by reading Éliphas Lévi, and by close encounters with the terrified mysticism of Huysmans and the charlatanry of the Rosicrucian lodges. I had too much good sense to give any credit to such crackpot notions as those put into his head by the moulding that he had found in my house. If everyone thought like that, the studios of sculptors would be populated by visionaries and the Academy of Fine Arts would be a branch-office of the School of Charcot—whereas all the sculptors of my acquaintance were happy souls with full beards, clear complexions and sturdy constitutions, far more interested in actual sensations than mere illusions. The kind of scare-stories contained in de Romer's daydreams would not prevent me, of all people, from sleeping peacefully.

※

A few days later, there was an evening when I had occasion to work late. I was beside the hearth, in the silence and solitude of my workroom; all the servants had gone to bed and I was the only person in the household still awake. I suddenly stopped writing, instinctively raising my head, beset by a troubling sensation that I was no longer alone, and that someone I could not see was in the room with me. I looked around, anxiously scanning the length of the four walls. There was no one to be seen, save for the vague inhabitants of an old tapestry, living their silent life of knotted woollen threads and eclipsed silks, and the heavy drapes hanging down in front of hermetically sealed windows. Here and there amid the shadows, illuminated by the intermittent glow of the firelight, there was the glimmer of a gilded picture-frame or the briefly-flaring scintillation of some trinket lodged in a display-case, but there was nothing else.

The sleeping house was located in a secluded quarter of a suburb blanketed by snow, and the silence was profound—still more profound since my pen had ceased to scratch upon the paper that lay before me. My breathing became ragged and hoarse as the conviction grew in me that there was someone there, if not in the room itself then just outside the door. I had the horrible feeling that the door was about to open, pushed by some creature or thing unknown, whose uncanny footfalls made no noise at all but whose presence was palpable.

Feeling that any revelation would be better than the anguish of doubt, I prepared to rise from my place and go to the door—but the intention was punctured and I fell back helplessly into my armchair.

The room had once had a second door, but it had been sealed up and hidden away behind a curtain of green Turkish silk embroidered with silver; now I perceived, protruding from behind that curtain, clearly outlined against he blue of the carpet, a bare foot.

The foot was alive. The extended toes were surmounted by pearly nails, the heel was pink and rounded, and the texture of the pale skin was so uniform that one might have mistaken it for a precious *objet d'art*—a piece of alabaster or jade placed on the carpet, but it was a real foot. Oh, the exquisite curve of that arch, the perfection of its flesh! The green silk curtain cut it off just above the ankle, but the ankle was so delicate that the foot could only have been a woman's.

I got up, and was propelled in spite of myself towards the lovely apparition—but when I reached the curtain, the foot was no longer there.

✻

Have you ever noticed the almost-imperceptible perfume of ether that emerges from fresh snow? Snow has an effect on me that is similar to the effect of ether: it unbalances and disturbs me. There are people who become a little crazy when it snows, and it had been snowing for three days when I had my vision. I attributed my experience to the effect of the snow.

I remained anxious for several days lest the apparition should return, but as time went by my anxieties were quieted, and I soon resumed my habit of working late into the night. A few weeks went by before my experience was repeated.

I had stayed up late to correct some notes, and had become absorbed by the task when I suddenly started up in my armchair, abruptly seized by the same horrible certainty that something strange was nearby, lurking somewhere between the tapestry and the wall. My eyes went instinctively to the curtain of green Turkish silk.

This time there were two bare feet, delicate and feminine, extended upon the carpet. Their toes were clenched as though they were excited by febrile impatience. Above their ankles the green silk hung modestly down, but it bulged here and there, filled out with the impression of a pair of hips and two breasts. The figure of a woman was outlined there: the figure of a woman standing behind the curtain.

I rose up as I had before, in the grip of some horrid enchantment. Some power far stronger than my own will drew me, and with eyes dilated by terror and my hands held out before me I moved towards the outlined figure. I had the impression of a young girl—lissom, lithe, cold—but it had already vanished. My impatient hands clutched empty space, my fingernails barely grazing the embroidered silk as it collapsed.

No snow had fallen that night.

※

Fatigued by conflict, I began to harbour suspicions regarding my curtain of pale green silks and silver arabesques. I had bought it in Tunis, in one of those bazaars they have out there, and I had always suspected that there was something peculiar about it. The matter of its origin began to cause me some disquiet, and I began to look for hidden meanings in its embroidered designs depicting birds and flowers.

I had the curtain taken away; the balance of the room suffered, but when it had gone I soon recovered my composure and was able to resume the normal course of my affairs, including my nocturnal labours, as if nothing had happened.

But it was all to no avail.

When some little time had gone by there came an evening when I became drowsy after dinner, and fell asleep in my armchair with my feet resting on the edge of the fireplace, bathing in the soft warmth of the friendly hearth. I woke up abruptly in darkness, shivering with cold and faint of heart, to find that the fire was out.

The whole room was plunged in darkness—a darkness so profound that it seemed to weigh upon me like a cloak, pressing my shoulders down upon the armchair in which I had awakened. It was opposite the place where the decorated plaster moulded in the form of the *Unknown Woman* hung on the wall, and I saw—O horror!—that the cut-off head shone strangely in the gloom. The fixed eyes were illuminated by a halo of light that bathed her, surrounding her golden hair with a radiant aureole. From those staring eyes—her terrible eyes, whose dead pupils I had myself outlined in ultramarine—darted two rays of light, directed at the sealed door, now laid bare by the curtain that I had removed.

There, in the embrasure of that sealed door, appeared a female body: the naked corpse, blue with cold, of a decapitated woman; a cadaver resting against the wooden door. Between the two shoulders there was a great red gaping wound, from which trickles of blood were still leaking.

And as the plaster head hanging on the wall looked upon the body, the cadaver drew itself up and away from the accursed door . . . and on the sombre carpet the two feet twisted and writhed, as though contorted by some atrocious agony. At that precise moment, the head turned upon me that frightful stare from beyond the grave, and I rolled over, collapsing upon the carpet, grovelling before those tortured feet.

An Uncanny Crime

"Protect us, O Lord, from the frightful things that walk by night."
      King David

"I TELL YOU, the things that can happen in a furnished hotel room on the night of Mardi Gras surpass all the horrors that the imagination can invent!"

Having topped up the chartreuse in his glass with soda, Serge Allitof emptied the glass in one go, and began his story:

"It was two years ago, when my nervous troubles were at their worst. I had recovered from the ether, but not from the morbid phenomena to which it had given birth: hearing things, seeing things, nocturnal panic-attacks and nightmares. Sulphonal and bromide had begun to alleviate the worst symptoms, but my distress continued in spite of medication. These phenomena were at their worst in the apartment on the other side of the river, in the Rue Saint-Guillaume, which I had shared with them for so long. Their presence seemed to have impregnated the very walls and fittings, by means of some pernicious sympathetic magic. Everywhere else my sleep was regular and my nights calm, but scarcely had I crossed the threshold of that apartment than some indefinable ancient malaise corrupted the atmosphere around me. Unreasoning terrors froze and shook me by turns. There were bizarre shadows huddling in the corners, suggestive folds in the curtains at the windows, while the door-curtains would suddenly be animated by some frightful and nameless semblance of life.

"Night itself became abominable there. Some horrible and mysterious thing lived with me in that apartment: an invisible thing, but one whose presence I could detect, crouched in the shadows, lying in wait for me; a hostile thing whose breath I sometimes felt on my face, and whose indefinable presence would nestle close beside me. It was a frightful sensation, my friends, and whenever I was forced by some nightmare to wake up I thought that I would be better off . . . but I shall pass on. . . .

"So, the time came when I could no longer sleep in my apartment, could no longer even stay there. Even though I had taken the lease for a year I took my leave of it, and went to a hotel. I could not, however, stay long in any one place. I left the Continental for the Hôtel du Louvre and the Hôtel du Louvre for others less salubrious. I was possessed by a vexatious restlessness, a mania for locomotion.

"After eight days spent at the Terminus, therefore, in all the comfort a man could desire, I was forced to descend to that mediocre place in the Rue d'Amsterdam—the Hôtel de Normandie, de Brest or de Rouen, or whatever it's called—next door to the Gare Saint-Lazare.

"Was it the incessant traffic of arrivals and departures that drew me to that place rather than another? I can't tell. My room, a large one with two windows on the second floor, looked out over the hotel entrance in the Place du Havre. I had stayed there for three days, starting on the Sunday before Mardi Gras, and I felt quite well.

"It was, I repeat, a third-rate hotel, though perfectly respectable: a hotel frequented by travellers and provincials, less out of their element in the vicinity of the station than in the city centre; a businessmen's hotel, empty one night and full the next.

"The faces I encountered on the staircase and in the corridors were all one to me; they were the least of my worries. Even so, when I went to the reception desk that evening, at about six o'clock, to get my key—I had dined in town and was returning to my room—I couldn't help looking, more curiously than was strictly necessary, at the two travellers I found there. They had just arrived, a black leather-bound trunk at their feet, and they were standing before the receptionist, discussing the price of rooms.

"'It's just for one night,' declared the taller man, who also appeared to be the older of the two. 'We leave again tomorrow. Any room will do.'

"'One bed or two?' the receptionist asked.

"'Oh, the sleeping arrangements don't matter. We'll hardly be sleeping at all. We've come for a costume ball.'

"'Give us two beds,' the younger intervened.

"'All right—one room, two beds. Do you have one, Eugene?'

"The receptionist rang for one of the porters, who came in. After some discussion, he said: 'Put these gentlemen in 13 on the second floor. You'll be all right there, gentlemen, it's a big room. Are you going up now?' When one of the strangers shook his head he went on: 'Are you going to dinner? We have a restaurant here.'

"'No, we're dining out,' the taller man replied. 'We'll be back about eleven to dress for the ball. Just have our trunk sent up.'

"'Shall I light a fire in the room?' asked the porter.

"'Yes, light it for eleven.' They were already turning away.

"I realised then that I was standing there staring at them, my lighted candle in my hand. I blushed like a child caught in some naughtiness, and immediately went up to my room. The porter came up behind me to make the beds in the room next to mine—I was in number 12 and number 13 had been given to the new arrivals, so our rooms were adjoining.

"I was still intrigued. When I went back down to reception, I couldn't help asking the receptionist about the new neighbours he had given me. 'The two men with the trunk?' he replied. 'Look—they've forgotten their receipt.' A swift glance was sufficient to read their details; they were Henri Desnoyels, aged thirty-two, and Edmond Chalegrin, aged twenty-six, residents of Versailles, both butchers.

"My two neighbours seemed too well-mannered and well-dressed for butcher-boys, their bowler hats and overcoats notwithstanding. The taller, especially, had seemed to me to be nicely gloved and, overall, to have a rather aristocratic bearing. They also bore a certain resemblance to one another. They had the same blue eyes, so deep as to be almost black, narrow and heavy-lidded, and the same rusty moustaches, emphasizing their abrupt profiles. The taller, however—who was much paler than the other—had a certain world-weariness about him.

"For an hour I thought no more about it. It was the eve of Mardi Gras and the brightly-lit streets were full of masks. I returned to the hotel at about midnight and went up to my room. Already half-undressed, I was going to bed when I heard the sound of a raised voice from the room next door. It was my two butchers, who had just returned.

"Why did that irrationally demanding curiosity, which had already bitten me once at the reception desk, take hold of me again? In spite of myself, I pricked up my ears. 'You don't want to get dressed, then? You aren't going to the ball?' the taller man said, loudly. 'We might as well not have bothered. What's wrong with you? Are you ill?' And when the other did not reply, the older went on: 'You're drunk. You're drunk again.'

"Then the other voice replied, thick and plaintive; 'It's your fault. Why did you let me drink? I'm always ill when I drink wine like that.'

"'All right, go on then. Go to bed!' said the louder voice, brusquely. 'Get your nightshirt out!' I heard the hinges of the trunk grate as it was opened.

"'So you're going to the ball anyway?' drawled the drunkard.

"'Oh, it's great fun to roll around the streets on one's own, in costume! I'm going to bed too.' I heard him punching his mattress and pillow angrily, followed by the sound of clothes being thrown across the room. The two men had undressed. I listened, breathless and barefoot, at the communicating door between the two rooms. The voice of the taller man broke the silence again. 'And such lovely costumes—not half bad!' And there was a rustle of silk and ruffled satin.

"I had put one eye to the keyhole. Candlelight alleviated the darkness and allowed me to make out what was happening in the neighbouring room while I got my breath back. The bed of the younger man was directly opposite the connecting door. Slumped on a chair beside the bed, he was quite still. He seemed extraordinarily pale, and his eyes were unfocused. His head had slipped from the back of the seat and was dangling on the pillow. His hat was on the floor, his waistcoat was unbuttoned and his shirt was open, He had no tie. He looked as if he had been strangled. I had to make a effort to see the other, who was prowling in his socks and underpants around a table strewn with bright silks and spangled satins. 'Zut! I have to try them on!' he exclaimed, heedless of his companion—and, setting his slim and elegantly muscular form before the looking-glass, he slipped on a long green domino cape trimmed with black fur, whose effect was so horrible and so bizarre that I could hardly hold back a cry.

"I was so overcome with emotion that I could no longer recognise the creature as a man. With his face secreted behind a metallic mask within the dark fur hood, it was as if that sheath of pale green silk had magnified him, even though it made him seem even slimmer.

"It was no longer a human being that undulated before my eyes; it was the horrible and nameless thing, the frightful thing, whose invisible presence had poisoned my nights in the Rue Saint-Guillaume. My obsession had taken form; it had had become a living reality.

"The drunkard at the corner of the bed had watched this metamorphosis with a distraught expression. He had been seized by a tremor. His knees were knocking and his teeth were chattering in terror. He pressed his palms together as if in prayer, shivering from head to toe.

"The green and spectral form gyrated slowly and silently in the middle of the room, by the light of two burning candles. I felt the glare of the two dreadfully attentive eyes behind the mask. Eventually, the creature went to set itself directly in front of the other, and with its arms crossed upon its breast it stared at him from behind the mask. The other man met that unreadable gaze, and there was a strange complicity in the exchange—but he collapsed from his chair to the floor, as if seized by a fit of madness. He lay there, prone. Reaching out to clasp the robe between his arms, he rolled his head in the folds, stammering unintelligibly. There was foam on his teeth, and his eyes were wild.

"What mysterious relationship could have existed between these two men? What irrevocable past was recalled in the eyes of that drunkard, that spectral robe and that polished mask? Oh, the pallor of that face and those two tensed hands delving ecstatically into the loose folds of the phantom's robe! It was a scene fit for a Sabbat rather than the banal setting of that hotel room! And, while the one gasped breathlessly, strangling a cry in the black hole of his mouth, the other—the mysterious figure—slipped away, retreating backwards and dragging in its wake the hypnotised wretch wallowing at its feet.

"How long did that scene last? Hours, or minutes? The Ghoul stopped again, placing its hands on the forehead and the heart of the insensible man. Then, taking him in its arms, it replaced him in his seat beside the bed. The man lay there motionless, mouth agape, eyes closed, head turned aside. Meanwhile, the green figure bent over the trunk. What was it searching for by candlelight, with such feverish ardour?

"I assume that it found what it was looking for. Although I saw no more, I heard the clink of glass over the wash-basin, and an odour that I knew very well—an odour that immediately went to my head, intoxicating and enfeebling me—spread through the room: the odour of ether. The green figure reappeared, softly and silently steering a course for the unconscious man.

"What is it carrying so carefully between its hands?"

"O horror! It's a mask made of glass: a hermetic mask, without eyes or mouth; and the mask is full to the brim with ether, poison in liquid form. See how the one bends over the defenceless other, his face inanimately offering up! See how it applies the mask to that face, and ties it in place, affixing it firmly with a red scarf. And as a laugh shakes the shoulders beneath the hood of sombre fur, it says—or so it seemed to me—'As for you, you won't talk.'

"The so-called butcher now undressed himself. He crossed the room, naked save for his underpants, his frightful robe having been discarded. He put on his everyday clothes, slipped on his overcoat, his clubman's kid gloves. With his hat on his head, he silently, and perhaps a trifle feverishly, replaced the two masquerade costumes and the little bottles in the trunk, closing its nickel clasps. He lit a cigar, took up his suitcase and his umbrella, opened the door and went out . . . and I could not contrive a cry. I made no sound. I did not raise the alarm."

"And you were dreaming, as usual," de Jacquels said to Allitof.

"Oh yes, I was dreaming—so cleverly that, even as we speak, there is an incurable etheromaniac in the asylum at Villejuif, whose identity has never been established. Consult the registration-book, if you care to. *Found on Wednesday 10th March, at the Hotel de whatever, rue d'Amsterdam*, it reads, *Nationality: French: presumed age: twenty-six years: presumed name: Edmond Chalegrin.*"

The Holes in the Mask

"IF you want to see for yourself," my friend de Jacquels said to me, "equip yourself with a sufficiently elegant domino of black satin, put on your dancing-shoes—and, for this occasion, black silk stockings too—and wait for me at your place on Tuesday. I'll pick you up at about half past six."

The following Tuesday, therefore, enveloped in the rustling folds of a long cape and wearing a velvet mask with a satin beard tied behind the ears, I was waiting for de Jacquels in my bachelor flat in the Rue Taitbout. I was warming my feet on the embers glowing in the fireplace, restlessly irritated by the unfamiliar contact of silk and skin. The confused sound of all the hoots and exasperated cries of a carnival eve drifted in from the street.

Looking back on it now, that masked figure slumped in the armchair in the eerily lit ground-floor apartment, cluttered with bibelots and muffled by wall-hangings, must have seemed rather strange, even disquieting. There were mirrors on the walls, the oil-lamp was turned up high and two long, very white slim candles, like funereal candles, were flickering—and de Jacquels had not arrived! The distant cries of the masked figures only served to emphasize the hostility of the silence. The two candles burned so steadily that I suddenly felt weak and afraid. Seized by a sudden whim I got up in order to snuff out one of the three lights.

At that very moment, one of the doors swung back and de Jacquels came in.

De Jacquels? I had not heard the bell, nor the opening of the door. How had he got into my apartment? I have often wondered since. But, at last, de Jacquels was there before me. Or was he? There was, at any rate, a long domino, a tall, sombre figure, veiled and masked, as I was.

"Are you ready?" he asked. His voice was so different I did not recognise it. "My carriage is here. We have to go."

I had not heard his carriage roll along the street nor stop outside my window. Into what nightmare, into what shadow and into what mystery had I begun to descend?

"Your hood is blocking your ears. You're not used to the mask," de Jacquels said, in a louder voice, having guessed the reason for my silence.

He was the one who knew what was required of us that evening, so he lifted up my domino to assured himself of the quality of my silk stockings and my slender shoes. The gesture was reassuring. It had to be de Jacquels, and not someone else, who was speaking to me from behind that domino. Another man would not have known or cared about the instructions de Jacquels had given me the previous week.

"All right, let's go," the voice commanded, and we went out into the passage that led to the front door, with a rustle of crumpled silk and satin. As we stepped outside and our capes suddenly rose up above our dominos, it seemed to me, that we must have looked like two enormous bats in flight.

Where did that gust of wind come from? Was it the breath of the unknown?

That Mardi Gras night was so mild, so warm, so humid.

※

Where are we going now, crammed into the shadows of that extraordinarily quiet carriage, whose wheels and horseshoes make no more noise on the paved byroads than they do on the macadam of the deserted avenues?

Where are we going, along the quays and unfamiliar riverbanks, scarcely lit here and there by wan lanterns reminiscent of days long past? Much time has already passed since we lost view of the fantastic silhouette of Notre-Dame, set against the leaden sky on the far side of the river. We have passed the Quai Saint-Michel, the Quai de la Tournelle, even the Quai de Bercy; we are far beyond the Opéra, the Rue Drouot, the Rue Le Peletier, and the city centre. We are not even bound for Bullier, the vice district, to which the lawfully-minded escape on the carnival nights leading up to Mardi Gras, cynically and almost demoniacally, hiding behind their masks.

But my companion kept silent.

As we passed along the shore of the grey and taciturn Seine, under the spans of the ever-more-widely spaced bridges, along the quays planted with tall thin trees, spreading their branches beneath skies as livid as dead men's fingers, an irrational anxiety took hold of me: an anxiety aggravated by the inexplicable silence of de Jacquels. I had again begun to doubt that it was really him, and believed that there was an unknown by my side. My companion had taken my hand in his own, and although its grip was gentle and exerted no force, it seemed to be a vice that ground my fingers together. . . . That powerful and determined hand held my protest in my throat, and within its embrace I felt any inclination to rebel founder and dissolve.

Now we have passed beyond the fortifications. Along highways flanked by hedges and the dreary shop-fronts of wine-merchants, suburban music halls long closed to new arrivals, we fly on beneath the crescent moon, which has finally emerged from a floating mass of cloud. It scatters its light upon that equivocal suburban landscape as if upon a salt-sprinkled tablecloth. . . .

At that moment, it seemed to me that the horseshoes suddenly resounded on the raised earth of the roadway, and that the carriage wheels, which had ceased to be mere phantoms, creaked as they disturbed loose stones and pebbles.

"There it is," murmured the voice of my companion. "We've arrived. We can get down."

When I stammered a timid "Where are we?" he replied: "The Barrière d'Italie, outside the fortifications. We've taken the long way round, but it's the safest. We'll go back another way tomorrow morning."

The horses came to a halt, and de Jacquels let go of me, until he opened the door and offered me his hand again.

※

A vast room with a high ceiling, its rough-cast walls whitewashed, its windows hermetically sealed by interior shutters. Along the entire length of the room, tables are set with tin-plate goblets secured by chains. In the background, at the head of three steps, there is a zinc counter loaded with liqueurs, and bottles bearing the coloured labels of famous vintners; behind it, hissing gas-lamps turned up high and burning bright. One could hardly find a cleaner and more spacious establishment in this district; business is obviously thriving.

"Not a word to anyone, now—that's vital. Don't speak, and don't reply if anyone speaks to you. They'll see at once that you aren't one of them, and we won't last a quarter of an hour. As for me, I'm known here." And de Jacquels pushed me into the room.

Some masked drinkers were scattered about the place. As we entered, the proprietor of the establishment got up and came towards us ponderously, dragging his feet, as if to block our passage. Without a word, de Jacquels lifted up the hems of our two dominos, and showed him the narrow dancing shoes on our stockinged feet. It was obviously the *Open Sesame!* of that strange establishment. The proprietor ambled back to his counter—and I noticed a bizarre thing: that he too was masked, but his mask was coarse coloured cardboard, painted with a caricature of a human face.

Two waiters—twin colossi with their shirtsleeves rolled up to expose the hairy biceps of wrestlers—circulated silently. Their faces were hidden beneath similarly frightful masks.

The disguised customers, who were drinking while seated around the tables, were masked in velvet and satin. With one exception—an enormous cuirassier in uniform, a brutish sort of fellow with a heavy jaw and a wild moustache, seated next to two elegant dominos in mauve silk, who drank with his face uncovered, his blue eyes already blurred by intoxication—none of the beings assembled in the room had a human face. In one corner sat two large workmen in velvet peaked caps, masked in black satin. Their suspect elegance was intriguing: both blouses were pale blue silk, and below their brand new trousers, they were stockinged in silk and their toes were clad in tapering dancing-shoes. I would have continued to contemplate that spectacle, as if hypnotised, had de Jacquels not drawn me into the back of the room, towards a closed glazed door with a red curtain.

Entrance to the Ball was inscribed above the door, in the decorative script of an apprentice painter. A military policeman stood guard beside it. That, at least, seemed to be a guarantee of safety—but as I passed him by, chancing to brush against his hand, I realised that he was entirely made from wax. His body was wax, as was his rosy face and his bristling false moustache. I experienced the horrible realisation that the only being in this place of mystery whose presence had seemed reassuring was a mere mannequin. . . .

❋

How long did I wander, alone, amid those silent masks, in that barn vaulted like a church? It was indeed a church, albeit abandoned and deconsecrated: a vast hall with Gothic windows, the greater part of its walls and its sculpted colonettes washed with a thick yellowish plaster, which clogged the flowers inscribed on the capitals.

A strange ball, where no one danced, where there was not even an orchestra! De Jacquels had disappeared, I was alone, abandoned in the midst of that unknown crowd. An ancient wrought iron chandelier suspended in the vault, its clear bright light illuminating the dusty flagstones—some of which, blackened by inscriptions, were rather reminiscent of tombs.

In the background, at the place where the altar should have held sway, feeding-troughs and racks were running half way up the wall, and there were heaps of harnesses and discarded halters in the corners. The ballroom was a stable! Here and there, large hairdressers' mirrors framed in gilt reflected, one to another, the silent promenade of masked figures—or, rather, no longer reflected them, because they were all sitting down now, quite still, ranged along the two sides of the ancient church, buried to shoulder-height in the ancient choir-stalls.

They had taken their places mutely and without a gesture, as if receding into mystery beneath long cowls draped with silver: a dull and unreflective silver. They no longer had dominoes, nor blue silk blouses. There were no Columbines, no Pierrots, no grotesque disguises. All the masked figures were alike now, sheathed in identical green costumes—a livid green, as if it were dusted with gold—with great black sleeves. All of them were hooded in dark green, with the two eyeholes of their silver cowls visible within the hollows of the hoods.

They might have been the chalky faces of some ancient leper-colony. Their black-gloved hands lifted up the long stems of black lilies with pale leaves—and their hoods were crowned, like the one that Dante wore, with black lilies.

And all these spectral figures were silent and motionless, and above their funereal crowns the Gothic arches of the windows stood out sharply against the moonlit sky, capped by transparent mitres.

I felt my reason darken in dread; the supernatural enveloped me. That awful, rigidity, the silence of all those masked beings! What were they? After one more minute of uncertainty, I went mad. I could no longer hold myself back. Anguish impelled me towards one of the masked figures with one hand outstretched, and I lifted up his hood.

Horror! There was nothing there.

My haggard gaze encountered nothing but the creases of the hood; the costume and the cape were empty. That living being was nothing but shadow, nothing but the void.

Mad with terror, I tore off the cowl of the masked figure seated in the neighbouring stall. The green velvet hood was empty—and so were the hoods of all the other masked figures seated along the walls. All of them had faces of shadow, nothing but the void.

And the gaslight flared up more strongly, almost whistling, the light in the great hall—supplemented by the moonlight streaming through the windows set within the Gothic arches—became dazzling, almost blinding. Amid all those hollow beings, vain apparitions of spectres, a new horror took hold of me. A dreadful doubt embraced me as I stood before all those empty masks.

Suppose that I too was like them? Suppose that I too had ceased to exist, and that there was nothing under my mask, nothing but the void!

I threw myself towards one of the looking-glasses. A dream creature stood before me, hooded in dark green, crowned with black lilies, masked in silver.

And the mask was mine, for I recognised the gesture of my hand as I reached up to my cowl.

Agape with terror, I let out a scream—for there was

nothing under the mask of silvered cloth, nothing in the oval of the hood, save for the crease of the material gathered about the emptiness.

I was dead and I . . .

"And you've been drinking ether again," the voice of de Jacquels muttered in my ear. "A fine way to keep ennui at bay while you were waiting for me."

I was stretched out in the middle of my room. My body had slid down upon the carpet while my head still rested on my armchair . . . and de Jacquels, dressed for the evening in a friar's robe, gave feverish orders to my bewildered manservant, while the wicks of two lighted candles, having burned themselves out, flared up as they fell into the wax molten in their trays, and woke me up.

The time had come.

The Visionary

In an old pewter ciborium,
Shedding its petals, dismal and dolorous,
An ochreous autumn rose,
Painted yellow as the sun.

Near to a large Venetian glass.
On a cloth of old damask silk,
The sick rose is dying
A slow and sumptuous decease;

Among the embroidered materials,
Weighed down by old gold threads
Seeming morbidly to reflect
The tones of its dry leaves.

In the depths, shadowed by curtains,
A large leaded window, limpid and bright,
Brings into view the masts
Of a fishing-port, a winter sky;

A tepid and gentle December sky,
Whose ashen grey is softening,
Makes of the rose shaded by decay

A transparent flower of amber;
And the proud death-agony
Of the flower amid ancient luxury
Is suited to the heart and the harmony
Of that patrician home;

That home, where under long veils,
Great saddened archiluths
Extend their necks, encrusted
With pearl and gold, like so many stars.

A gentle air of frangipani,
By means of an unhealthy gentleness,
Discreetly mounts and emanates
From a corner where a harpsichord rests;

And the poor and ugly thing,
That is the foliage of a flower,
Becomes an exquisite sorrow
In that high and tepid room.

In an old pewter ciborium,
Shedding its petals, dismal and dolorous,
An ochreous autumn rose,
Painted yellow as the sun.[1]

DE JACQUELS had not heard me come in. I had closed the door quietly and approached the table stealthily, on tip-toe, the generous pile of the Smyrna rug muffling the sound of my footsteps. I leaned over his

---

1. Lorrain had published this poem, "Effeuillement", in his 1887 collection *Les Griseries*. A ciborium is a sacred vase; an archiluth is an antique stringed instrument resembling a large lute.

shoulder to read these morose stanzas. They seemed to me to be etiolated by spleen—and so did he.

"Monsieur is under the weather today," the manservant had told me, regretfully, when he let me in. I had forced an entry, invoking the authority of a ten-year friendship. It was as an intruder that I had come to disturb the silence of his study.

"So you're not well, old friend?" I said, placing a hand on his shoulder.

De Jacquels started, his entire body seized by a sudden tremor. He looked up at me, without getting up from his armchair. In a voice that was faint and infinitely weary he said: "Oh, it's you. Cyprian let you in. That's all right . . . I was getting nowhere with this rubbish." He closed his blotting-pad with a flourish.

"Rubbish?" I said. "I read your verses over your shoulder. Anemic flowers and world-weary roses! You've got a full-blown case of the autumn blues. No one sees you any more, because you don't go out. What's up with you?"

"It's . . . it's just . . ." His voice was distant.

His long-fingered hand, astonishingly slender—and, on that particular day, more bloodless than I had ever seen it—pointed towards the window. His gesture took in the leafless branches of the trees in the deserted avenue and the hard and chalky surface of the roadway: all the cold and miserable decor with which November routinely furnishes the junctions of Paris.

He got up and went to the casement.

"Oh, that dull yellow sky that lies upon the city like a lid; the phantoms of the denuded trees; the rooftops half-hidden by the drizzle—and that grotesquely garish billboard exploding out of the column, clashing with everything, and that cab-rank down there on the corner . . . and the ugliness of the passers-by, fewer here than elsewhere, but still present. . . .

"I'm dying, do you see? Dying for want of the unexpected. Dying of the sheer banality of that poor and ugly thing that is a Paris street."

"And of this too, a little?" I suggested. I let my gaze wander around the large but cluttered room, which was furnished and decorated in a fashion as bizarre as it was luxurious. My eyes settled briefly upon a green bronze vase in the shape of a face with eyes of burnished silver, posed on a marble pillar, then on a more distant painted wax figure on top of a cupboard, whose haggard eyes and parted lips suggested a delicious agony, as charming as it was frightful.

"Can you seriously maintain that all this art-work is healthy?" I demanded. "I tell you, there's a sorcery in these accommodations that would play havoc with anyone's brain." Having noticed a strange severed head—of Sappho or Orpheus—floating between water lilies in a greenish-gold pond, set in an antique silver frame embossed with fruits of agate and cornelian and signed by Jeanne Jacquemin, I went on: "And that corruption—that theatrical flower in that haunted landscape. Do you think that you can live for any length of time with all these severed heads without suffering a nervous breakdown? The colour-scheme is enough in itself to be the author of moral infirmity! For example, where have you ever seen chrysanthemums like these?"

I put out a finger to touch a bouquet of fleecy flowers, their greenery speckled with scarlet and russet lint, like dead roses stained with blood. "No one but you could abide such monsters. I tell you, it only needs a few stuffed bats, dangling here and there from purple tapestries, to complete the effect. Sick, sick, sick! And your choice of reading-matter! Maurice Maeterlinck's *Serres chaudes* and *La Princess Maleine*. Catulle Mendès, Jules Laforgue, Henri de Régnier and Marcel Schwob—the complete works, of course. Too much dreaming, my friend. Too much dreaming drags one down if one isn't careful."

The servant brought the lamps in. De Jacquels, his face obstinately pressed to the windowpane, maintained his silence—and in the gathering dusk his stillness and his pallor took on a quality so strange that I was deeply disquieted. I had to whisper "Maxime!" in his ear, to assure myself that he was not asleep.

But he only said, in a distant voice, as if he were indeed lost in a dream:

> *"In the depths, shadowed by curtains,*
> *A large leaded window, limpid and bright,*
> *Brings into view the masts*
> *Of a fishing-port, a winter sky."*

Having said that, however, he finally decided to favour my observations with a response. "You see, what is lacking in these horizons, the cause of my distress and despair, is that landscape of masts and yard-arms. My eyes can no longer discover anything out there that is familiar. Oh, that little fishing port of my childhood, where I was always so bored! When I was there, my eyes were always turned towards Paris or somewhere else—but how it filled my eyes and my heart! How I loved its stinking, crawling quays, littered with barrels of pickles; its herring-tuns and fishing-boats, perpetually outward bound; the sailors bundled up in shining yellow cloth, waddling ponderously along the quays in their great muddy sea-boots; ships' boys hauling themselves from one longboat to another; caulkers suspended midway down the sides of the ships, repairing the hulls; and brown frizzy heads leaning out of open port-holes toward the women clinging to the iron bars of the railings on the quay.

"It reeks of the departure, the dream and the eternal adventure: in the evening, the tremendous gaiety of mariners on the spree, rolling around the streets at dusk; the odour of alcohol and salt, strong enough to take you by the throat; and, behind all the heavy doors set ajar, on the slippery thresholds and from the depths of the damp corridors, a noise rises up of coarse voices, coarse kisses and lumbering footsteps, which fills my heart with joy and health.

"Many a time, sitting in the smoky depths of an inn with thick windows, yellow as horn, in the midst of the card-games and the oaths of drunken sailors, I blossomed in that heavy atmosphere, among primitive brutes who are happy in their purpose, whose filthy and naive children are enraptured by their hearty traditional songs, and the beautiful patches of gold that the lamp is illuminating on the bellies of fish, turbots and red herrings suspended from the ceiling, and the smoky lamp that strikes sparks from the blonde hair of the young girls, beneath their woollen bonnets, and makes the bald heads of the old men gleam. Outside, the streets were always full of shouting, and the thick November mud. An excise-man came in, dripping with rain, and announced that he was coming to fleece someone—and everyone in the crowd shook his head, laughing loudly and declaring that *there's no need to get mixed up in other's people's business*. And I was laughing too, in my corner, in recognition of the celebrated Norman prudence....

"But the best evenings of all were the stormy ones, when the unleashed sea ran the length of the harbour, and the hail and the rain were swept by gusts of wind over the old deserted jetties.

"The inns overflowed with the tall figures of all the tradesmen, saddened by the idea of the evil sea and entered therein to blunt the sensation. On evenings like those, the pots and the pitchers were emptied in earnest, and the conversations were gravely serious, and I felt myself enraptured as I listened to those brave and simple men talk of tempests at sea and ships in distress, of collisions and castaways. While the rain redoubled its assault upon the windows and the sea went *hou, hou, hou* as the squall battered the cliffs, the old salts would say that it was 'blowing like Robillard's doll tonight.'

"Robillard's doll was a meaningless local phrase of unknown origin, of the kind that the lower classes of every land invent—but in my unquiet imagination, on very windy nights, I could see a giant and misshapen phantom doll drifting on the tide, with its head in the rain-clouds and its feet underneath: an immense mannequin, hideously pale and stuffed with rags. A dislocated spectre with long still hands, she ran, that doll, upon the crests of the waves, all the way to the entrance of the harbour, whirling around in the squall with her head slumped as if in death. She was all dripping with foam, sparkling strangely in the fugitive rays of sunlight that penetrated openings in the clouds, high above the cliffs. Her bewildered silhouette danced on the waves, slapping at ships in peril with the backs of her heavy hands, causing them to founder under her blows or to break up on the distant reefs.

Oh, that Robillard's doll! What a delicious and terrible vision! How she quickened my heart and made it leap! And there were other legends and other nightmares, no less sweetly frightful and no less beautifully horrible. My memory was full of them—and when calm returned and I was back in my own room, I only had to look out of my window, at the masts and yard-arms in the port, to see my phantoms again . . . to smile and salute the distant sails . . . down there, down there. . . ."

Down there!

De Jacquels' voice was fading away. Still motionless at the corner of the window, one might have thought that he was narrating a dream—and when I went to stand next to him, I saw that his eyes were fixed and his features set.

He was sleeping standing up. He was entranced.

Down there, down there, in the little fishing port, whose quays and masts he missed so much, were the ashen skies and the stormy nights, full of rattles and cries.

He was asleep.

I called his servant and we put him to bed, fully-dressed.

The Possessed

"YES," Serge told me, "I must be ill. I can no longer live here—and it isn't because I'm still feverish in spite of all the blood that the doctors have given me. My chest is much better, thank God!, and I can keep the bronchitis at bay if I'm careful—but I can't spend the winter here, because as soon as the November weather sets in I begin to hallucinate and I become prey to a truly frightening obsession. To put it bluntly, I'm too terrified to stay."

He read the thought in my eyes, and was quick to contradict me.

"Oh, don't blame it on the ether! I'm cured of that habit—completely cured. Besides which, it's poisonous. For two painful years it spread its poison through my being and filled me with I don't know what delicious sensations, but we know nowadays what it can do to one's arms and legs, and I began to notice an actual deformation in my limbs. It's been a year now since I last took ether.

"Anyway, why should I want to take it? I don't suffer from insomnia any more and my heart's all right. All that trouble with my lungs, and the atrocious pains that used to strike so suddenly in my left side while I lay in bed, making my flesh creep—all that is no more to me now than some far-off nightmare, like a vague memory of the tales of Edgar Poe that were read to me when I was a child. Honestly, when I think about that awful period of my life it seems more as if I dreamed it than actually lived through it.

"Nevertheless, I do have to go away. I'd be sure to fall ill again as soon as November arrives, when Paris becomes fantastically haunted. You see, the strangeness of my case is that now I no longer fear the invisible, I'm terrified by reality."

"Reality?" I was a little disconcerted by what he had said, and could not help but repeat that last word questioningly.

"Reality," repeated Serge, stressing every syllable. "It's reality that haunts me now. It's the creatures of flesh and blood that I encounter every day in the street—the men and women who pass me by, all the anonymous faces in the hurrying crowds—which seem to me to be horrid apparitions. It's the sheer ugliness and banality of everyday life that turns my blood to ice and makes me cringe in terror."

He perched himself on the corner of the table.

"You know, don't you, how I used to be afflicted with visions? When I was a miserable wretch addicted to ether, I changed my apartment three times in two years, trying to escape the persecution of my dreams. I would literally fill my rooms with the phantoms of my mind; as soon as I found myself alone, behind closed doors, the air would be filled with the gibbering of ghosts. It was as if I were looking down a microscope to see a drop of water seething with microbes and infusoria; I would see right through the curtains of shadow to behold the frightful faces of the invisible beings within. That was the time when I couldn't look around my study without seeing strange pale hands parting the curtains or hearing the patter of strange bare feet behind the door. I was slowly being destroyed by my incessant struggle with things unknown: half-mad with anguish, dreadfully pale, cringing away from shadows and nervous of the slightest touch.

"But all that was long ago! I'm cured, thank God! I've recovered my appetite and I sleep as well as I did when I was twenty. I sleep like a log and I eat like a horse, and I can run up hills with all the enthusiasm of a schoolboy—and yet, despite that I feel so healthy, I must be ill—the victim of some vile neurosis that watches out and lies in wait for me. I know only too well that the fear is still lurking inside me—and I'm afraid of that fear!"

Serge stood up again; he began to pace back and forth across the room, taking great strides, with his hands crossed behind his back, his brow obstinately furrowed and his eyes fixed on the deep pile of the carpet. Then, suddenly, he stopped.

"You've noticed, I suppose, the remarkable ugliness of the people one encounters in the street? All the little people, openly going about their business: the petty clerks and their managers, the domestic servants. You must have observed how absurdly exaggerated their mannerisms are, and how oddly fantastic they look whenever they ride on a tram! When the first chill of winter descends upon the city they become quite terrible. Is it their everyday cares that make them so? Is it the depressing weight of their tawdry preoccupations, or the anxiety they feel at the end of every month, when they can't pay the debts that fall due, or is it the apathy of the penniless, who feel trapped by a life that is stale and devoid of surprises? Is it that they live with such troubles, without their minds being able to entertain a slightly more elevated thought or their hearts a slightly broader desire? It always seems to me that I have never seen such wretched caricatures of the human features!

"What gives them their hallucinatory quality, I wonder? Does the sensation arise because one is brought abruptly face to face with their ugliness? Is it because of some relaxation brought about in them by the warmness of the benches or the deleterious influence of the stale air? Whatever causes it, there's a sudden increase in their evident bestiality: all the people huddled together on the seats; all those struggling against one another in the gangway; the fat women collapsed in the four corners; the old ones with pinched and green-tinged faces, and knotted fingers whose knuckles are turning white with the cold, and thinning hair, always looking meanly sideways at one another from beneath their flabby eyelids; the dubious characters with their coats buttoned up to the neck whose shirts one never sees. . . .

"I ask you, could there possibly exist beneath the grey November sky any more dismal and repugnant spectacle than the passengers on board a tram? When the cold outside has stiffened all their features, solidified all their characteristics, hardened their eyes and narrowed their brows beneath their caps, their glazed, empty expressions are those of lunatics or sleepwalkers. If they're thinking anything at all, that only makes it all the worse, because their thoughts are always low and sordid and their sideways glances always thievish; if they dream at all they only dream of self-enrichment, and that by venal means—by cheating and stealing from their fellows.

"Modern life, whether lived in luxury or in hardship, has imbued men and women alike with the souls of bandits and blackguards. Envy, hatred and the hopelessness of being poor are remaking people in new images, flattened about the head and sharpened about the features, like crocodiles or vipers; avarice and selfishness give others the snouts of old porkers or the jaws of sharks. Whenever one boards a tram one steps into a bestiary where every base impulse has imprinted its brutal stigmata on the surrounding faces; it is as though one enters a cage where frogs and snakes and all manner of repulsive creatures are together entrapped, grotesquely dressed up as if by some clever caricaturist, in trousers and coats . . . and since the beginning of the month I have been forced to make such journeys daily!

"Because I don't have an income of twenty-five thousand francs, I have to take the tram, just as my doorkeeper does. Every day I have to share the vehicle with the men who have pigs' heads and the women with birdlike profiles, the lawyer's clerks like black crows with a wolfish hunger in their eyes, and milliners' errand-boys with the flat features of lizards. I'm forced to mingle promiscuously with the ignoble and the unspeakable, unexpectedly reduced to their level. It's beyond my powers of endurance. I'm afraid of it.

"Do you understand what I'm saying? *I'm terrified.*

"The other day—it was Saturday, still quite early—the nightmarish impression was so very strong that it became quite insupportable. I'd taken the tram from the Louvre to Sèvres, and the distressing effect of the suburban landscape, perhaps exacerbated by the desolation of the Avenue de Versailles, brought me to such a pitch of anguish while I watched all those ugly faces, that I had to get off near the Pont-du-Jour. I couldn't bear it any longer. I was possessed, so sharply that I could have cried out for merciful relief, by the conviction that all the people facing and sitting to either side of me were beings of some alien race, half-beast and half-man: the disgusting products of I don't know what monstrous copulations, anthropoid creatures far closer to the animal than to the human, with every foul instinct and all the viciousness of wolves, snakes and rats incarnate in their filthy flesh.

"Sitting between two others of the same kind, right in front of me, there was a cigarette-smoking hag with a long, mottled neck like a stork's, and hard, widely-spaced little teeth set in a mouth that gaped like the mouth of a fish. The pupils of her staring, startled eyes were extraordinarily dilated. That foolish woman seemed to me to be the archetype of an entire species, and as I looked at her, an unreasoning dread took hold of me that if she should open her mouth to speak, no human language would emerge, but only the clucking and cackling of a hen. I knew that she was in truth a creature of the poultry-yard, and I was seized by a great sorrow and an infinite grief to think that a human being might degenerate so. To cap it all, she wore a hat of purple velvet, secured by a cameo brooch.

"I had to get off!

"Every day on the tramway, inside the tram, in that same carriage, the horror of the faces of all those living spectres emerges, further increased in the evening by the harsh light of the streetlamps. The same animal profiles are slowly set free from the glimpsed faces, for my eyes only, visible to no one except myself.

"It's a kind of possession, don't you see?

"But I know that I play my part too. I make that dreadful hell myself; I, and I alone, provide its trappings."

The Double

AS she came down the staircase of the palace, she met the great shadows that rose up in the opposite direction. They were the figures of knights in metal helmets, women in conical head-dresses and monks in penitents' hoods, with mitred prelates, mercenary foot-soldiers and pages mingled among them. The outlines of banners, lances and the turned-up rims of helmets were silhouetted in black on the hanging tapestries, but they were only shadows and they made not the slightest noise.

Gerda stopped, not daring to pass through that silent company. "Fear naught," croaked the raven perched on her shoulder. "They are but Dreams, no stronger than smoke. They overrun the palace every night when the lights are put out."

I have always adored folktales and I was comfortably stretched out in a circle of lamplight, pleasantly intoxicating myself with the delicate opium of one of Hans Christian Andersen's most poetic fantasies,[1] when the drowsy

---
1. The lines are from a French translation of the story known in

silence was dispelled by the sudden invasion of my room by my servant. As he presented me with a card set upon a plate, he explained that there was a gentleman who had brought a book and had asked that he be allowed to convey it to Monsieur himself. He had been firmly told that Monsieur was not receiving visitors—was not even here, having gone out—but the visitor was insistent.

I saw that I had been poorly defended, and I took the card resignedly.

Michel Hangoulve.

The name seemed vaguely familiar, but I could not place it.

"Young or old?" I asked the servant.

"Young," he replied. "Very young."

In that case, I thought, it must be some debutant to whom I had been recently introduced in an editor's office—unless I had seen the name attached to an article in a magazine.

It is our duty to encourage the young. I signalled my readiness to receive the visitor.

I had no sooner caught sight of the man than I regretted allowing Michel Hangoulve to come in. He was entirely devoid of hair and goggle-eyed. His skin was ruddy. He hopped forward hesitantly, his long, sloping back bent obsequiously towards me. His was an ugliness so tame and servile that I reacted with the instinctive aversion one feels toward a coward or a madman.

He excused his insistence on seeing me with excessive politeness, which made me suspicious of the great admiration that he professed for my talent. He had seized the rare opportunity of a publication to force his way through my door to lay it before me, and also ask my advice. . . .

English as "The Snow Queen."

He proceeded to wax lyrical upon the difficulties nowadays piled up before every debutant; upon the indifference of the press to literary matters; upon the degradation into which journals overflowing with interviews conducted by whores and pimps had sunk; upon the great authority of my pen in matters of artistry (and he had the temerity to look at me without laughing); upon the crash of the book-market and the deserved death-agony of the novel of the sewer . . . and after several blows of the fist aimed at Zola and amusing diversions on the subject of Great Exposition, the Parc de Bouteville and symbolist painters, he finally came to dwell upon the great service that a man like me might render to him with a few well-chosen words—hardly anything at all, two or three lines in an article, perhaps—and upon my benevolence, so well-known to everyone.

In the meantime, he had discreetly deposited his book on my table. It was an octavo volume, rather luxurious, ornamented with a frontispiece by Odilon Redon.[1] Its first page carried a considerable list of names from the worlds of business and the arts, flattering and reassuring the vanity of its subscribers.

I took it up politely. While leafing through it, I watched the excitable Michel Hangoulve from the corner of my eye, interested by his awkward combination of real effrontery and pretended timidity.

He was a real curiosity, not so much because of his

---

[1]. The artist Odilon Redon (1840-1906) was one of the contemporaries praised highly by Jean des Esseintes in Huysmans' *À rebours*. He produced a series of charcoal drawings and lithographs between 1879 and 1888, including illustrations of works by Baudelaire and Poe, which made him as much a hero of the Decadent Movement as Gustave Moreau.

prognathous face and menacing teeth as by virtue of the care that he took to belie the audacity of his demands, the myriad affectations of his furtive gestures and the manner in which his hands were incessantly rubbing against one another, caressingly. His speech was oddly restricted, his announcements undermined by reticences, as if he were always at pains to correct himself but always too belated to achieve that end. His expression seemed virginal, the eyes lowered, but I sensed the presence within them of an evil gleam suggestive of a desire to strangle and kill. There was something of both the anarchist and of the student in the young man—but taking everything into account, it was the student who tainted the anarchist by making him interesting; hypocrisy is such a hateful defect, though easy to find. It was disgraceful that the twenty-three years that the young author had lived had not provided him with a better reason to rail so proudly and so rancorously against a society whose greatest crime, in his eyes, seemed to be that it ignored his work.

It was, however, no longer the particular mixture of ugliness, envy, servility and bad temper manifested by my visitor that intrigued me.

The longer I looked at him, the more I became aware that he was prey to a peculiar agitation. He literally could not stand still. From time to time he would stand up abruptly and go to sit in another chair, only to vacate it almost immediately and return to the first one. Eventually, these perpetual comings and goings were further supplemented by a sort of conversation, as if someone were continually speaking into his ear. His entire body was continually turning towards some invisible presence, of what kind I could not tell. He would greet it with gestures and facial expressions, inclining his head and stretching his neck to receive some mysterious counsel.

The warm and peaceful atmosphere of the large room, shadowed by mystery and ancient tapestries, was measurably disturbed. Certain kinds of decor are very prone to aggravation by supernatural aspects once darkness falls, and in the equivocal light of the single lamp, blurred by a bluish haze and supplemented by the ruddy glow of the embers in the fireplace, I could not help but feel a particular terror creep up on me.

At length, the confrontation became deeply distressing. The presence of this Michel Hangoulve, with his perpetual restlessness and his continual shifts of position, oppressed me like a nightmare.

Evidently, he was not alone. He had brought someone with him: someone who talked to him, to whom he replied, and whose presence obsessed him, but whose form escaped my eyes, lost in the shadows, stubbornly invisible.

The passages of Andersen's tale came back to haunt me, as tenacious as conscience:

> As she came down the staircase of the palace, she met the great shadows that rose up in the opposite direction. They were the figures of knights in metal helmets, women in conical head-dresses and monks in penitents' hoods, with mitred prelates, mercenary foot-soldiers and pages mingled among them. The outlines of banners, lances and the turned-up rims of helmets were silhouetted in black on the hanging tapestries, but they were only shadows and they made not the slightest noise.

Eventually, I had to follow the man with my eyes every time he got up, always hoping—and, at the same time, dreading—that I would see some frightful and hairy shadow appear behind him, silhouetted against the background of the tapestries: his double.

How did it come about, I wondered, that this Michel Hangoulve moved within the oppressive and bizarre atmosphere of the tales of Hoffmann and Edgar Poe?

To the extent that the sound of his voice still impressed itself upon me, it seemed shrill, like the creaking of a pulley, continually broken by abrupt, almost derisive, titters. Was it really him laughing, during those frightful minutes, or the other? Waterfowl, gathered on winter nights on the banks of frozen rivers, make those same strange whimpering sounds.

And the horrible man went on and on, redoubling his volubility and amiability. The more I looked at him, the more his phantasmal aspect came visibly to the fore, filling me with terror. It came to the point when I no longer dared look into the shadowed corners of the room or the dead transparency of the mirror; I was too fearful of seeing some nameless figure loom into view.

He had not entered my abode alone; that was more and more evident. What atrocious presence had he allowed to follow him into my now-ensorcelled room? The wretch made the very air hallucinatory, so that it cast a spell on objects and persons alike. He was a spectre in the service of some evil spirit: the ghost of a man, or some mandrake changeling animated by occult will-power, an inane homunculus that dislocated itself from its host before my very eyes.

It reminded me of something out of Péladan.[1]

---

1. Joséphin Péladan (1858-1918) was the most prolific and most colour-

But there was still the scenery of the tale to reassure me:

> Gerda stopped, not daring to pass through that silent company. "Fear naught," croaked the raven perched on her shoulder. "They are but Dreams, no stronger than smoke. They overrun the palace every night when the lights are put out."

Perhaps, after all, it was nothing but a dream, nothing but powerless smoke.

At last my equivocal visitor took his leave. He retired with copious expressions of reverence and forceful protestations. He would never forget the cordial welcome I had extended to him, his gratitude was boundless, etc. etc.

Finally, I had the joy of seeing the door close behind him.

I immediately rang for my servant.

"I shall never be in to Monsieur Michel Hangoulve—never, do you hear?"

And reaching out towards the fireplace, I took up the fire-shovel and I set a little incense upon it to burn.

---

ful of the Parisian lifestyle fantasists inspired by Éliphas Lévi. He combined his pose as a scholar-magician and master of a Rosicrucian Lodge with the production of a long series of novels entitled *La Décadence latine* and a long series of scholarly fantasies entitled *Amphithéâtre des sciences morts*. Although he railed against the decadence of contemporary Paris, crying out for its salvation by a spiritual Renaissance led by a great Magus (himself), the lubricious delight he took in chronicling the perversions of his contemporaries and their Roman forebears was obvious, and many of his novels appeared with obscene frontispieces by the Belgian artist Félicien Rops, who was firmly established in the public eye as a Decadent Symbolist in the same camp as Gustave Moreau, Odilon Redon and Fernand Khnopff.

SOUVENIRS

The Toad

IT must have been of the most frightful sensations of my childhood and it remains the most tenacious of all my early memories. Twenty-five years have gone by since that little misadventure of the school holidays, and I still cannot think of it without feeling my head reel and the bile of horror and disgust rising into my mouth.

I had attained my tenth year, and with it the two-month-long vacation of a schoolboy recently elevated from a humble village school to one of the best in Paris. I spent it at the house of one of my uncles, whose surrounding acreage was a parkland of deep shadows and sleepy ponds, at the foot of a hill whose sides were covered by a beech wood. It was a charming landscape with an even more charming name: Valmont. I was to rediscover those two Romanesque syllables in an evil book, the cruelest and most dangerous of the eighteenth century.[1] Valmont: whose tender and melancholy image, compounded out of tall trees, spring water, long and silent walks along covered lanes, is still mingled in my memory with the

---

1. Valmont is a village near Fécamp, the town where Lorrain was born. The "evil book" in which the narrator rediscovered the name is *Les Liaisons dangereuses* (1782; tr. as *Dangerous Liaisons*) by Choderlos de Laclos, whose viciously cynical male lead is named Valmont.

chromo-lithographs of Tony Johannot, Scottish lakes surrounded by forests, castle-dominated valleys beyond the Rhine and musical fragments drawn from my mother's piano twenty years before!

My uncle Jacques owned a considerable property in that part of the country. It had once been the estate of an abbot, in whose convent—now converted into a country house—he lived. The former cells had become so many neat and narrow rooms, the refectory a dining-room, and the parlour a drawing-room. There were more than a dozen family members resident there that summer, including various male and female cousins and their parents, and parties went out every day for the amusement of the children.

These expeditions pleased my little cousins—there was much excited hand-clapping and joyful capering—but I always took care to avoid them. I was already enamoured, even as a child, of solitude and daydreaming, and I had an instinctive distaste for the noisy games the boys played and the newly-coquettish teasing of the girls. To noisy parties on the beach, picnics on the grass or in the woods, fishing for crayfish and all similarly delightful amusements, I much preferred wandering randomly in the great park, with no company but my own.

The lawns and meadows seemed mysterious to me, bathed by a dreamlike clarity between the tall crowns of poplars, beeches and birches. Some of the gilded aspens beside the ponds were trained into spindle-shapes and I loved their eternally unquiet foliage, although I could not watch it without a certain fluttering of the heart. I was equally attracted and fascinated by a summer-house with tinted windows, half-hidden among the osiers of a little artificial island surrounded by tranquil water. There I dreamed the long hours away, stretched out on my back in a little boat secured to the bank, with my arms folded behind my head and my eyes following the clouds as they fled across the clear blue sky.

Oh, the somnolent torpor of warm July days I spent in that corner of the shadowed park, when all the gentlefolk of the estate retired to their cool rooms, listening to the quiet hum of insects, interrupted from time to time by the monotonous noise of a rake scraping on the sand of the pathways! Then, when the first rusty tints of September showed through, the leaves would fall from the plane-trees to form translucent amber-yellow plaques on clotted ponds the colour of tin!

How far away it all seems now. And yet, it is present within me even to this day—and how I wish that all those yesterdays were tomorrows!

When I sneaked off on expeditions of my own during the somnolent siesta hours of summer and the afternoons of autumn, I embarked on veritable voyages of discovery across the unexplored hinterlands of the estate, whose mysteriously alternating light and shade so intrigued me. There were long pauses by ant-hills, enraptured contemplations of frogs sitting stock-still on lily-pads, prudent inspections of beehives: all the pleasures, in sum, that children take in the study of creatures who do not know that they are under observation. Finally—perhaps strangely, given my age—there was a particular sensuality to be obtained from the rapt contemplation of water.

Water has always attracted, seduced, captured and enchanted me. It bewitches me still, and God knows that I was served according to my desires on that estate, where a succession of islets, rustic bridges and ponds were laid out in a chocolate-box landscape. It was the first English park to be created in the entire country when the romances of Rousseau became fashionable. All these marvellous water-features were fed by a lazy river, which was swelled in its turn by four or five little springs, which the original owner's vanity had provided with as many chapels. They were spread out along the length of the park, like so many paved and cemented bathing-pools set beneath slate roofs, each with four or five steps descending into the transparency of the cold green-tinted water produced by the wellspring.

These, I admit, were the principal objects of my elective pilgrimages. One of them, sometimes called "the ferruginous," pleased me most of all. Situated on the edge of the park, at the foot of a stand of pines whose blue shadow drenched it with a lunar twilight, it was quite still and deliciously cold, like a block of ice embedded in a quadrilateral of walls. The limpid spring welled up in such a leisurely manner that it scarcely seemed to be moving, although a few bubbles of quicksilver continually burst upon its surface. Surrounded as it was by wallflowers, ground-ivy and slender ferns, the spring no longer seemed to be water at all, but a mass of molten rock-crystal set at the bottom of a reservoir.

One of my pleasures—I already preferred those that carried a slight edge of guilt, refined by the attraction of forbidden things—was to slip swiftly away after the midday meal and run straight across the park in order to arrive hot and sweating, completely out of breath, at that favourite spring. Once there, I would drink madly and deeply of the blue and glacial water: the water that was never allowed to us at table, although our eyes drank in the mystery of the carafes misted by condensation.

I rolled my sleeves up to my shoulders in order to plunge my two shivering hands into the water, scooping it up by the handful, filling my mouth and gullet with sensual gurgling, I poked my tongue into it as if into an ice-cream, and I felt a sharp coldness descend into my being, penetrative and yet as gentle as a flavour. It was a kind of frenzy, utterly sensuous, tripled by the consciousness of my disobedience and by the scorn I had for others who did not dare to do likewise.

And afterwards, it felt so good to be in that retreat, in the calm and seemingly eternal shadow of the great conifers, resting my eyes on the velvet of mosses!

Oh, the ferruginous well of the old park at Valmont! I believe that I loved it just as passionately, and possessed it just as sensuously, as the most adored mistress—at least until the day came when, by virtue of a cruel revenge of circumstance, I discovered the most degrading of punishments there.

One day, when I came, as was my habit, to drink slowly and deeply of the intoxicatingly cold water, supporting myself on the palms of my hands—that day, indulging my gourmet sensibility, I was lying on my stomach in order to lap at the spring like a puppy—I noticed on the tiles of the surround, crouched in a corner, a motionless black form that was watching me.

There were two round eyes with membranous lids horribly fixed upon mine, and the figure was flabby, as if collapsed into itself. The mere idea of touching something as nearly-black and limp emasculated me. Its immobility, too—the immobility of a monster or a ghost—filled me with anger and terror as I gazed across the transparency of the well into the toothy shadows of the ferns.

Then the gelatinous brown mass stretched its limbs slowly, and two palmate and miserably thin feet took a tentative step towards me,

The toad moved—for that was what it was: a filthy toad, pustulous and grizzled. It had come out of its corner now, and the light filtered by the conifers fell on its back, displaying its entire form. It dragged its milky white belly between its feet, enormous and inflated, like a boil about to burst. It moved painfully, each crude forward movement full of effort. The heaviness of its low-slung hindquarters was loathsome.

It was, moreover, a monstrously large toad, whose like I have never seen since: a magician toad, at least a hundred years old, half-gnome, half-beast of the Sabbat; one of those gold-crowned toads that one hears of in folktales, set to watch over hidden treasures in ruined cities with a deadly nightshade flower beneath its left foot, nourishing itself on human blood.

The toad moved and I had drunk the water where that monster lived and swam!

And I felt in my mouth, in my gullet, in my entire being, a taste like dead flesh, an odour of corruption.

And to heap horror upon horror, I saw that the pupils of the toad's eyes, which had seemed at first to fix themselves upon me, had burst, tinting its eyelids with blood.

I understood then that it had taken refuge in the spring, tortured and breathless, in order that it might die there.

Oh, that blind toad! The agony of that mutilated beast, in that clear water with the taste of blood!

Night-Watch

MY mother was very ill.
We were living at that time in Fécamp, in a large detached house of the Louis XIII era situated a little way out of the town. With a single projecting wing and high slate roofs, it stood at the bottom of a large garden whose treetops were always rustling, never allowed a moment's rest by the sea breeze. Under that relentless assault, the firs, chestnuts and birches ended up permanently inclined in the direction of the valley: a charming landscape whose charm seemed to be further increased by the name of Fécamp. Beyond a bridge that was immersed twice a day by the high tide, the bell-tower of Saint-Etienne and the roofs of the village could be seen. A major road ran alongside the property, from which we were separated by a high wall.

The restlessness of the eternally tremulous foliage of that ancient domain gave birth to one of the anxieties of my childhood. I felt isolated there, too far removed from normal activity, becalmed by life in a coastal town: a little fishing-port that was only fully awake in the winter months, when the boats from the New World returned, falling back into torpor once they were gone. If I now parade before the world a slightly unhealthy nervous restlessness, and if my life since turning thirty has been nothing but a long convalescence, I am convinced that it is because I listened too closely to the wind moaning in the huge trees of that profound and isolated garden.

My instinctive fear of all that wild greenery, late to heed the call of spring but all-too-soon rusted in autumn, was further aggravated by the anguish that my father and I had already suffered for two months by my mother's bedside. I was a very capable sixteen-year-old, a delicate but independent boy who had grown up a little too quickly in the charge of a private tutor. The doctor, afraid that the sight of a nun's habit might have a bad effect on the morale of the invalid, had put his trust in me to serve as one of her guardians. She was completely in the grip of typhoid fever, constantly delirious, so my father and I took turns to sit beside her all night, in a big bedroom with three windows situated in the projecting wing of the house. My heightened imagination lent a sinister significance to trivial things.

I had never seen my mother, nor anyone else, in such a state of prostration. Ever-alert and animated, I could do nothing save for moving restlessly around her bed, with tears in my eyes, convinced that the time would soon come when I would never see her again. I camped beside her bed, never taking my eyes off her, riffling through the pages of a novel without reading them, with my heart so full that I had not even the strength to stifle my sobs—which, fortunately, that dear creature could not hear.

Whenever my father took over, forcing me to go to bed in the next room, whether by day or by night, I remained in the grip of terrible anxiety throughout the period when I was removed from her side.

That night, it was my turn to stand watch.

My father, while embracing me before going to his own bed, had hugged me more closely and more urgently than was his habit, and there was a catch in his voice as he said: "Go on, my child. If there is any change at all, call me." And I realised, although he had drawn me into the shadows, that he too was choked with tears. So I returned to my station beside the bed and took her poor burning hand in my own, and I fixed my eyes on her dear face.

I only got up once, to put another log on the huge fire that burned night and day in the huge sad room—for it was the middle of winter, and the stars were shining brightly in the clear cold sky. The garden was still for once, becalmed by the dead air. There was not a sound to be heard in the sleeping house. There seemed sure to be a heavy frost. I quickly returned to my patient's side.

I do not know how it came about that I fell asleep, but the sound of the clock striking two woke me up.

A feeble night-light was burning in the room, which was as quiet as the grave. Nothing could be heard but the painful, slightly raucous, breathing of the bedridden woman, the faint crackling of the fire and the simmering of the water heated by the bedside for infusions.

Was it really the chimes of two o'clock that had punctuated the night, I wondered—for I had been sound asleep—or was it an increase in the pressure exerted by the hand still clasped within mine? I came abruptly to my feet, and then leaned over the distressed body, looking down at that poor exhausted face. She too was asleep. A log spat out a jet of flame, suddenly illuminating the room; the light died away almost immediately, but not so quickly as to prevent me from perceiving something that terrified me.

We were not alone in the room.

Someone was there: an unknown whose face I could not see and whose presence held my voice fast within my throat. I had no way of knowing whether it was a man or a woman. Installed in the chimney corner, in the large armchair where I often went to sit while supervising the infusion of a tisane, the unknown figure presented its back to me. In the half-light of the room, however, I could distinctly make out the two hands that it extended towards the fire; they were silhouetted in black against the glowing embers. The figure was motionless and mute, as if held at attention in the familiar pose that all old women adopt when they huddle before their fires—but I knew it was no mere delusion of my over-excited brain because, given a moment's pause, the hands reached out to take up the firetongs, prodding the embers so forcefully that a few spilled out on to the carpet.

A frightful dread seized me by the throat. I stood up straight, unable to help looking at her—for she was a woman, albeit a very large one. When the fire blazed up again I could plainly see the little knot of grey hair twisted over her meagre neck. I could neither speak nor cry out, so great was my fear, so strong my conviction that this strange presence could bode nothing but ill for the patient over whom I watched.

I was frozen thus for three minutes, a cold sweat forming on my forehead, but I finally contrived to move towards the terrible unknown woman. With the carpet muffling my footsteps I threw myself towards her. I planted my hands on her shoulders—but the spectre had vanished.

I had been the victim of a hallucination, a dream.

Distraught, I let myself fall into the armchair in which, a moment before, I believed that I had seen an emissary of

Death. Having reflexively extended my arms towards the fire, in the same pose as the phantom, I had scarcely begun to recover my spirits when the silence of the room was split by the strangled voice, suddenly and raucously raised, of my patient. My mother was delirious.

"Jean, do you hear them coming up? I don't want them to come up! You mustn't let them in!"

Sitting up in bed, she pricked up her ears in distress, probing the shadow with two frightened eyes, their pupils wildly dilated. I hastened to take the delirious woman's hands in mine and leaned over her, trying to reassure her.

"Oh, how near they are! And still climbing. The staircase is full of them, one upon every step. How did they get into the house? You mustn't let them in here!"

Oh, what an infinite terror distressed the voice of the sleeper—who had lain feverish through all the long nights of our vigil—as it echoed in the silence of the sleeping house. My poor mother had communicated her terror to me, and I felt that I too was sinking into the nightmare, into the supernatural realm—but I had to be strong.

"Who's there on the staircase? You're dreaming. I can't hear anything."

"Who's there? The storks! I tell you that there's one on every step. Oh, those long beaks, with their flabby sacks!" She clutched my hands violently.

"No, no. Poor Mama, you're having a nightmare. It's all in your head. Do you want me to go see?"

"Oh no, no, no—they'll come in. The door's firmly shut, isn't it?"

Seized by the same anxiety, I went to make sure that the door-catch was properly engaged, straining my ears for the least sound—and I heard for myself the sound of footsteps on the staircase. The piety of my early youth reasserted itself then, and I remember vividly that as I braced myself against the threatened door I made the sign of the cross.

The footsteps moved away then—or so, at least, it seemed to me—and I soon returned to my mother's side.

"They're gone," I told her. "Gone—and they're not coming back."

And she, in her turn, said to me: "Who's that?"

"You know very well. The storks—the evil storks. I've chased them away."

"Ah yes—the storks!" Her voice, already sleepy, softened and became childish; the hideous nightmare had released her at last.

I pulled the covers over her bosom, sighing: "If only she can sleep!"

That was one of the most terrible nights of my life. I passed the rest of it sitting in the large armchair, keeping the ailing fire going, my ears straining, my heart fluttering and my entire body shivering with inexpressible anxiety. I was the one who was haunted by the storks now; three times before the sun rose I heard something beating at the shutters, like frightful wings.

My torture did not end until the day was fully dawned, when Sosthène brought my breakfast.

"Ah, Monsieur," the servant said, sadly. "The gardener's wife died last night. She was so young—only twenty-three—and the cause is unknown. She was perfectly well yesterday. The doctor is mystified—but how is Madame this morning?"

"No change—she's hanging on. Thank you, Sosthène."

Death had been prowling around us all night.

The Spirit of the Ruins

SHE only appeared to me twice.
The first time was in Roumanin Castle, where Mistral had already brought the beautiful Stéphanette de Ganthelme to life for me, causing her to emerge from the crenellations of the battlements at sunset, calling in so melancholy a fashion to the gentle spirits of yesteryear, the illustrious swains and the laughing lady-loves of the beautiful land of Provence: Pierre de Châteauneuf and Jeanne des Porcelets; Guy de Cavaillon with Hugonne de Sabran; Guilhem de Baux and the Tender Beatrice; the Dame de Porcairargues and the Dame de Moustier; Alix de Mayrargues and the Comtesse de Die, with Blacas le Grand and the brown-haired Pierre Vidal, the last troubadour.[1]

---

1. The Provençal narrative poet Frédéric Mistral (1830-1915) was later to win the Nobel prize (in 1904). He was a leading figure in the Félibrige Movement, which attempted to raise awareness of Provençal language (Occitan), history and tradition. Founded in 1854, the movement remained vigorous until the *fin-de-siècle*, when it went into a long decline. The ruined castle and the "spirits" listed here are appropriated from Mistral's poem "Romarin", which had appeared in an edition of *Les Îles d'Or* published in Paris by Alphonse Lemerre in 1889, in which Provençal and French versions of each text were printed on facing pages (Lorrain would presumably have been unable to read the Provençal version).

They kept on coming, the souls of the departed, and Mistral said: "Is it a dream, or am I bewitched?" And will-o'-the-wisps ran lightly one-legged across the moor, and the melancholy swarm of poor pale ghosts said, as they passed by: "Fair or dark, we are dead, but Laure d'Avignon lives on because love has preserved her name." Another, already effaced, said: "The dream of love burns within me even in the tomb." Blanchefleur de Flassant (for Mistral recognised all of them) sighed: "It is lovely to hear the birds singing in the blue skies of May, when spring returns." The Friar of the Isles of Gold said: "Remember that life is but a dream"; but Pierre Vidal the troubadour shook his head, and declared in words aflame: "There was a very particular sweetness in the love of Provence, O brothers of the Midi, of which others must be told!" And they all joined in to plead: "Remember us!"

But none of those spirits was the spirit of the ruins.

By leafing through the pages of Mistral and old chronicles of the region, I too came to know them all, eventually: those fugitive visions of the queenly lovers of the ages, each the cynosure of so many eyes, each the cause of so many tears and smiles, both of joy and of pain; all gone to dust now, their names remembered only by poets. I came in the end to know them and to love them, those beautiful Provençal heroines. I came to hold them in the same affection that I, as a man of the North, had always lavished upon the epic figures of the women of Celtic legend: Guinevere, Melusine, Elaine, Vivien.

"You are in the land of Faerie here," my friend Rouquérolles—who was amused by my enthusiasm for the past—never ceased to remind me. "In our beautiful Provence there is not a stone upon the road, not a curbstone on a well, not a ridge upon an ancient wall, that does not speak of some nymph or lady of olden times; you only have to look at the archives of Nîmes or Aix-la-Jolie. Given that you're an imaginative man, I haven't the slightest doubt that you will run into the Comtesse de Die or Blanchefleur de Montferrat one fine evening, as our lovely twilight fades. Admit that you find it alluring: the old Castle of Roumanin, up there on the burnt hill, beset by wild almonds and dwarf olives."

The old crenellated tower was visible from one of the windows in Rouque's country place, like an upraised finger set on the horizon, above an uncultivated valley that was blue with rosemary and black with brambles, perfumed by juniper and thyme. I was certainly tempted by the prospect of a walk in the ruins that Mistral had made famous. Above the ditches heaped with the rubble of ancient landslides, only the bulky keep remained standing: an attentive and menacing silhouette, sole survivor of events long past. But some superstitious fear always made me put the anticipated adventure off, until the next day.

How, then, did I eventually come to make my expedition through the seared and strangely lonely valley to the brushwood and the broken stones, under the clear sky of a June afternoon?

Always making fun of my enthusiasm, Rouquérolles no longer seemed to be eager to take me to the ruins, but my curiosity became gradually more obsessive. On certain days, when the azure sky shone through the loopholes and gillyflowers blossomed on the walls, the light would play tricks, making them seem to be very near at hand. One would almost have thought that one could reach out a finger and touch them. On other days, by contrast, they appeared to recede into the distance, as though retreating towards infinity, hundreds of leagues away in the landscape of a dream: not merely unreal but almost spectral in their unreality.

One evening, as was my habit, I was loitering in Rouque's little dining-room, resting my elbows on the window-sill, gazing at the old keep whose former masters were roasting in the fires of Hell.

"Well, I can see that I'll have to take you there tomorrow, Monsieur Parisian," Rouque said, his piercing voice mocking me. "You'll fall ill otherwise, and then I'll certainly have to introduce you to the spirit of the ruins."

"The spirit of the ruins!" I echoed, slightly alarmed.

"The very same—and you should listen to this for your own good. She's an old woman, who has been seen continually among those broken stones during the thirty years that I've had this place: you might say that she's their guardian. No one hereabouts knows where she came from; they call her Fuldrade and she's thought to be something of a witch. The village children used to throw stones at her, so she never goes down there any more. Months go by without a sight of her and then, one fine morning, her meagre silhouette is seen prowling around the almond-trees with her herd of goats and her big dog. Three years ago, she sold milk to the sight-seers and filled them in on all the details of the château's remains, which she knows better than anyone. She slept underground, so rumour had it, and was said to be a hundred and ten years old. She knew all the stories and legends connected with Roumanin, and more, and yet more, and she spent the summer telling them in return for small payments— but for a year the hussy's been unable or unwilling to say anything at all. Her life is a mystery. She's Fuldrade, the teller of tales—that's all anyone knows. The old folk say that she's always been there, and that she was already old when they were children, posing as the last descendant of the old Counts. One tale told throughout Provence holds that on the day the old nag dies, the last keep that's still standing will finally cave in and fall into the valley. So, shall we attempt the adventure tomorrow?"

"I believe we shall, my dear Marius. Nothing would give me more pleasure."

I seized both his hands in mine, but he pulled away.

"Good, Good. I'll have to take you there myself, Monsieur the lover of antiquities, because you won't find anyone among the local peasants who'd dare to accompany you. The reason for that is rather amusing. Legend has it that out of every party that visits the ruins, one will die by the end of the year—at least one. Everyone who goes there goes in a group, even now—they all hope that the curse will fall upon one of the others, you see. Tomorrow, if there are only two of us, there won't be much choice. I am, as you see, a very devoted friend."

"My dear Marius!"

"Let's leave it at that. When the time comes that one must die, one must wish his friends well—and the time will come, whether you've been there or not. Let's hope the old lady doesn't make us fall into a hole—but perhaps we won't even see her there. I expect that she detests Parisians, and as she has a fine nose she's bound to sniff you out. We probably won't see anything at all."

※

The next day, at about five o'clock in the afternoon, after walking for a Provençal league (which is worth a good four of Normandy's) we stood mopping the sweat from our brows at the foot of a hill. The hill was bare of vegetation and strewn with stones; the two of us were sorely fatigued and as red as tomatoes, which my friend Marius always calls love-apples.

We had been walking since lunchtime in strong sunlight with no company but junipers and mastic trees. That evil ruin, which had seemed to be so close when seen from Rouquérolles' country cottage, seemed to be playing a malicious game of tag with us, teasing us and then running away. For every hundred paces by which we approached, it retreated at least a kilometre. It was as if it were animated by some strange elfin life of its own, taunting us and then taking refuge on the horizon, level with the moor where Roumanin Mount abruptly plunged into the almonds and grey olives. Dazed by the heat and the impatient chirping of cicadas, we had come to the end of our tether. Marius had abruptly fallen silent, and we had been walking side by side, saying nothing, for two long hours.

Then, as soft as the drone of bees in flight, strains of Gothic music rose into the air. Voices were laughing lightly, set against the hum of stringed instruments. I stopped dead in the middle of the path.

The music was coming from the edge of a little wood of fir-trees and white Italian poplars away to our left, about fifty metres from the path. I thought, may God forgive me, that I could distinctly see a group of young women and handsome young men sitting on the slope, in the shadow of the conifers. They were slender, stretched out in delightful poses at the feet of three noblewomen, forming a highly attentive circle around them. Their brightly-coloured costumes were bizarre, the shades curiously softened; they were very similar to those worn by princesses and lordly donors depicted in old stained glass windows.

I told Rouquérolles something of what I had seen. He immediately went very pale and whispered through clenched teeth: "I told you that you are in the land of Faerie here. What you've encountered is the Comtesse de Die, the beautiful Phanette de Gantelme and the Lady des Porcelets, listening to the aubades of their lovers. Don't look at them. Don't turn around. It's always dangerous to displease the dead. You're not the first to see such things, but it just goes to prove that you've had too much sun. You'll have to lie down when we get back. Do you want to go on?"

"More than ever," I replied, although I was considerably disturbed.

"Let's go then—we're practically there."

Indeed, Roumanin Castle—or rather its debris—had all of a sudden loomed up before us. A great wedge of shadow descended all the way from the foot of the keep to the bottom of the hill. The exasperated song of the cicadas was as strident as a band-saw.

With our shirts steeped in sweat, we set our feet on the narrow winding path that zigazagged up the hillside.

The sun was low on the horizon, as red as a beacon fire to which the torch had just been put. The enormity of the ruins stood out against it, seemingly suspended now above our heads. Huge ivy-covered blocks of stone and tall nettles hampered our every footstep and we were submerged to the waist in warm brambles. We were forced to put our hands high in the air to avoid being pricked, and we laid about us with our walking-sticks, breaking the branches blocking our path.

We marched into the shadow of the castle, while trails of wild clematis dangling from the giant walls brushed our faces

The entire landscape exhaled a powerful odour of juniper, bitter almonds and burnt dust. It was a veritable land of Faerie: chimerical, equivocal, disquieting. It extended to the limit of vision, a hundred feet below. The faint strains of the Gothic music, though very distant now, still sounded from the edge of the evergreen wood. Having turned around in spite of Rouque's advice, I thought that I could still make out that echo of the past in the ruddy light of the setting sun: the beautiful noblewomen and their lovers, chatting and making music on the grass.

There now seemed to be a vast brazier set behind Roumanin, setting the castle on fire. The old tower was limned in jet black, each of its loopholes a long *I* of incandescent embers. It was grandiose and extraordinary.

Then old Rouque pinched my elbow and whispered in my ear, in a voice so changed it stopped me in my tracks: "Look at that! There's no use going any further. Look!"

Two hundred metres above our heads, outlined in black against the red sky, was the silhouette of an old woman. She was so thin, angular and desiccated that she looked like one of those owls sometimes that perch on a farmgate. She stood out, strangely magnified, in the hollow of a breach at the very foot of the tower. To either side of her was the silhouette of a goat's head, its horns and long beard black against the red sky.

It was terrible, diabolical.

In the valley, the cicadas had fallen silent. A profound silence had taken over the landscape.

We stood where we had stopped, hardly daring to breathe.

"It's her! It's Fuldrade!"

A stone disturbed by our feet rolled down the hill, waking echoes in the abyss. The shadow of the witch leaned forward, so suddenly menacing above our heads that, in spite of ourselves, we closed our eyes.

When we opened them again, she and her goats had disappeared.

Thus it was that the spirit of the ruins appeared to me for the first time.

※

We never went back to Roumanin. By some tacit accord, the question never even came up again. On sunny and somnolent days, when the old keep seemed to come very close, almost to the window of our dining-room, we made the sign of the cross. In the limpid blue of early morning or the greenish gold of sunset, we avoided looking at it altogether. Its name was never spoken aloud in the cottage.

My reward for our adventurous expedition was a bad case of sunstroke, which put me in bed for a week and a day with a raging fever. Throughout those eight days the faint Gothic signature-tune of the lovely ladies and their lovers manifested itself in the rosy twilight. The laughing voices and the songs of that handsome group I had encountered beside the evergreen wood persecuted me, in so cruel a fashion that my good friend Rouque was firmly convinced that I would have a stroke.

My convalescence was long drawn out, and I retained an irrational fear of the sun and cicadas, which prevented any and all excursions for fifteen days. I no longer dared to go out alone in the neighbourhood of the cottage, as I had before.

It is a shameful thing to have to admit, but I was not only afraid of a second encounter with those phantasmal beauties, who left sight-seers with such implacable headaches. I had also begun to feel terribly bored in the intimate company of my old fried Rouque, to that poor fellow's great distress.

"Oh, what the devil's up with you? You need distraction. You need to be shaken up. You've only caught a little sunstroke."

Little! I consigned him to the devil; what would he need then!

Marius, it must be admitted, was a hero. It would have been so easy for him to shut me up. It was, after all, me who had insisted that we undertake that deplorable escapade. But he exhibited a delicacy that was hardly in character, given that he is a talkative Southerner much given to drivelling on. He did not crush me with common sense, did not poke fun at me, and spared me all that abominable good humour that the Midi produces, liberally seasoned with garlic, to set against the perpetual disquiet of the imaginative men of the North.

Touched by the sun or not, the days began to drag behind the closed shutters of my room, to the extent that one morning I took my courage in both hands and informed my friend Marius that I had been recalled to Paris. I expressed my deepest regrets, but I had received letters, there were affairs demanding my attention . . . the newspaper . . . my editor. . . .

"Yes, you're bored. I understand that—but it's your own fault. You don't want to do anything. You don't want to go out. You just lie there like a hearth-cricket in the cinders, and all because . . ."

I stopped him with a gesture. "Yes, because . . . you're quite right. It's me who wants to go. It's all my fault. Your cuisine is worthy of Saint Monica herself, your wine is excellent, and this place has air and sun to spare—but I'm going anyway."

"That's all right then—go. I'll order a cab for the end of the week."

"The end of the week! You're mad. It's only Monday. I'm leaving tomorrow."

"Tomorrow!" He seemed so utterly downcast that I couldn't help smiling.

"Oh well—the day after tomorrow, then. Poor Marius!"

"Oh yes, poor Marius. You promised me you'd stay here for two months, and you're going after scarcely a month."

"Scarcely a month? But it's July the sixth and I arrived here on the twenty-ninth of May."

"Are you sure it was the twenty-ninth?"

"Definitely. I'll be leaving on the eighth. May has thirty-one days, so that's forty-two days that I've been a burden to you, my friend."

"A burden to me for forty-two days! You've kept count. Your stay here must have been very boring indeed." And with a stifled sob, which caused his voice to change completely: "Yes, you're right, it'll be better all round if you leave tomorrow. My conscience would never let me rest if I refused to release a friend who's bored stiff. I'll order the cab."

"Marius, Marius!" I cried after him—but he no longer wanted to listen. He was already on his way to the village.

I felt a pang of remorse. Poor fellow—how devoted and faithful he was. Our friendship dated from our fifteenth year, when we had both been pupils of the Dominicans at Arcueil.

But the kindly impulse was short-lived, and the selfishness that underlies all human action soon reasserted itself. "Bah," I said, with an insouciant gesture. "It's everyone for himself in this world. This poky little place is boring me to death."

※

I was awakened at eight o' clock on the following morning by the noise of little bells. The driver and his rig were beneath my window, and friend Rouque, aided by his old housekeeper Alix, was hoisting my brass-bound trunk on to the cart. It was tightly fastened, the buckles and their tongues so brightly polished that I hardly recognised it. I could hardly believe my eyes.

"Have you gone mad?" I demanded of Marius, when he caught sight of me leaning out of the window. "It's eight o'clock and we're off already? We're catching the half-past-six express this evening, and it's only five and a half hours from here to Marseilles by cab. So you're treating me to dinner at Roubion's, are you?"

Rouque lifted his head. "Roubion's? We'd be dining at half past two. No, I'll lay on a picnic." And as he saw my expression change: "Not in some ruin, have no fear. You can't refuse to spend one last day with me, in the good air and the beautiful sunlight of Provence. You no longer like it because you've suffered for liking it too much, Parisian that you are. Look what I've packed for dinner!"

Leaping up into the cart he raised up almost to the height of my nose an immense basket crammed to bursting with loaves of white bread, sausages and various tinned goods, plus an enormous ham, ready-sliced.

Dumbfounded, I said nothing.

"I've got five bottles of that wine you told me about cooling in the straw," he said, "with some Mazargue greengages and a pâté. Go on, get down here. Finish what you have to do and let's get going. I don't want you denigrating Provence when you get back to Paris. I'll take you to a spot that I know you'll love."

Good old Marius had taken full advantage of my slumber to pack and buckle my trunk, with the kind of affectionate care one would expect of an older brother. I didn't take long to complete my toilet and pack my personal effects.

An hour later we were rolling along at a fair clip behind the driver's trotting horse, through a scorched landscape perfumed with honey and wild mint. The morning was clear and blue. A gentle wind, freshened by the sea from which it blew, shook the crowns of the Italian poplars planted along the side of the road.

"But where are you actually taking me?" I asked, at the end of an hour of jolting in and out of the dried-up ruts. The silence of my friend Rouque had begun to disturb me. Our previous excursion had left me with too many bad memories to allow me to contemplate another dangerous escapade without trepidation. Marius's constant reminders that "we are in the land of Faerie" had not reassured me at all.

But he, with a certain malice in his eye, replied: "Where am I taking you, Monsieur the Amateur Antiquarian? Why, to the seaside. But we won't be eating any shellfish there. There's neither village nor fisherman to be seen—but the cicadas will sing, accompanied by the music of the waves. It's one of the prettiest headlands in Provence. You'll see; you'll see."

And when the driver had cracked his whip his gallant horse began to gallop; we blazed a fine trail across the sun-baked landscape, between the clumps of short and patchy grass.

There was neither lie nor exaggeration in what Rouque had promised.

On a long beach of yellow sand, burnished with gold, an agglomeration of blackened cones—which might have been tents of animal hide, or enormous beehives—stood at the limit of vision, their innumerable silhouettes striping the horizon. Beyond them was the gleaming Mediterranean, like a sheet of boiling lead extended beneath a sky so darkly blue as to be almost violet.

"It's a gypsy camp!" I exclaimed, silently cursing my friend for having dragged me to such a lonely spot. "Is it prudent for us to go there, Marius?"

"Gypsies! No wanderers these! All those figures you see in the distance, disporting themselves on the seashore, are bells. Yes, bells, brought down from their towers and silenced: old chatterboxes rendered mute. This place is known as the Bells' Cemetery. There are some among them some that date from thirteen or fourteen hundred years ago. It's quite a story."

I stared at him, and he continued: "It goes back to very ancient times, to the time of the war against the

Albigensians.[1] Didn't those heretical dogs seize the bells of towns and villages for more than thirty leagues around? And didn't they proceed to submerge them out there in the Mediterranean, convinced that they would never see the sun again? But after hundreds and hundreds of years, it turned out one fine morning that the sun had retreated. All the bells that were supposed to have been forgotten reappeared, populating the strand with their brazen spirits. They're silent now, and their silence is respected. This isn't Brittany and the lost city of Ys.[2] We're in an entire city of bells!"

And they were indeed bells. Now that we were coming closer, I could easily make out the great scattered herd. There were hundreds of them, sleeping in the sunlight on that serene strand. There were massive ones, tall ones, slim ones, ones so squat that they seemed to have caved in on themselves: every possible Gothic and barbarous form. They were all black, by virtue of their years-long sojourn under the sea. Seaweeds had once turned them green, but then, having been leprously eaten away by the waters, they had blackened under the open sky.

They were deeply embedded in the sand, driven deep by their weight. Some scarcely extended above the level of

---

1. The "crusade" against the Albigensian Cathars, launched by Arnold of Citeaux and Simon de Montfort in 1208 at the behest of Pope Innocent III, was one of the bloodiest episodes in French history.

2. The Breton folktale telling of the inundation of the city of Ys following the seduction of the king's daughter and the consequent loss of the key to the gates holding back the sea had been recently repopularised, when Lorrain wrote this story, by the successful opera *Le roi d'Ys* (1888) by Edouard Blau (1836-1906) and Edouard Lalo (1823-1892).

the strand, like drowned corpses floating half-submerged upon the surface of the water. Others were like great purple flower-heads—a purple that had once been bronze red, until it was tinted with blue and sadness—springing up here and there, stripped from their stems by the perpetual battery of the sea breezes.

It was the gloomiest spectacle that any human eye had ever seen. Beyond the bronze stampede the Mediterranean extended its silver silk, and the burning air freshened slightly, as if stirred by the flapping fronds of invisible palms.

"It's said that the angels sometimes stay the night here."

We had dismounted from the cart, and were making straight for the city of bells, when the outlines of a few skinny goats suddenly appeared between the purple flower-heads. We planted our feet, coming to a halt fifty metres away.

I couldn't help murmuring: "Fuldrade!"

"You're rambling," said Rouque. "Roumanin is ten leagues away and Fuldrade never leaves the ruins.

My only response was to point out the tall but stooping figure of the teller of tales. She had emerged into view within the city of bells. The sunlight bathed her meagre carcass; thanks to the transparency of the air, I could see her distinctly. Wrapped in a dress the colour of ash, she extended above the profound blue of the horizon the gaunt neck of a vulture. Two or three locks of white hair poked out of a little bonnet of black horsehair, in the form of a conical head-dress, which was posed on her bald forehead. In spite of the beak-like nose over her thin lips and the thousand wrinkles of her poor grey face, it was evident that Fuldrade had once been very beautiful.

She walked slowly between the black bells, pausing from time to time to use her staff to scrape at the stains and mosses, so as to read the old inscriptions engraved upon them. Her fantastic goats were capering before and behind her, picking at the purple flowers with their teeth. At other times, the old woman halted in order to look long and hard at the horizon, and the sea. When she did that, her attitude was suggestive of regret and ecstasy. One sensed that the wandering spectre was entirely lost in the Past; she was a sister to the bells.

We kept her in sight for as long as we could, but the bells soon hid her from our eyes.

I never encountered the spirit of the ruins again.

RÉCITS

Dolmance

"SADISTIC, sadistic . . . everyone seems to think that everything had been said once that epithet was pinned on the back of the first maniac. . . . I wish I could say the last maniac. . . . Word of honour, I don't know whether to shrug my shoulders or to roar with laughter?" And as he began to set down the hand of cards that he was challenging the rest of us to beat: "The English are far worse than us on that account."

With his lips drawn out in an equivocal smile, our host Gerard Asseline continued to lay his cards out on the green cloth. The king of hearts and the ace of spades secured his claim of victory.

Outside, the wind blew in gusts and the sea was streaked with foam. Green and white beneath a sky the colour of oyster-shells, it hurled itself about with a dull roar between the two high cliffs, its surface rippled by the rain that had been pouring down since morning, and was still continuing as evening fell. For two days we had been trapped in the Villa des Saules by the torrential equinoctial downpour. Thus confined to quarters, we were miserably, almost desperately, trying to kill time, keeping boredom at bay with endless rounds of baccarat in the villa's drawing-room, temporarily transformed into a games room.

The only diversion from the monotony of our occupation came when the postman arrived, throwing a few personal letters into the midst of our lassitude, along with the somewhat adulterated gossip of the newspapers. Now, he had arrived just as the night-watch began; avid for new distraction, we feverishly turned the pages, while Asseline indifferently began to lay out a hand of patience with the cards left behind by our hastily-abandoned game of baccarat. Georges Moor, Jacques de Tracy and I, preoccupied with the Bloch affair had gone into a tight huddle to read the verdict—and that was the judgment we were discussing in loud voices, echoing from one end of the hall to the other, from the various divans where we had extended ourselves. Our discussion had become impassioned in spite of ourselves, and it was all that quivering indignation that the phlegmatically indolent Asseline intended to douse with the coldness of his mocking sentence.

"The English are far worse than us on that account."

But how am I to render the weariness of our host's casual gesture and the somnolent disdain of his voice? And when we all protested that we would be only too happy—flattered, even—to concede that particular superiority to subjects of Her Gracious Majesty, he went on tranquilly: "You've all read *La Faustin*,[1] I suppose?"—a question to

---

1. Edmond de Goncourt's *La Faustin* (1882). The passage quoted was excised from the bowdlerized English translation by G. F. Monkshood and Erenest Tristan, thus leaving Annandale's behavior devoid of even a suggestion of explanation. Goncourt, convinced that homosexuality had to be seen as a pathological condition, introduced George Selwyn into the novel as a predator blamed for the corruption of the young Annandale, which makes him the wrecker of Annandale's happiness and, indirectly, that of the actress who loves him. Lorrain's description of the passage read by Asseline as "charmingly evocative" is sarcastic; had Asseline continued he would have read out La Faustin's harsh

which Georges Moor replied with a vibrant: "Of course. What do you take us for?"

Asseline put on a mysterious smile and said, while shuffling the cards: "Then you all remember the honourable Lord Selwyn, the disquieting character who puts in a fleeting appearance at the end of the novel—and the scandal that was raised, when the book appeared, around that name!"

All four of us fell silent, not knowing where Asseline was going. He got up, went to his library-shelves and took down a book beautifully bound in pigskin. He leafed through it for a minute, then read from it while leaning his shoulder on the corner of the shelf. His voice became mordant, extracting the full meaning of the words:

> "*What, in essence, is your friend Selwyn?*"
> *Lord Annandale, occupied in lighting his cigar and taking a leisurely puff, looked his mistress full in the face and said:*
> "*George Selwyn . . . is a sadist.*"
> *And under the mute interrogation of Faustin's eyes, he exclaimed: "Yes, a man who has the desires and appetites of a deranged and morbid sensuality . . . but what is it that you . . . what is his life to us?" And as he began to walk across the room, he mumbled; "A great . . . a very great intelligence . . . immense knowledge . . . and an old childhood friend."*

---

judgment of Selwyn, based on her "instinctive repulsion". In this story, therefore, Lorrain's memories of Lord Arthur Somerset—and, more pertinently, of the rumours about Swinburne that continued to circulate long after his departure from France—are being ironically filtered through Goncourt's speculations regarding the possible origins of Lorrain's homosexuality.

A silence followed.

"Are you going out today Juliette?" he said, after a few moments.

"No!"

On hearing that, Lord Annandale headed for the stables.

And with a dull sound, Asseline reclosed Goncourt's novel. The evocative charm of those few lines had taken effect. We all remembered now, in every detail, the louche and mysterious friend of Lord Annandale. We saw every inch of him, from the rose in his buttonhole to the pigtail hidden inside the back of his coat: the hydrocephalic forehead, the figure like an old woman's; the pretentious but stained clothing; and the desiccated hands whose two little fingers ended in two nails enclosed, in the Chinese fashion, in a metal case.

In the meantime, the rain had ceased to fall. Through the large bay window of the studio, we saw the beach bathed in sunlight. The two convergent cliff-faces—one upstream and one downstream, seemed to have become luminous and transparent, and the open sea was suddenly blue.

"And to think that in this comic-opera setting," said our host and lecturer Asseline, laughing mockingly, "one might easily to run into the semi-reassuring spectre of the honourable Georges Selwyn! What? Here, at Etretat itself, between the once-romantic silhouette of Hamlet Faure[1] and the living memory of Guy de Maupassant . . . oh yes, oh yes," Asseline paused, with a wink of the eye directed at me, and then went on:

---

1. The baritone Jean-Baptiste Faure (1830-1914); he played Hamlet in Ambroise Thomas' opera in 1868.

"Some thirty years ago, a man of strange gait came to establish himself at Etretat. That was not the Etretat of today, where women come to bathe in the sea in colourful costumes, but a simple hamlet of fishermen, tumbledown cottages and orchards—and it was in an authentic thatched cottage, with a thatched roof, in the middle of a plantation of apple-trees, that this unknown person installed himself. There was nothing for the eye to see, extending to the horizon in every direction, but a land of steep slopes planted with beeches and ash-trees, of sunken roads that were always shadowed and always cool, even in the middle of summer. Surrounded by greenery, as I am here, half way up the valley, already far from the sea, it was a perfect artist's retreat in which the great lord became enamoured of solitude.

"No change having been made by the new proprietor, the exterior of the cottage stayed exactly as it was. Only the interior blossomed, it was rumoured, with the luxury of bizarre furniture and wall-hangings: a luxury born of sorcery, or at least of pure hysteria. The rumour was, however, based on furtive glances through open windows, for no one in the district—not even suppliers of merchandise—penetrated into Dolmance.[1]

"Dolmance was the name inscribed in black letters on the front door of that mysterious place. Dolmance: I leave it to you to consider for yourselves, messieurs, the choice of that name by a visitor from abroad. We have all read—or at least tried to read—the work of the divine marquis.

---

1. Dolmance is a character in the Marquis de Sade's *La philosophie dans le boudoir* (1795; tr. as *Philosophy in the Boudoir*). He is the slightly effeminate but vicious cynic who orchestrates and presides over the sexual and sentimental education of the innocent Eugenie, who is transformed under his tutelage into a matricidal monster of depravity.

"Among other marvels, it was said, there was the skeleton of a winged child, posed upright like a laughing Eros, with its head crowned with myrtle, veiled in black gauze, set in the middle of a tangle of flowering laurier-roses, in a long, narrow and high-ceilinged room decorated in violet silk. In another room—this one as bare as a corridor in the catacombs—there was a green bronze bust with eyes of burnished silver encrusted with emeralds: the head of a Renaissance woman with a stony expression, emerging from a wave of bright brocade and rustling material, with a conical head-dress.

"Elsewhere, there was a painted wax head with inanimate eyes and lips half-agape—the bleeding head of some decapitated saint, hanging from a hook on the wall above a large copper basin bordered with red lilies, like a cascade of blood. Finally, in another part of the room, a huge portrait of a woman set in an antique frame encrusted with agate grapes and onyx raisins, worthy of da Vinci, offered you the enigma of her smile. And, everywhere, veils and thrown gauzes complicated the presence of these troubling and mysterious objects. Hostile and symbolic flowers maintained an eternal vigil in the hieratically-formed vases: lilies, anthuriums and orchids, all the flora of mourning, were placed like sacrificial offerings at the foot of every statue . . . an entire interior imprinted with a sombre mysticism that was both Catholic and pagan: a realm of madness, in which the old Coppelius could be glimpsed at rare intervals, via narrow window-panes of archaic design, against a glaucous blue background sanded with gold.

"And no one was seen in the environs of the house . . . no one but the man with the strange gait, showing off his sloping shoulders and his ancient mocking figure behind the high hedge of the courtyard—and, occasionally, two other beings strayed from some dream or nightmare, both at least as disquieting as their master: a child, and a monkey.

"The grimacing and simpering monkey was almost feminine in its attitudes and coquetries. Possessed of an almost human ugliness, it cowered in the half-light of sumptuous rooms in various enamoured poses. It wore a collar of metal embossed with turquoises about its neck, and bracelets around its little black hands. It was really a macaque, but it walked like a child and like a child, knowing that it had to clothe itself, it wore a Spanish dress with puffed sleeves and was always playing with a fan.

As for the actual child, he was a marvel of beauty: a veritable Memling page, fourteen or fifteen years old— one of those boys that Ireland alone can produce, with florid blue eyes and fair hair surrounding the head like a halo of silk: a veritable feast of blond hair and fresh flesh . . . but he lived a wild and solitary existence, even more invisible than the coquettish monkey, jealously and carefully detached and hidden from every eye, like some captive Ariel or some imprisoned princeling of legend.

"All sorts of things had been supposed, imagined and rumoured of that trio . . . but it was the monkey starred with jewels and simpering, rigged out in crisp material, that raised the indignation of the entire neighbourhood.

"What was the truth of the matter?

"One night, the cottage of Dolmance, normally surrounded by silence, was filled with a clamorous uproar. There were exasperated oaths, voices raised in anger, sobs and groans, then a noise of argument and heart-rending appeals, and then a raucous grunting, a death-rattle. . . . All the villagers spent that night standing at their open windows, throats constricted in anguish as they craned their necks in the direction of Dolmance.

"The next day, the local carpenter was summoned to the cottage. He received from the owner an order for a child's coffin, hewn in heart of oak. When the coffin was delivered he was paid twice his asking price. Three days afterwards, the cottage was closed up, its shutters locked and its door nailed shut—and the honourable gentleman disappeared. A post-chaise had come in the night to take him away.

"As for the Memling and the monkey, since the night of groans and appeals, neither one had been seen! Who was the coffin for? The blond child? The macaque? It was a mystery! A crime had undoubtedly been committed, and there was talk for a long time afterwards of jealousy and vengeance. What ties could have bound those three bizarre individuals together? What sinister caprice could have torn them apart?"

"A tale worthy of Hoffmann," de Tracy concluded.

"Or a farce by Vivier,"[1] Georges Moor suggested. "London is a land of fun: fun and cold farce, sinister and exasperating. England is the fatherland of those gaieties, as sharp and cutting as a razor-blade. The honourable George Selwyn was probably just a macabre hoaxer, having mugged up on his Swift and his Poe."

"It's always the way," Asseline took up the story again. "Two months afterwards, a removal van came to take away the movable effects of Dolmance. The name of the domain disappeared from the front door and the hovel, the

---

1. Eugène Vivier (1817-1900) was a leading comedian in late-19th century Paris.

meadow and the surrounding orchard were all put up for sale by Master Réparon, the notary at Criquetot, whereby my father acquired it. The Villa des Saules is the old Dolmance; you are, my friends, on the site of the mystery...."

We all looked Asseline in the eyes. He had calmly taken his place at the gaming table. The rain began to fall again, even harder than before, and the great beeches in the garden, shaken by the squall, bent their rustling boughs madly.

One January Night

"I BELIEVE that you are developing quite a taste for fantastic stories!"

So saying, Guillory—who had surprised me *in flagrante delicto*—took up an old Elsevier edition of the *Tales of Hoffmann*. I had come across it while ferreting around in a sort of attic, which served as Guillory's library.[1] I had gone into it in his absence, with the authorisation of Madame Guillory—and comfortably installed in a large winged armchair, I had spent at least an hour leafing through the tasty and intoxicating stories of the German fantasist, delighted by the godsend of a story that I had not previously read in any edition of his works: "Albertine's Wooers".[2] Guillory's

---

1. The character of Guillory was introduced in an earlier and slighter story, "Chez Guillory", likewise reprinted in *Un démoniaque*; he is an antique-dealer whose private collection of rare first editions—including most of the texts that inspired the writers of the Decadent Movement—is not for sale.

2. With one exception I have substituted the English titles by which the cited tales by E. T. A. Hoffmann are usually known. The French title of "Albertine's Wooers" cited by Lorrain, whose English equivalent would be "The Choice of a Bride", is slightly more faithful to the original, "Die Brautwahl". "The Lost Reflection" is also known as "A New Year's Eve Adventure". The exception is "Doctor Cinnabar", which I have translated straightforwardly from Lorrain's "Docteur Cinabre". The reference is to Hoffmann's märchen "Klein Zaches gennant Zinnabar" (1819); I have been unable to trace any English

arrival had interrupted me in the middle of the stirring adventures of the private secretary Tussmann, waltzing in spite of himself in Spandaustrasse with a dirty broom in his arms, with a thousand other Tussmanns dancing around him, all with brooms for partners.

"Yes," I replied. "I love them, and I have the highest opinion of the master of 'The Golden Pot'. How the devil did you dig up this volume? You'll let me have it, won't you? I'll buy it from you, if that's all right. How much do you want?"

"Not at any price, even for you. That edition's impossible to find—but you can carry on reading it, and you can come back any time you like. My, how red you've gone. You look as if you're about ready to have an attack of apoplexy—that's what you get for keeping company with Krespel and old Coppelius; they're the sort of people you shouldn't visit too frequently, Monsieur Jean. You'll end up seeing the heads of foxes on the shoulders of your friends, just like poor old Tussmann. At least you didn't mistake my servant for an ostrich—the gigantic and deceptive ostrich that opened the door to visitors and startled the Mock family with its beautiful manners in 'Doctor Cinnabar'."

"Ah, 'Doctor Cinnabar'—a masterpiece of the fantastic, how very original! Hoffmann is the veritable master of the nightmare. A single word, a single detail within the simplest and most naturalistic story, and boom! It's like striking the gong of madness; you lose your footing and fall into the supernatural. When that ostrich in 'Doctor Cinnabar' comes to open the door and coolly welcomes

---

translation of this story—or, for that matter, a French translation under the title Lorrain cites, although it had certainly appeared in French as "Petit Zacharie, surnommé Cinabre".

flabbergasted visitors to his master's house—myself, I find that simply marvelous."

"With good reason, Monsieur Jean. Among nightmarish works, that's the finest, the very best—but there's no need to go so far afield to find the strange and the supernatural. That beer-swilling Hoffmann was well-served by his brilliant imagination, I'll grant you that, but his circumstances were a great help too. In the smoky environment of those old Heidelberg drinking-dens, surrounded by all the ugly faces of those bewigged lawyers, dressed in the fashion of the last century, the scary silhouettes of 'Cardillac the Jeweller' and 'The Sandman' virtually foisted themselves on his intoxicated eyes. Hoffmann was a heavy drinker, as you know, and a heavy smoker too. In the dead of night, as he left whichever bar he'd been loitering in, with his head reeling from the effects of tobacco and English beer, he'd doubtless have had the most mysterious encounters in the Medieval and quasi-fantastic streets of Spandau and Heidelberg. Have you noticed the obsessive frequency with which he reproduces nocturnal scenes set in inns in the majority of his tales? It's always in such places that his heroes encounter the ambiguous characters who undergo sudden metamorphoses, who dog their footsteps thereafter and never let up."

"It is after leaving the cafe where he habitually passed his evenings that the private secretary Tussmann approaches the terrible Leonard. It is in a tavern, where the stranger is having supper, that he witnesses the frightful juggling of the old Jew and Cardillac the Jeweller. Finally, in 'The Lost Reflection' it is while leaving a dance held in Master Thiermann's dive that Hoffmann himself makes the acquaintance, between a tankard and a tobacco pipe, of General

Souwaroff, the man who has lost his reflection, and of poor Spricken, the man who has sold his shadow. It always happens there, between eleven o'clock and midnight on moonless nights, after drinking, while everything is shaken by gusts of wind and the weathervanes on the roofs creak and screech like cats in heat.

"But the nights of modern Paris are just as full of inexplicable apparitions, unexplained and terrifying—even though, God knows, the environment scarcely lends itself to such manifestations, with our wide and dead straight streets, brightly lit by gas and electricity. Bah! Under the influence of a vivid imagination, overexcited by a good dinner, aided and abetted by the memory of things he had read, confronted by an utterly trivial incident, even the most well-balanced of men, healthy in body and in spirit—Guillory himself—may become a visionary."

"What? Even you, Guillory!"

"Even me—my very own adventure of the kind from which the fantasist Hoffmann would have profited. It has been imprinted on my memory ever since. It was something more than chance that I saw what I saw that night; it was almost like a revelation from the afterlife—those who know about such things would call it a communication from Beyond. Now, the Guillory family has no truck with spirits that I know of; to tell you the truth, all this has been troubling my head for a long time, all the more so because there were coincidences. . . . But you don't want to be here all night, so I won't bore you. This is the story:

"It was two years ago, at the end of January. The hard frost that had suddenly descended on Twelfth Night had lasted for a fortnight; not a day went past without some miserable soul being found frozen to death and the Seine was full of drifting ice. I had dined in Paris, at a kind of annual banquet of old. . . . I would tell you that they were old librarians, but you wouldn't believe me . . . old, at any rate . . . you know what I mean: retired to live in the sun, as men of means, producing wine and raising dairy-cattle, jolly fellows all. A great deal of fine wine had been drunk, without regard to the expense—there were two or three of our number with exceedingly good cellars.

"To be brief, at about one in the morning I found myself on the pavement at the upper end of the Pont-Neuf, a little worse for wear but steady on my feet—and, of course, a long way from Auteuil. No more omnibuses, no more trains from Saint-Lazare. I hailed a carriage with green lanterns—its driver was on his way back to Grenelle.

"'A hundred sous to take me to Billancourt,' I said to the coachman. 'It's a straight run, along the river by the Route de Versailles.' So there I was, rolling along the quays, tossed about on the cushions, with the winter moon full and white against a grey sky, which put me in mind of a vast expanse of iron filings. Eventually, I dozed off.

"I was sound asleep when it seemed to me that the cab stopped.

"Bah! I told myself. It's just a dream, sleep on—but no, we were no longer on the move. That's bad, I told myself. Does this hack take me for a mug? And I suddenly woke up, and opened the door.

"'Hey, Coachman!' I said. 'Are you messing me about?'

"But the man, whose long scarf was wrapped around his face, so that only his eyes showed above it, said: 'Excuse me, squire, but I can't go any further. My horse has lost the shoes from both forefeet and you'll have to get out. Anyway, you're half way there—it's not far.'

"'What? Only half-way!'

"We were just above the Passy footbridge, outside Doctor Blanche's establishment[1]—a nice spot to be at two in the morning, between the parapet of the quay and that set of high walls.

"'Tell you what, squire, if you'd rather sleep, I'll let you use my cab—but it'll be three francs an hour. Me, I'll unhitch Cocotte and lead her back to the depot.'

"I gave in, grumbling. I gave two francs to the coachman and he took off for the Pont de Grenelle with his limping horse and rig. So there I was, all alone, on the Quai de Passy, a castaway, not even the shadow of a policeman in the distance, all the cafes on the quay dead as a doornail, their shutters closed—and how cold it was! The night-shelters, if you recall, were overflowing that winter.

"I set my feet to march briskly, in order to warm myself up, when I suddenly found myself in front of a detached house with brightly-lit windows: a two-storey Louis XVI house wedged between higher walls. The ground floor was raised above a basement, with wrought iron balconies at its French windows. A petty tax-farmer's house, abruptly looming up before me on the quay—how odd! I had never really noticed it in broad daylight. Was I sure that I had ever seen it at all?

"I was seized by a devilish curiosity. I approached the house, clutched at the iron railings of one of the balconies, and used the strength of my arms to hoist myself up

---

1 Antoine Émile Blanche (1820-1893) was a noted alienist. His clinic at Passy had been established by his father in 1846. Guy de Maupassant had died there in July 1893 having been a patient there since January 1892, and Lorrain presumably had this in mind while writing the story.

and look inside . . . and I saw, as clearly as I see you, a panelled room illuminated by a candelabra; and a totally naked woman stretched out on her belly on a table, arms and legs akimbo, her hands and her feet strapped to the legs. A man clad as a Marquis, in purplish velvet, was cutting into her flesh with a scalpel. A veritable nightmare!

"The man had his back turned towards me; I barely had time to see his wig, but I had seen quite enough and I was already on my way, as you may well imagine. . . .

"I must have been dreaming, for the next day I went back along the entire length of the Route de Versailles, but I found no trace of that little Louis XVI house. It had vanished—and at the place where I had seen it on the evening before rose the walls of the Sanfourche veterinary hospital.

"It was nothing but the hallucination of a man who had had a little too much to drink—so, some time later, having bought an old guide-book of Paris, with views of various districts, I could not have recognised in one of the engravings the little house of my visionary night! But it was the spitting image, with the railings at the windows. And do you know what the guide-book had to say about that criminal house?

"It was the Pavillon de Sablons, the home of Monsieur d'Hérauville, sold in May 1778 to the Marquis de Sade."

The Spectral Hand

WHEN the world was rocked by the scandal of the murder of the Comtesse d'Orthyse, my friend Jacques and I were by no means as astonished as everyone else. We had known for some time what a tragic end that adorable woman was destined to meet, for an irrefutable sign had been shown to us—although had we told anyone else what we knew we would probably have been deemed mad. We even knew, by virtue of the revelation vouchsafed to us, whose brutal hand it was that would put a revolver to her heart and destroy her.

※

It all happened two years ago, when the woman in question had not yet become the second Comtesse d'Orthyse. She was the widow of the Marquis de Strada. She was still in the full flower of her enduring beauty, and was famed in Parisian Society for her taste, her flamboyance and her elegance. A portrait by Whistler shown at Champ-de-Mars had made her the most fashionable woman of that season. Her gowns—made up by a theatrical costumier from fabrics obtainable only from Chez Morice in London, in accordance with unpublished patterns by Burne-Jones—

wrought a revolution among the couturiers of Paris. In all the clubs and boudoirs of the city people discussed reports of her dressing-room, whose lacquered green chairs were each encrusted with a trefoil of diamonds, and whose Dresden china bath-tub, supported by three bronze Japanese frogs, was the epitome of symbolic extravagance.

The luncheons and dinner-parties the Marquise held—where artists, poets and painters gathered, and from which other women were virtually excluded—were also a perennial topic of conversation. Her little town-house in the Place des États-Unis, and its antechamber with white enamelled walls and carpets like snowdrifts, was the centre of attention of the entire tribe of society reporters. The Comte de Montesquiou was regularly to be seen there, with his ornamental cane and his blue hydrangeas. The smart set had quite forgotten the road to Versailles; the fashionable pilgrimage of the day was to the drawing-room of the Mansion Strada, with its drapes of rose-coloured Pékin and its furniture by Riesener.

On the evening with which my story is concerned there had been an intimate dinner at the home of the Marquise. Apart from Jacques and myself the only guests were Henry Tramsel and the poet Pierre de Lisse. The Marquise was deliciously displayed in one of those close-fitting and flexible gowns whose secret only she knew. To surprise her, we had bedecked her dining-table with yellow tulips; there were tulips in clusters about the candelabras, tulips in sheaves in the silver centrepiece, tulips scattered like rushes about the tablecloth. The conversation—whose principal topics were art and literature—was sparkling; it extended from the new illustrations for Grimm's tales done by Walter Crane to the recent acquisition by the Louvre of nightmarish paintings by Breughel and Hokusai, taking *en passant* Maeterlinck and the Goncourts, Ibsen and Outamaro.

Afterwards, we retired to the drawing-room, following in the wake of the rustling train of the marquise's gown. The train was the colour of mauve hydrangeas, a mauve that was almost pink, like the rosy hue of a dewy dawn, but which became blue when it was shadowed. We sat down again, the marquise stretching herself out among the cushions of a narrow couch, delicately nibbling the long stem of a tulip she had picked up from the table. She told us all about some strange and mysterious event that she recalled from childhood. While she related the story, it seemed that she became again the little girl that she had been, rather than the young woman she now was, all a-shiver with the thrilling fear of the supernatural.

Once the subject had been broached, the conversation took up the occult theme, sliding easily into a discussion of magic, spiritualism and all the mysterious sciences that so fascinate our tired and enervated *fin-de-siècle*. Someone mentioned the phenomenon of table-turning, and the marquise immediately came to her feet, rang for a servant and demanded a small round table. She was suddenly animated by a fervent interest that coloured her pale features; the superstitious aspect of her child-like personality had been stirred up by the notion of invoking the spirit-world and bringing about some incursion of the marvellous. She paced back and forth, her hands fluttering wildly. Her former indolence had turned into a fever, and she continually glanced about the huge ruddily-illuminated drawing-room, as if expecting spirits to manifest themselves at any moment.

Unfortunately, the marquise's home was furnished in such a manner that a table of the necessary size could not be found—all the tables she had were in the English style of the previous century. After a few fruitless attempts to persuade the spirits to tilt a little copper stand we were compelled to abandon that particular line of enquiry. In any case, the marquise, with her eternal tulip lodged between her lips, kept interrupting the circle in order to make sure that the flower was still secure. This failure irritated our beautiful but short-tempered hostess, so much so that Henri Tramsel proposed that we should try another method of evocation, which he called "the spectral hand".

We asked him what he meant by that, and he assured us that it was one of the most certain means by which the living might enter into communication with the dead. It required, he said, a very particular set of conditions—but the marquise's drawing-room, which was connected to the dining-room by a large curtained bay, was ideal. He warned us solemnly, however, that the experiment was dangerous, and that it would require stern courage and strength of character.

"Dangerous?" responded the marquise. "Oh, how delicious! What must we do?"

Henry Tramsel put out all save one of the shaded lamps that illuminated the huge chamber, and he required all five of us to sit down before the soft silk curtains that hung in the bay separating the drawing-room from the dining-room.

"The first necessity," he said, in a very solemn voice, "is to believe. None of us has the least doubt as to the immortality of the soul, isn't that so? We all accept the reality of spirits and other invisible beings that exist all around us, and the possibility that there is a world beyond our own, existing in parallel with it, into whose mysteries we desire to be initiated.

We all nodded our heads in acquiescence, a little discomfited by the profound silence that had suddenly taken possession of the room. Only a moment before, it had been filled with luminous gaiety, but now it had been invaded by a host of shadows, which stirred strangely in the flickering light of the one remaining lamp. That lamp had a shade of bluish gauze with a design representing the head of an owl, and it surrounded us with a curiously lunar light. The billowing pleats of the great awning of soft silk that separated us from the pitch-dark dining-room acted strangely upon our imagination. The five of us sat side by side, facing the drapes, as if they were the curtains of a theatre, and the imperial harp that the marquise had set to stand in an alcove beside the bay confirmed the impression of a dramatic spectacle.

"This is what must be done," Henri continued. "I shall attempt to invoke an invisible presence, requesting it to manifest itself by means of a sensation of coldness. Whichever one of us experiences that sensation most keenly is the one who is chosen to be summoned. His duty is to get up, and extend his hand into the gap between the curtains, into the dark void beyond. There he must wait until his hand is gripped by another, at which point he may ask questions of the spirit that has come."

With a slight shiver, Henri Tramsel addressed his brief prayer to the spirits, invoking the souls of those departed whom we had held most dear. The strangest thing happened! It was as if a sudden current of air blew from the deserted dining room. It brought us briefly to our feet.

Was it an illusion born of apprehension? For myself, I distinctly felt a chill in my blood, and a constriction in my heart, but none of us dared make the decision to step forward until Henri accepted the responsibility himself. Approaching the bay, he dared to stretch out his hand and insert it into the gap between the curtains of pale silk.

Several minutes passed, during which interval we scarcely allowed ourselves to breathe, but in the end Henri said: "My hand feels a little heavy, but nothing more. Let someone else try."

Pierre de Lisse took his turn to extend his hand into the shadowed room, and then the marquise took hers. I replaced her, feeling the hairs stand up on the back of my hand as I did so. The sensation of cold increased; I reported, as the others also had, that my hand became heavy—but no obvious contact was made, nothing touched my flesh.

Jacques was the only one who refused to take his turn, which he did with determined obstinacy. We were amused by his fearful reluctance, and had just begun to carry forward the experiment by taking our turns again, in a far lighter mood, when we suddenly saw him grow pale. He lifted himself from his seat and took a few steps forward, his eyes huge and round—and then he fell down at the foot of the harp, whose strings gave out a muted groan.

He had certainly seen something; the invisible had undoubtedly made itself manifest. We immediately crowded around him and lifted him up.

The lamps were relit, filling the room with a roseate glow. We harassed him with questions regarding his experience, but he said that he had seen nothing, that it was an ordinary dizzy spell without any evident cause. Plainly, he did not wish to reveal what he had seen.

Some time afterwards, I visited Jacques in his studio.

"You have known the family of the marquise for a long time, have you not?" he asked me, rather brusquely. "You used to visit her home when you were a child, did you not?"

When I answered in the affirmative, he went on: "The other evening in the Place des États-Unis, when I had a fit of dizziness during that imprudent spiritualist séance, I did, in fact, see something—but I dared not say what it was at the time, for fear that I might strike terror, perhaps irremediably, into someone's heart."

"What was it, then?" I asked. "What did you see?"

"As soon as Henri Tramsel took up his station for a second time," he said, "a female figure—which was at first as faint as smoke—appeared plainly to me, leaning against the frame of that imperial harp. She was dressed in a manner that was fashionable five or six years ago, and she stared fixedly at the marquise."

"The Marquise de Strada?"

"Exactly. And you know, don't you, what it signifies when a spectre of that kind looks long and hard at one of the living?"

I did not, and said so.

"It is," he said, "an infallible indication of approaching death. The figure appeared, moreover, to have an expression of infinite sadness and infinite pity. That face has haunted my dreams ever since, and I have painted it from memory, in order that I might show it to you. You knew the Duchesse d'Esparre, who was the mother of the marquise, and you will be sure to recognise her, if that is who the spectre was."

He abruptly turned around a canvas so that I might look at it. It held the image of a young girl, dressed in white—but there was not the slightest resemblance to the Duchesse d'Esparre. The name of another woman, whom I had also known quite well, sprang instead to my lips.

"The Comtesse d'Orthyse!"

It was the first wife of the man whom the marquise was later to marry—although we did not know that at the time. We could not understand, then, why that particular spectre should have sought to communicate with the elegant and charming young widow of the Marquis de Strada. But the inexplicable vision acquired a terrible significance six months later, when the marquise announced that she was to marry the handsome Émery de Montenor, whose several titles included that of Comte d'Orthyse.

※

I will never forget the circumstances in which the proposed union was announced to us. It chanced that we had come together again, Jacques and myself, at an afternoon gathering at the home of our beautiful friend. She was dressed in white, as though she were already a bride, and while the hot tea was poured from the samovar she nibbled—as was her habit—a red rose with a long stem, which was on the point of shedding its leaves.

While she told us of her forthcoming marriage, making the announcement with such a mischievous insouciance, as if she were announcing a dinner party, three petals detached themselves from the rose and came to rest like three large spots of blood upon her corseted bosom; at precisely that moment she pronounced the name d'Orthyse, and Jacques and I each experienced a sudden constriction of the heart. Jacques went eerily pale, and I thought that I would be compelled to prop him up—but the marquise's salon was very crowded that day, and we were able to leave without attracting too much attention.

"He will murder her," Jacques said to me, as soon as we were outside. "That etheric phantom, of the first Comtesse d'Orthyse, was behind her again today. He will kill her, with a revolver shot to the heart. Did you see the three drops of blood shed by the rose? They did not fall by chance!"

Subsequent events, alas, showed all too clearly that we were not deceived.

Prey to Darkness

HENRI TRAMSEL had been asleep for four days. His sleep was extraordinarily calm and profound; his face was relaxed, his breathing regular, his strength utterly annihilated. Some treason of the nervous system had put him into a kind of coma, or suspended animation.

It had taken hold of him one Saturday night—or, more accurately, in the early hours of Sunday morning—after his return from a spiritualist séance organised, as something of a lark, by a friend from the salon. Tramsel had gone to bed, according to his habit, but on the following morning neither his valet nor, eventually, his mother had been able to rouse him from that strange sleep. A doctor was called, then two; a cautery of wormwood had been burned on his skin, which was then cut by a scalpel. The blood had run red and clear, but the patient had not responded. His face remained calm and white. His lips were scarcely stirred by the rhythm of his respiration but the teeth that displayed a thin line of enamel between them were curiously clenched. When the doctor's fingertips gently lifted his eyelids the whites of his eyes looked like tarnished silver, the two pupils being withdrawn as if departed who knew where.

His limp hands, which Madame Tramsel continually lifted in order to take his temperature, remained warm and gentle as they lay, inertly, outstretched on the coverlet—but the quality of that softness began, in the end, to raise gooseflesh on the arm of anyone who touched him. This was neither lethargy nor hypnotism, but rather a suspension of vitality, which became deeper and deeper as the hours went by. The young man's breast rose and fell like a blacksmith's bellows, in long and measured beats, and the resultant breaths resonated in his bronchi as if in an organ-pipe.

The doctors were mystified.

Madame Tramsel had already kept vigil in the bedroom for three nights. An intolerable odour had seeped into the air, irritating the nostrils and the throat: a savage and strident odour of the wilderness, like burnt mastic; a musky stink reminiscent of an animal's den, or hides in a tannery, or a cage in the zoo where lions were kept—or all of these things at once. The windows had been opened wide and the fixtures sprayed with scent, but to no avail. The foetid stink continued to permeate not merely the room but the entire apartment in the Rue Michel-Ange, as if it were some evil and pestilential menagerie. Strangely enough, it was the slumbering body—although it seemed perfectly healthy—that was emitting the heavy and infamous odour, which sickened the doctors and made Madame Tramsel's vigil seem ill-advised. Ammonia had now been recruited to fight it—one evil odour against another—but the warm perfume exhaled by the prostrate Tramsel was so strong that it continued to hold sway, like a deadening miasma suspended above the drawn and distressed faces. It was that same odour, born of Tramsel's sleep, that was gradually deepening his unconsciousness, poisoning him by slow degrees.

The doctors had no more suggestions to offer. In the extremity of her desperation, Madame Tramsel's maternal intuition urged her to make her own inquiries at the house where her son had taken part in the séance, in case he had lent himself to some dangerous experiment in suggestion. Perhaps, after all, the unnatural sleep that was killing her son was an effect of animal magnetism.

On the fateful evening, Henri Tramsel had dined at the home of the Marquise de Strada, the eccentric and seductive young woman of whose tragic and mysterious end I have already related to you.[1] Madame Tramsel did not know the woman who would become—and would die—the Comtesse d'Orthyse, but that did not lessen her determination to go to her. The information that she received in the Place des États-Unis confirmed her suspicions. There was a mystery, if not an active maleficence, in Henri Tramsel's sleep.

On the evening in question, Henri had temporarily taken his place in the medium's seat around a turning table. In the presence and under the direction of Marcius de Gorre, the well-known thaumaturge, the spirits had deigned to manifest themselves in the Marquise's home that evening. The very tables had talked. Warm breaths, silky and gentle, had caressed the faces of the participants. The names of known demons, such as Beelzebub and Belphegor, had been spelled out by the tapping feet of the pedestal table.

---

1. In "The Spectral Hand". Lorrain seems to have intended these stories to be elements in a continuing series but it proceeded no further, although the novella "Un démoniaque" took up some of the themes of Tramsel's visions. Lorrain's split with Jeanne Jacquemin must have happened soon after this story was written, and that might well have had something to do with his loss of interest in the pretensions of fashionable occultism.

The exceedingly over-excited Henri, identified by the mage himself as a centre of nervous energy, extremely sensitive to the action of the spirits, had stayed until the very end.

The reflex action of the invisible must have continued when her son went home; that was the cause of the unyielding sleep that now afflicted his eyes.

A telegram was immediately dispatched to Marcius de Gorre, bringing the thaumaturgical scholar to the patient's bedside that same evening. As soon as he set foot on the threshold the particular odour of the apartment had warned the seer what to expect.

"As I expected," he said to the unhappy mother, "your son has fallen prey to Assyrian demons; the spirits of the night have possessed him. Do you smell that odour? It is the odour of the wilderness, of the dismal deserts of Babylon and Nineveh. There, it is the perfume of the spirits of Asshur, which generates the laughter of hyenas and jackals in rut amid the rubble and the fallen columns of dead cities." Then, having taken the soft pale hand of the stricken man, he said: "It's the fourth day, isn't it? I've arrived just in time." Turning to Doctor Simpson, he added: "Why didn't you send for me sooner, doctor? It's obvious that what we have here is a case of mesmeric sleep."

The Englishman only shrugged his shoulders, but the thaumaturge was no longer paying attention. He took the precaution of closing the windows, and carefully distributed nine candles on the chest of drawers, placing three incense-burners among them. Then he went into the next room, declaring his intention to purify his hands and prepare the necessary aromatic spices. He came back almost immediately, his hands anointed with verbena, dressed in a long white robe with a breast-plate studded with beryls and magical stones secured about his neck. Having called for silence, he approached the bed and placed a hand sparkling with rings upon the forehead of the sleeper.

Then, in the uncertain light of the room, illuminated like a memorial chapel, a faint and distant voice that was no longer that of Tramsel, but rather its oh-so-distant echo, let loose a plaintive sigh.

"Quiet! He's going to speak—and you, Madame, write down what your son says. As soon as we have recorded the vision by which he is obsessed, the patient will be delivered."

De Gorre released the sick man's hand for a moment in order to set odorant powders to burn in the glowing embers of the incense-burners. He returned to Tramsel's bedside and placed his hand on the sleeper's forehead for a second time.

Within the smoky chamber—which already seemed half-filled with moving blue gauze as the odours of incense, cinnamon and myrrh swirled around the white-robed mage, creating an atmosphere suggestive of the temple of some ancient Oriental cult—the distant voice began its lament anew, chanting in a monkish fashion.

※

"Why has she put on such a strange dress this evening, and why does she always smile when she looks at me? I love that V-shaped cleavage, opening like the calyx of a flower, the embrace of all that blue jet, rustling and coruscating like armour. Her eyes have the same gleam in them . . . so why is she looking at me like that? I don't like that smile, and if I were alone with her this evening I think that

I would cry out in anguish—but fortunately, the others are here! Why have the tables not been turned? I haven't come here for her to stare at me with those two cold blue eyes, piercing as a gimlet. What's Marcius de Gorre doing, then? She's standing before me now. De Lisse and de Romer have made her lift up the hem of her dress so that they can better admire the serpents of blue jet that she has embroidered on it. They are lifting it higher, holding the scintillating richness and laughing, affording a glimpse of the bust and slender figure enclosed within the gauze, and it seems as if she is at the centre of an enormous, sinister and glittering spider's web. Oh, I don't like that at all!

"Asmodeus, the spirit of disquiet and disturbance, the demon of great cities, of morphine-addicts, of neurotics, of weary orgiasts, of curious sensualists, the demon of all occult researchers, men and women alike . . . and the demon of ether too. Ether! It's three years since I last took any: why has that table said that it is Asmodeus, that he loves me tenderly and that he will never leave me?[1] See here, de Gorre, tell me that this spirit is nothing but some miserable larva. But then, all this is just for fun—I've seen de Romer pushing the pedestal table, the table isn't moving of its own accord. . . .

"Where am I? Where did those stumps of ancient porticos and long fragments of column come from? My God, what a mess! And those old mutilated statues, their pedestals buried in the sand! How did they get here—how did I

---

1. Asmodeus was the demon most familiar to French writers and readers, having played the starring role in Alain René le Sage's *Le Diable boiteux* (1707; tr. as *The Devil on Two Sticks*). Released from a bottle after the fashion of the captive djinn in the Arabian Nights, Asmodeus lifts the lid on the follies and hypocrisies of contemporary Paris by raising the roofs of the lightly-disguised "Madrid".

get here! Where have I seen this ruined city before? Not a blade of grass, nor a leaf of ivy . . . sand and more sand, everywhere . . . such a strange wilderness. Not a bird in the sky . . . how quiet it is! But how sweet the air seems! I love this dead city bathed in moonlight. How brightly it reflects from the porphyry of those columns! Oh! Something moved close by, in the darkness. There's an arch there whose shadow is threatening me, truly . . . and where could those ruffling feathers have come from, since the city is dead and devoid of birds?

"Oh! Oh! That time I saw eyes within the shadows . . . points of flame, no, diamond studs . . . stars reflected in some watery pool . . . but there's not a drop of water in the desert and the stars have fallen from the sky. . . . I love those murmurous words whispered in my ear, I love the attenuated consonants and soft vowels of that language, which I don't understand. . . .

"The portico and the steles are inhabited now. Is it the caryatids that animate them? But I have never seen such gentle female faces. Oh! They're coming closer, forming a circle around me! No, they're immobile now; they're the colour of ash, wearing conical head-dresses and tiaras like the priestesses of Indra. I'm not afraid, and yet I'm shivering. I've seen these figures before, somewhere—but where? I recall now: in Gustave Moreau's famous watercolour of Salome dancing . . . no, it's Sarah's smile.[1]

"Take me away from those two figures in Chinese porcelain who are mocking me, laughing at me from the mantelpiece. In the thousand years since they first shook their heads and stuck out their tongues they've made my head go soft. Don't you see that with every movement of their

---

1. Presumably Sarah Bernhardt.

porcelain heads my own head tosses and turns? Oh, my head, my head! Throw them in the bucket—yes, the toilet bucket into which I just emptied all the old flowers from my study, the black irises and the guilder-roses . . . but mind the spun-glass frog that I put in the bottom to keep it fresh: if you break it, I shall die.

"She's under my bed, I tell you. I hear her roaring and marching back and forth: she's a dreadful spider, a death's-head, a frightful laughing death's-head, who runs back and forth on long hairy legs, the legs of a giant crab, all red . . . she has drunk so much blood! I hear her, I tell you, as she darns her web with the thread from her spinneret beneath my bed; if you don't chase her away, she'll come out when you're gone and climb on top of me and bite my neck. Aaah. . . !"

And with a loud cry, the sleeper awoke.

"The spirits have departed," said Marius de Gorre. "Quick! Open the windows and light all the candles to banish the darkness from the room. Madame, your son is healed." And he favoured Madame Tramsel with a deep bow.

She put down her pen and mopped her forehead, still all a-quiver.

CONTES

The Princess of the Red Lilies

THERE was a cold and austere child of kings. Scarcely sixteen years old, she had the grey eyes of an eagle set beneath raised eyebrows, and her skin was so white that one might have thought that her hands were made of wax and her face of pearl. Her name was Audovere.

The daughter of an old warrior king, who was always occupied in distant conquests when he was not defending the borders of his realm, she had grown up in a convent, among the tombs of the kings of her race. She had no memory of her mother or her birth; she spent her early childhood in the charge of the nuns.

The convent in which she had spent the sixteen years of her life was situated in the shady silence of a secular forest. Only the king knew the path that led to it, and the princess had never seen the face of any man other than her father. It was a harsh place, hidden from highways and by-ways alike; nothing penetrated its depths but the sunlight, which was considerably weakened as it made its way through the dense overarching foliage of the oaks.

At vespers, Princess Audovere sometimes went outside the convent wall and strolled at a leisurely pace, escorted on either side by two groups of nuns, each in single file. She was serious and thoughtful, as if she were oppressed by the weight of a secret trust, so pale that one might have thought that she would soon die.

A long robe of white wool, whose hem was embroidered with large gold trefoils, hung down to her feet. A light veil of blue gauze fastened to a circlet of engraved silver about her head subdued the shade of her blonde hair. Audovere was as blonde as lily-pollen, and her lips were slightly paler than the ruby-red of old altar vases.

And that was her life. Patiently, with her heart full of hopeful joy—as another woman might have awaited the return of her intended bridegroom—she waited in the convent for the return of her father, the king. Her favourite pastime was to devote her thoughts to imagine the battles he fought, the perils he endured, the armies he commanded and the princes he massacred in the wake of his triumphs.

In April, the surrounding slopes were covered with primulas. In autumn, they were bloodstained by bare clay and fallen leaves. And in April as in October, as eager in June as in November, always cold and pale in her white woollen robe embroidered with gold trefoils, Audovere walked beneath the green or russet oaks, in perpetual silence.

In summer, she would sometimes pick the great white lilies that grew in the convent garden; she was so frail and white herself that she might have been taken for their sister. In autumn, it was the foxgloves that she twirled between her fingers—purple foxgloves plucked at the edges of forest glades—and the sickly pink of her lips came to resemble the wine-redness of the flowers. Strangely enough, she never pulled the petals off the foxgloves, although she kissed them often, as if mechanically; on the other hand, her fingers seemed to take pleasure in shredding the lilies. A cruel smile would then draw her lips half-open.

It was as if she were performing some obscure rite—as if her actions corresponded, after the fashion of a distant echo, to some dark and bloody ceremony that was happening elsewhere.

Which, in fact, they were.

Each gesture of the virgin princess was connected to the suffering and death of a man. The old king knew that perfectly well. He was in distant possession of the eyes and the baleful virginity hidden in that unknown convent. The complicit princess knew it too: hence her smile, when she kissed the foxgloves or crushed the lilies slowly between her beautiful fingertips.

Each lily spoiled was the corpse of a prince or a young warrior killed in battle, each foxglove kissed an open wound, a gaping cut giving vent to the heart's blood.

Princess Audovere no longer kept count of her distant victories. In the four years that had been fully aware of the charm she had become ever more prodigal in lavishing her kisses on the poisonous red flowers and increasingly ruthless in her destruction of the guileless lilies. Giving death with a kiss and taking life with an embrace, she was her royal father's mysterious executioner and funeral aide-decamp. Every evening the chaplain of the convent, an old blind Barnabite,[1] heard her confession and absolved her of her sins—for the sins of royalty only work to the damnation of the common people, and the odour of cadavers is incense at the foot of the throne of God.

---

1. The Order of Barnabites was founded by Antony Zaccaria in 1530, in honour of the apostle who introduced Paul to the other apostles and undertook the first missionary journey in his company.

The Princess Audovere was devoid of remorse or sadness. No sooner was she made aware that absolution had purified her than death-rattles sounded in the fields of battle and the nights of destruction and severed limbs were brandished at the red sky. Princes, mercenaries and beggars offered up their pleas for mercy to proud virgins, but virgins do not react to blood with the anguished horror of mothers—mothers forever trembling for their much-loved sons—and Audovere was, above all else, her father's daughter.

One night, having reached the unknown convent by some freak of chance, a wretched fugitive beat on the door of the holy shelter, crying like a baby. He was drenched in sweat and black with dirt and his wretched body was bleeding from seven wounds. The nuns took him in, cleaned him up and lodged him among the tombs in the crypt, more out of fright than pity. A pitcher of iced water was placed beside him so that he might slake his thirst, along with a sprinkler of holy water and a crucifix, to ease the passing of his sinful life—for he was already at his last gasp, his breast congested by the onset of his final anguish.

At nine o'clock, in the refectory, the superior recited the prayer for the dead on the wounded man's behalf, and the nuns, somewhat distressed, returned to their cells. Then the convent fell asleep.

Audovere alone remained awake, thinking about the fugitive. She had scarcely caught a glimpse of him as he crossed the garden, supported by the arms of two aged sisters and a single thought obsessed her: the agonised man was undoubtedly an enemy of her father, some deserter who had escaped a massacre, a cowardly and panic-stricken derelict run aground at last at the convent.

The battle must have taken place in the neighbourhood, much closer than the nuns suspected, and the forest must at that very moment be full of other runaways. An entire host of bleeding, whimpering wretches, suffering and pustulant, with stumps where arms and legs once would be laying siege to the convent walls by dawn, waiting to receive the charity of the nuns.

It was the middle of July, and the long flowerbeds were perfumed by lilies. Princess Audovere went downstairs and across the garden, advancing upon the tall moonlight-bathed stems, upstanding in the night like moist spears—and she began, slowly, to strip the petals from the flowers.

But the flowers, by some mystical means, exhaled sighs and emitted death-rattles, weeping and pleading. Beneath the pressure of her fingers, the petals acquired the texture and resistance of flesh. Something warm fell upon her hands, which she took at first for tears, and the scent of the lilies, strangely transformed, suddenly became disgusting, heavy and insipid. It was as if their cups were full of noxious incense.

Although she was near to fainting, Audovere stuck to her task, continuing her murderous work, decapitating the calices without pity, shredding the corollas without respite—but for every flower that was cut down, more than one was regenerated, and the host became innumerable. There was now an entire field of tall rigid flowers, sprouting in a hostile manner beneath her feet: a veritable army of four-petalled pikes and halberds blooming in the moonlight. Desperately weary but gripped by a vertiginous destructive rage, the princess went on and on shredding, murdering, pulverising everything before her, until a strange vision stopped her in her tracks.

From a spray of taller flowers, bluishly translucent, the cadaver of a man emerged. With his arms extended as if on a cross and his feet clenched one atop the other, he displayed in the darkness the wounds in his left side and his bleeding hands. There was a crown of thorns splattered with mud and pus about his head. The frightened princess recognised the wretched fugitive who had been taken in that same evening: the wounded man dying in the crypt.

He raised a swollen eyelid painfully, and cried out in a reproachful voice: "Why have you struck me? What have I done?"

Princess Audovere was found dead the following day, her eyes retracted, with lilies between her hands and pressed to her heart. She lay across a pathway at the entrance to the garden, but all the lilies around her were red.

They never produced white flowers again.

Thus died Princess Audovere, of having breathed the scent of lilies by night, in a convent garden in July.

The Princess at the Sabbat

PRINCESS ILSE loved nothing but mirrors and flowers. There was nothing in the entire palace but reflections of flower-heads and petals; huge water lilies bathed, day and night, in the water of great alabaster vases, while all manner of fixed foliage, moist and pale, maintained an eternal vigil in high-ceilinged hallways ornamented with marble and green bronze. Princess Ilse had never really looked at another human being, man or woman; she only saw herself reflected in every eye, as if in the deepest and bluest ocean. The eyes of her subjects were, to her, so many living and smiling mirrors.

Princess Ilse loved nothing but herself. Standing for long hours before pewter-backed sheets of plate glass, having already set herself within silken robes designed at her command by Ethiopian weavers who would never see their homelands again, wrought and brought to bloom in gold, she passed her time plaiting the golden threads and living silken pearls of her hair or setting rings and bracelets against the bare flesh of her slender arms.

Princess Ilse was nonchalant and indolent, her grace slowly and carefully cultivated before her precious mirrors. Her sumptuous existence was entirely dedicated to bathing herself, perfuming herself, combing her hair, dressing herself up, trying on jewels, undergarments and veils, smiling at herself and dreaming of yet more new dresses made of unknown materials and cut in unprecedented styles, which would made her stand out from the crowd and distinguish her from other women.

She was, in sum, an entirely idle little creature, ferociously egotistical and madly enamoured of herself—but when she was clad in transparent tunics from the Canary Islands and necklaces of shells from the Far-East she was perfectly ravishing, and no one else in the kingdom had so supple a figure.

Princess Ilse loved nothing but mirrors and flowers.

One morning, while she rested her delicate limbs in the icy water of a bathing-pool, she looked more curiously than usual at the two bronze monsters crouching on the edge of the basin, whose scalloped mouths vomited forth perpetual jets of water. She had never taken much notice of them before. They were two enormous frogs with almost human features. Their bodies were coloured by the unique green patina of time-weathered bronze, save for their gold-rimmed eyes: two eyes of glass, illuminated by a yellow glow! To decorate the immense bathroom in this manner had been the fantasy of one of Ilse's ancestors. Sculpted by a prestigious artist whose name is now quite forgotten, the two motionless monsters sat upon their marble steps, seemingly alive—or, better still, possessed of that intense and chimerical life that only masterpieces have.

Princess Ilse immediately fell in love with these monsters. Her delicate beauty became even more refined in the presence of their hideousness and, instinctively, she resolved to fill the rooms of her palace with monstrous frogs of metal and earthenware, cast in the image of those beside the bathing-pool.

The princesses of legend and the queens of mythology were invariably depicted in the company of fabulous animals. Leda laid herself down beneath a swan. Europa sprawled naked upon the rump of a bull. A hind with golden horns reared up beneath the hand of Diana. Queen Mellissinte was portrayed leading a lithe greyhound on a leash. Princess Ariadne extended her beautiful body across the loins of a tiger. A peacock spread its tail of sapphire eyes behind Queen Juno. Blanchefleur sat upon her throne with her bare feet placed upon a lion. Blismode's arms embraced a unicorn. Saint Catherine was crushed by the claw of a monster. She, Princess Ilse, would have a frog beside her. Well, Lady Venus had her doves and the virginal Athene an owl![1]

A frog! The frailty of her flesh, set with samite and orphrey, would be brought out even more exquisitely by the nearness of such a monster—so goldsmiths and sculptors were summoned to fill the entire palace with fabulous batrachians.

There was a veritable plague of frogs. There were frogs in every room, frogs as green as new shoots and frogs as blue as the sky. There were frogs of iron, frogs of copper and frogs of glazed earthenware made to order by potters. They were baked in every ceramic furnace in the realm, in all the colours of the rainbow. There were frogs the colour of the moon, frogs seemingly covered in duckweed, frogs

---

1. Most of the names in this list are familiar legendary figures. Of those that are less well-known, Blanchefleur is the heroine of Boccaccio's prose romance *Il Filocopo* and Blismode is the central character of another of Lorrain's *contes*, "Légende des trois princesses" (1894); Queen Mellissinte does not appear anywhere else, so far as I can tell.

as milky as Venetian glass with sides striped in gold. The monster in her bedroom was of burnished silver with eyes of emerald and the one in her chapel was of an unknown material, translucent as jade, with eyes of turquoise—and beside each and every immobile monster, Princess Ilse struck her lithe and languid poses, always certain that her beauty was enlivened and magnified by the ugliness of the frog crouched at her feet. Clad in improbable gowns, embroidered with splashes of water, irises and anemones set against a background of oceanic green, and crowned with river-grass, she seemed more naked than if she had actually been unclothed, and thus she lingered, delightedly, before the dead pools of her mirrors.

She was said to be an enchanted princess—and she was happy to think so because, more enamoured of herself than the Narcissus of olden days, she liked to imagine herself a godchild of the fairies, whose diminutive delicacy inspired an infinite respect in them.

Well, the fairies played a trick on her.

One warm day in September, as she walked among the trimmed yew-trees in the park, following a waterside path decorated at intervals by marble frogs—whenever she paused in the course of a long walk she liked to lean her elbows on the shiny back of some such monster—she perceived, floating on the surface of the canal, some large blossoms whose pale blue colour she had never seen before: a species of lotus with petals like blue enamel and pistils like shafts of sunlight. Enormous leaves were arrayed in the shape of a heart around these marvellous blooms, and Princess Ilse wanted to have them. . . .

She hurries down some steps and bends down to pick them. The blue blossoms are out of reach of the bank but there is a boat idling at its mooring whose prow is in the midst of the azure flowers. Ilse does not hesitate. She climbs into the boat—but the mooring-rope comes undone, the dream-flowers and their leaves sink out of sight, and the boat draws away, drifting into a landscape that Ilse no longer recognises. The current carries her across country, to an immense plain bordered with poplars.

Ilse wrings her hands fearfully. How far she has already come from the ancient garden, the city and her ancestral castle! Towards what enchanted land is the boat carrying her?

Ilse, who believes in fairies, is seized by dread of what they might have in store for her—but a chain of islands soon appears, where the trunks of willows are distributed among the water-weeds.

A grotesque child is sitting on the shore of one of the isles, wearing a scarlet hood, with a long hazel wand in his hand. The dwarf child watches over a herd of croaking frogs whose hopping is becoming agitated. "Quiet, rainettes!"[1] the little herdsman quavers, in a monotonous voice. Princess Ilse is afraid when she sees her boat draw close to the island's shore, because she remembers a legend about a child sorcerer who keeps frogs, but the evil isle is already receding into the distance as the boat drifts on, moving faster and faster.

The boat coasts between the willows to another islet, where strange haymakers are foraging with pitchforks among their pale stacks. They are great grey-haired women with haggard faces, dressed in rags; they insult Ilse with

---

1. The French "rainette" signifies both a tree-frog and an apple; the population of the second islet is also based in a double meaning, an alternative meaning of the French "grain" being "squall".

mute laughter as the violence of their labour throws scattered hay up towards the sky—and the sky is soon striped to the horizon with hostile clouds sparked with lightning and clattering with thunder. There is a torrential downpour, tepid and icy at the same time; the marvellous gilded dress is ruined and the rain redoubles its force upon the shoulders of the shivering princess.

The isle of the haymakers is already far away.

Ilse, soaked through, is thrown to her knees in the bottom of the boat. The boat swings from side to side, tossed by huge waves and shaken by the sudden downpour, and the outline of yet another island appears out of the mist: an island planted with sombre chestnut trees. A small thatched cottage is nested under the branches.

As the boat comes closer, a kindly little old lady watering a large hood decorated with hollyhocks comes trotting out of the cottage to meet Ilse.

The rain has stopped and the good woman welcomes the unfortunate Ilse; brandishing her crutch, she takes the lovely girl into her home. It is a riot of sunflowers, pierced by little windows, like dwarfs painted on the yellow background.

As the old woman undresses Ilse and dries her with a towel before a huge fire, Ilse does not notice her shaggy chin, or the club-foot that she hides under her dress.

Night falls, and the princess, standing naked before the fireplace, feels herself being anointed and massaged with a strange ointment. She thinks that the odour will make her faint, but is reanimated by terror at the sight of her hostess squatting down, also naked upon the hearth, likewise anointing her shrivelled breasts, scrawny thighs and flabby stomach.

"Up the goat! Up the goat!" Voices break out on the roof, the logs in the fireplace crackle and flare up—and two capering broomsticks fall with a loud clatter from who knows where or by what means, snorting and whinnying: "Up the goat! Up the goat!" And the barefoot princess, frozen by fear, is lifted up by her hair.

Beneath the rainclouds, illuminated by a green moon, witches are in hectic flight. Young and old, thin and fat, mournful and delighted, naked bodies bound, dive and swirl about, howling wildly, and then come hurtling down upon the forest. Animals are also flying through the air. An owl brushes her with its wing; an ape with a hen's beak spirals around her head; a dung-beetle passes overhead, wing-cases clattering. Below her, following the tracks along the ravines, a swarming crowd is wending its way through the wood. There are cripples and hunchbacks, ventriloquists and highwaymen; it is as if the entire population of the region is hastening upon some pilgrimage, a mass movement of jugglers and acrobats towards some frightful fête.

"Sabbat! Sabbat!"

It is the Sabbat. All nature's outcasts are marching across the land in serried ranks, a surging tide drawn by the moon; the lame hopping like toads along the pathways, showmen with dancing bears at the crossroads.

Princess Ilse feels that she is dying. A flock of strutting turkeys closes around her, a rat's tail strokes her, a fox sniffs at her, a viper with the wings of a cock whips her. . . .

And, raked by claws, kissed, bitten and ridden by a thousand invisible beasts, Princess Isle wakes up with a loud scream.

She is in her bedroom, surrounded by stucco and panes of glass.

Ilse jumps wildly from her bed. The burnished silver frog with emerald eyes lies in pieces on the carpet. Scarcely reassured, Princess Ilse runs in alarm to her mirror.

What horror! Is she still in the grip of that frightful nightmare? The tall glass reflects a disordered bed and an empty room. Princess Ilse can find no trace of herself.

She flees from the accursed room and runs through the palace to interrogate all the other mirrors. Each and every one displays a shattered frog of metal, china or baked earthenware—and nothing else.

Princess Ilse never recovered her image; she had left it at the Sabbat. The fairies had played a trick on her, to punish her vanity.

One should never trust flowers that float on water and faces that smile in looking-glasses. Princes Ilse loved mirrors and flowers a little too much.

Narkiss

ON my table, the open mouth of a heavy sandstone fish spews forth English irises: irises so white that they seem blessed by the light, like transparently nacreous azaleas; white irises more beautiful than orchids, luminous, fierce and temperamental. The hectic gush of the floral fountain also includes the long trumpets of arums and the effusive efflorescence of white peonies: flowers with the semblance of flesh and silk. Among them, here and there, are meadow-grasses and the yellow stigmas of star-like honeysuckles.

In the dappled light that seeps into the high-ceilinged room when the blinds are closed these flowers, as if vomiting forth from the monster's mouth, are possessed in their immobility by a supernatural life. They are no longer flowers but works of art, endowed with and animated by a curious occult power. The irises have the appearance of being carved in jade, and the stout peony-buds, swollen by massive petals, open out into large cups like white lotuses. In truth, they are supernatural, in the silence of the study, these gushing flowers solidified in all their splendour, reminiscent of all things white and precious. There is a mystery within them: the mystery of vitality and the mystery of moisture. They also exude a strange clarity: the whole gloomy vault of the room is illuminated by their translucent corollas.

Ah, those flowers! They know all the secrets of springs and pools, all the pastoral poems of woodlands and all the idylls of the prairies. They know, too, all the mysteries and debaucheries of the most ancient religions; their symbolic corollas have decorated the altars of so many gods, and their perfumes have intoxicated so many death-agonies, from the long processions of victims that troop to the funeral pyres of Vedic India to the hecatombs of Sicilian bull-worshippers. They have garlanded every festival and every torture, flourished among the ceremonies of Isis-worshipping Egypt, the ancient temples of India and the Roman circuses of the Caesars. They are savage, triumphant and cruel; they are nourished by blood and by blood they replenish themselves—but by the same token, they are divine.

They are lustful too; every one of them is the form of a sexual organ: every one, from the peonies whose petals yawn like open mouths, to the arums whose long golden pistils stiffly protruding from their enfolding bells possess the kind of phallic obscenity that is revered by the men of the Orient . . . and it is an ancient tale of the Orient—a story of the Egypt of antiquity—which is imposed on my memory by the pale and ostentatious apotheosis of the tall irises of long jade, the rigid arums and huge lotus-like peonies. As they spring forth thus, in a malign tumult of leaves and stems, these lilies of snow, these nacreous irises cannot help but remind me of Narkiss and the monstrous water-lilies of legend . . . and of all the other sinister and luminous calyces, nourished on the blood of sacrifices, which floated like vegetal vampires on the stagnant water of the Nile, at the foot of a great staircase leading down from an old temple—where the young Pharaoh, his unclothed body radiant with gems, flowers and ornamental ivories, came to tread his leisurely paces in the twilight.

Yes, Narkiss! Narkiss, the Egyptian Narcissus, whose story had been told to me that winter, by an Arab dragoman: a legend far more tragic and far more beautiful than the familiar tale of the Greek youth in love with his reflection, who died—indifferent to the loving appeals of nymphs—leaning over a stream of water, spellbound by his own image prisoned in a mirror.

> *Narcissus, son of Cephissus and Liriope, was so handsome that all the nymphs loved him, but he could not hear any of them. Echo, powerless to seduce him, was withered by her anguish. Tiresias prophesied to the parents of the young man that he would live only as long as he did not see himself. As he returned one day from the hunt, he caught sight of himself in a fountain and became so enamoured of himself that he languished and died, and underwent a metamorphosis into a flower.*

That is the Narcissus to be found in the dictionary of fables and the *Metamorphoses* of Ovid. Sculpted and painted images of the frail and sickly adolescent are owned by all the museums of Germany and Italy, including our own Luxemburg: plaintive images of all the graces of frailty, compounded of androgynous charm and consumptive languor.

What artist could not be tempted by the piquant enigma of a human being who became a flower? So many have been attracted by the livid quality of that care-laden brow, that head swelling like a bud from the narrow stalk of the neck, its mass beginning to bloom, already becoming vegetal upon those shoulders drained of blood and the sturdy stem of the emaciated torso. The myth is so melancholy, its representations are never less than heartfelt; its sadness is bittersweet, mingling tears and smiles—but the terrible tale of the Egyptian Narkiss is another matter.

※

Narkiss, prince of Egypt, the descendant of innumerable Pharaohs, was superhumanly beautiful. The blood of Isis flowed within him, as it had flowed within all his ancestors for many centuries, but in him—the last descendant of a sumptuous bloodline—the divinity of the great Ancestress had been replenished with such awesome splendour that it was said that his mother had bowed down in adoration before his cradle. No sooner was he born than he caused crimes to be committed; his nurses strangled one another out of jealousy.

Even the animals were sensible of his beauty. Lions prowled around the city, having followed the caravans from the depths of the desert—for the nomads were now permanently encamped beneath the walls of Memphis, night and day alike, in the hope of seeing one of the little king's smiles. At a greater distance, troops of jackals and hyenas were halted by prudence on the surrounding heights, where they lay in wait, attracted in their turn by the marvellous presence, waiting for the slightest opportunity to descend upon the city and pass through its gates. Now that the child was there, flocks of pink ibises swooped down upon the gardens of the rich; from dawn to dusk they preened their feathers with long strokes of their beaks, and the domestic palm-trees seemed to bathe in the light of a neverending dawn.

The sentinels on the city-walls had to be doubled in number; four watchmen were posted on each of the towers—and always, from the sands of the desert and more distant lands, crowds of beasts and crowds of men filed towards Memphis. The entire plain was covered by tents, and ships constantly disembarked along the river.

At night, by moonlight, the crocodiles of the Nile took to creeping from the mire and climbing the steps of the terraces, weeping. Their voracious elongated mouths rapped upon the bronze gates and their scales rustled strangely in the murk as they moved along the deserted parapets. Even elephants would not follow in their footsteps, because the odour of crocodiles is so foul that it makes the greatest of wild beasts recoil—and dread spread throughout the palace.

There was butchery in the city; intrigues stained the temples with blood. Without, there was a state of siege; within, there was rioting in the streets. The wife of Pharaoh, shot through and through by arrogance, had strangled her husband and proclaimed the infant king; all women and common people sided with her against the opposing party of priests and elders. The dead Pharaoh had been jealous of his son and it was to save Narkiss that his mother had been forced to the hazard of horrid murder.

The child lived, and his fabulous beauty was magnified hour by hour amid the tumult comprised of the cries of the various factions, threats and imprecations, conspiratorial whispers and the brandished pikes of rebellion. He became handsome and strong amid the horrors of a siege that was aggravated as much by a plague imported by the nomads as by the famine generated by the vast and diverse crowds camped beneath the city's ramparts. The sky, above the city and to the extent of ten leagues beyond, was black with the flocks of birds of prey; even wild beasts were dying of hunger and every night was beset by the frightful lamentations of the crocodiles prowling on the terraces, interrupted now and again by their sinister laughter as they snapped up some passing slave—for crocodiles do not nourish themselves merely on carrion.

That was the first part of the tale the dragoman told me.

※

The time came when the priests dedicated to the service of the goddess Isis took charge of the ill-starred child. They stole him away from the queen and—having hidden his wondrous beauty under a long black cloak—they took him into their own company. Then, under the pretext of a pilgrimage to one of their temples required by a religious festival, they smuggled the Pharaoh out of Memphis, evading the surveillance of his guards. By stages they conducted the descendant of Isis to a safe haven: an ancient sanctuary previously consecrated to Osiris. Its sprawling ruins comprised the remains of three temples, which had been returning to a natural state for eight centuries, already partly-buried by creepers, horsetails, acanthus and the tall papyrus-grasses of a stagnant backwater of the Nile.

On returning to Memphis, the priests told the people that Isis had appeared to them and that the goddess had recalled the boy Pharaoh to be close to her. Narkiss would be given back to them when he was twenty years old. The mother of the king, dethroned now that she no longer had a son, entered a college of priestesses. The usurpers governed in her name, as they were later to govern in the name of Narkiss.

The intention of the priests of Isis was to take control of they boy's life, to raise him in their own fashion in their isolated temple, remote from his people and the counsel of great men. Once the child had been formed according to their plan, having become their instrument and their possession—his royal soul having become, at length, manipulable and pliable, so that the child of the goddess had become their child—they would have created the ideal Pharaoh; then they would replace the exile on the throne and continue to reign over Egypt in the name of the pious and religious Narkiss. The descendant of Isis would be the slave of her priests; thus Isis would govern Isis.

So Narkiss grew up in the shadow of the ancient temples, in natural surroundings. Hundreds of leagues of sand now separated him from Memphis. The sanctuary of Osiris was on the very edge of the desert; beyond the third temple there was a marshy region extending from the dead arm of the Nile. Narkiss lived wild there; as naked in his resplendent beauty as the idols that were ranged on the slopes and terraces. When he passed them he touched them lightly; polished by the centuries, they resembled him strangely. Like him, they were svelte and straight in their lapidary immobility and turquoise-incrusted scarabs ornamented the granite of their breasts. They seemed to watch over Narkiss as if he were one of their own children—and Narkiss was, in effect, nothing but a little idol!

Narkiss had the large hypnotic eyes of Isis: immense eyes with night-black pupils, where the water of springs and the fire of stars seemed to shimmer. He had the long narrow face of Isis, the accentuated jaw and the sacred pallor: the transparent, almost radiant pallor that revealed the goddess, even when she was veiled, to her initiates.

At night, beneath the tall palm-trees stirred by the breeze, the nudity of Narkiss brightened the shadows. The hawk-headed images of Anubis smiled on their pedestals when—to the rattling sound of their long ear-rings—the little Pharaoh approached, slowly and reverently. Narkiss was always sparkling with jewels and made up like a woman. In cultivating his terrible beauty, the ancient eunuch priests who were committed to his guard and charged with effeminating the tyrant he might otherwise become, were not so much obedient to their order as to the occult power of a fateful and intoxicating gift of the gods. Narkiss embodied in his person the sum total of the beauty of a race.

Lithe and slender, with straight shoulders and a lean figure, his tapered hips widened out beneath the torso to provide his loins with the shape of a lyre. He was Grace and he was Strength. Braided with elliptical pearls and acutely-faceted gems, three girdles of different lengths ran around his waist. To this loincloth, instinct moved him to add sprigs of leaves and flowers.

Clad thus in moving jewels and moist petals, Narkiss would sometimes pause in the twilight on one of the ruined temple-platforms, to breathe in the wind and contemplate the sands that the night rendered blue as the sea. The undulant roots of old trees filled the oasis and whenever the breath of the wilderness was fresh upon the child's brow, it became the wind of the open sea, as if paying homage to a young god of the desert.

※

By day Narkiss slept, sprawled on mattresses in one of the paved halls of the first sanctuary. The walls were tiled with mosaics and decorated to the height of a man with symbols and hieroglyphs lined in gold, which shone in the shadows like splinters of slick enamel. Massively thick pillars tinted with vermilion still supported the vaulted roof, but there were places where the ceilings had collapsed, where creepers and lianas slid through the fissures. Here and there, in the life-giving light, cascades of flowers hung like soft winged stalactites all a-tremble with colours; where the sun's rays fell obliquely there were swirls of buzzing flies. And Narkiss, propped up on piles of cushions, eyelids half-closed beneath the silken caress of mosquito-nets, would watch the sunlight streaming in the cascades and listen to the flies whose humming disturbed the silence. At one time he might pluck berries from an amber cluster; at another he might crush the cold calyx of a lily against his artificially moistened skin; and thus it was, in the torrid heat of the long Egyptian summer, that the exhausting, somnolent and empty days of the little Pharaoh passed.

The days were all alike: monotonous and interminable, suffocated and enervated by a superabundance of perfume and torpor; the college of Isis had decided it. Only rice and peeled vegetables were provided for his nourishment, so that the heat of his blood should not be dangerously stirred. Narkiss had no idea how to read the scrolls of papyrus that were consulted night and day by the priests. His eyelids painted with antimony and his teeth rubbed with Suakin gum, he lived in sublime ignorance of his birth and his destiny. Night and day, the vigilant eyes of his guardians kept watch on him; night and day, their listening ears were alert. They cultivated nothing but his beauty: his beauty, and his unconsciousness. And, like a well-fed idol, Narkiss allowed himself be adored and served by the attentive and timid troop of ancient eunuchs who were his gaolers.

They approached him only rarely, moved in spite of themselves by his terrible beauty; the blood of Isis was in him, after all. Although they were obedient to the High Priest, it felt vaguely sacrilegious thus to render effeminate the descendant of the gods—but naked beneath his armour of jewels, his flesh quivering at the touch of cold gems, Narkiss languished throughout the warm hours of day amid the chiaroscuro of the ruined halls, instinctively in love with the luminous tresses of flowers streaming through the holes in the vaulted ceilings, seduced by the intimate caresses of the cool mattresses upon his propped-up body. The idle existence of a young and precocious animal, deprived of all exercise, depraved him by degrees.

Sometimes, during those hours, his pre-pubescent reveries were disturbed by other dreams, when unexpected images rose up before him: visions recollecting his celestial heritage. In order to hold on to them Narkiss clenched his fists and closed his eyelids, his chin raised and his lips taut in anticipation of the unknown mystery of the kiss. Then the sounds of the harp, the calls of the flute would resound, voluptuously tender; delicate arpeggios would extend like caresses, prolonging his ecstasy and making his visions more precise—and Narkiss, exasperated, would wake up with a start, and every time, at the moment of his awakening, there would be a flurry of flaxen robes in some corner of the hall, the rapid flight of guilty footsteps, the reverberations of smothered harps, the panic of surprised musicians.

As the guardian priests extended their vigilance over

the young Narkiss, his siestas became longer and longer; his strength withered under the oppression of the burning days, and the young Pharaoh could find no hint of freshness and calm until the fall of dusk, when night approached and the desert would turn blue. Then, Narkiss would leave his sanctuary, all a-glitter with flowers and jewels, and venture forth on to the terraces. He would prowl there until night fell. Night had, for him, the appeasing delicacy of maternal caresses. Divine, as he was, the night loved and consoled the child. Throughout the torrid and dazzling days, Narkiss instinctively felt like a prisoner in the halls haunted by music and perfumes, but at night he felt free. By night he became himself again and loved those ancient temples, which seemed by day to be a country of exile.

Those temples! The enchantment of moonlight reclothed them with such beauty, in the darkening blue of the Egyptian nights. It was as if unknown edifices loomed up from their ruins; the colonnades were raised again, the porticos extended to infinity across the sands that glistened like a sea of metal. The palm-trees sprang up as if made of bronze, having become chimerical. At the limit of vision, between the desert and the Nile, there were arrays of sphinxes and idols of hawk-headed Anubis, immeasurably magnified. Twisting spiral staircases climbed upwards, leading no one knew where; others descended from terrace to terrace, idols with silver eyes standing on every step, asleep or on watch. Flowers became reminiscent of faces, and there were gestures in the motionless curves of the vegetation—and scents that were greener and more lingering revived Narkiss instead of numbing him. In the sky, the moon, as distinct as a globe of jade, orbited so softly in the silence that Narkiss, while watching it, felt as if he were relaxing beneath a gentle caress: a powerful and profound caress; an immense caress, which ran through his being like music and a cascade of honey.

At night, too, the bleak solitude of the desert was repopulated; hyenas and jackals, attracted by the remains of sacrifices, came to prowl beneath the ruins. Their velvet footfalls brought them as far as the foot of the terraces, and the corpse of the oasis was filled with dull rustlings; then the wandering silhouette of Narkiss led them much nearer to the temples and their yellow eyes lit up the night like so many topazes. Narkiss watched them fearlessly and fixedly. Sometimes, a tiger ventured forth, or even a lion, and the stink of the wild beast filled the shadows—and Narkiss would look upon the tiger exactly as he looked upon the lion. He felt that he attracted and fascinated the beasts, and he was intoxicated by a great arrogance and a great strength: the consciousness of his power and dominion.

After the wild beasts, women came: slow and supple veiled figures with large dark eyes that shone like water beneath the transparent gauzes. At first they came alone, one by one, then collected in groups of five or six, then all in a crowd they came to stand at the foot of the terrace. Motionless beneath the moon, they watched him for a long time. Were they nomads or ghosts? Narkiss, in his turn, studied them for a long time; they recalled the visions of his somnolent days. He liked them while they kept their veils—but when, one after another and with grand gestures, they discarded the drapery that made them mysterious and revealed the smoothness of their bodies, Narkiss turned his head away and disdainfully refused to look at them any longer.

They came again the next night and the next; for a whole month they persisted in returning and the moans of hyenas and amorous women filled the oasis with poignant wailing—and then, one evening, they came no more. Occasionally, now and then, a shrouded form would prowl around for two or three nights, but then would vanish, tiredly, into the desert. The indifferent Narkiss preferred to match stares with the beasts; his hypnotic eyes attracted both women and lions. Isis was revealing herself, and asserting her authority, through him.

Isis!

Narkiss had never seen her. If Narkiss had been able to behold his own reflection, he would have seen the face of Isis, and the priests—who wished to govern for Isis but did not wish to be governed by her—dreaded the moment when Narkiss would come to know himself, delaying from one day to the next the moment of revelation. In discovering his beauty the Pharaoh would discover his strength, his origin and his power; it was necessary to drain away all his energy before his fateful encounter with his own image, necessary to make an idol and not a king of the young Pharaoh. It was with this end in mind that he had been removed from his mother, withdrawn from his people and hidden from the councils of the aristocracy.

The great mirrors of steel, which had once been suspended from the columns of the temple by day and by night—sacred mirrors where Osiris and Isis came in turn to catch sight of their glory, Osiris by day and Isis by night—had been carefully removed and taken down to the crypts. The ambition of the priests had emboldened their sacrilege. Beneath the porticos deprived from that moment of the august reflections of the gods, Narkiss had been able to live for fifteen years without once encountering his own image, lest he see shining within it the beauty of his ancestress, which would have informed him of his power.

In similar fashion, sacrifices—the bloody holocausts of bulls required by the cult of Osiris—had always been hidden from his sight. It was feared that the sight of blood would surely awaken in the son of the gods the instincts of domination and murder that are the prerogative of kings. Those sacrifices of which the Pharaoh needed to be kept ignorant were held in the third temple: the oldest of the sanctuaries and also the most dilapidated, whose foundations bathed in the waters of the Nile, enmired in a bog whose already foetid mud was further enslimed with carrion. It was amid those ruins, between twenty collapsed pillars overrun with wild vegetation, that the ceremonies of the altar were celebrated henceforth. It was there, in the hottest hours of the day, during the cunningly-prolonged siestas of the child, that the only male priest in the company of eunuchs would cut the throat of a ram or a bull—and sometimes a human captive—demanded by Apis, and the stagnant arm of the Nile would become putrid with blood. Spices were burned, night and day, in the four corners of the temple in order to drown the miasma of the swamp and a hedge of figs concealed the entrance; lest the powerful odour of the charnel-house be insufficient to deter the child, the only direct order that he had ever received was that he was never to pass beyond the second temple.

Narkiss was quite indifferent to the remainder; he had the arrogant incuriosity of savages and animals. The hedge of figs seemed to him to be wild and ugly; an unpleasant smell of decay emanated from the forbidden ruins. Narkiss preferred the scent of flowers and the pleasant odours of cosmetics and essences, the glitter of sparkling gems and the cool moistness of great fleshy lotuses. Narkiss was equally ignorant of the power of his gaze and the colour of blood. . . .

※

At this point, Ali the dragoman squatted down beside me to remove the amber mouthpiece of the hookah from my lips, then stood up with a flourish, scattering the cushions on which we had been smoking, while he told his story and I lost myself in the dream.

"Enough *kif* smoked today, sidi! It is twilight: the hour when the desert turns blue, as blue as in the story of Narkiss. Come make a tour of the oasis. There never was a sight in Tripoli more beautiful than the oasis at sunset!"

"And that is all you have to relate? It is not finished, your story!"

"I will tell you the rest later. You are all pale—you have smoked too much *kif.* It is necessary to take the air. The horses are saddled, Kadour has come to the door and given the sign. I know—I will tell you later this evening, if you wish, how Narkiss died on the bank of the Nile, in the ruins of the third temple, amid lotuses and the lilies whose stems were swollen with blood."

※

One night, while he was wandering about the ruins from colonnade to colonnade and from terrace to terrace, Narkiss—without even being aware of it—came as far as the surrounding wall of the third temple. The hedge of figs concealed the foundations from his eyes and the tall pillars of green marble supporting the heavy entablatures of the porticos that suddenly sprang up before him, without any apparent base, seemed to be an artifact of a dream, an enchantment of the moonlight, a desert mirage blossoming on the instant.

Narkiss went into the temple.

At first, he felt faint: a pestilential atmosphere reigned there, heavy with the odours of blood and carrion—but it was heavy with the scents of flowers and the perfumes of spices too; detached lotus petals strewed the paving-stones, mingled with the large red petals of a flower unknown to him. Tripods of bronze were distributed about a great table of onyx; spikenard, benzoin and myrrh were slowly burning away in them, and long spirals of blue smoke were swirling like veils in the warm air.

Narkiss came to a halt. The great onyx table was red in places: red and moist, as if heaps of strange purple flowers had been crushed thereon—flowers whose cascading blooms Narkiss had loved, their inner surfaces luminously glossy and gloomy but as clear as the gems of his necklaces. Although it had been washed in white spirits by the priests, the entire altar exuded into the spice-saturated air a particular stink that caused his nostrils to flare. A new emotion lit up his eyes, expanded his breast and clasped his heart; he had always wanted to be here beneath the high-flying colonnade that spread out so boldly in the bluing shadows, always belonged here amid the purplish-blue vapours of the tripods, drinking in these perfumes of murder, lotus-blossoms and incense.

Narkiss moved around the altar, circling it three times. He placed his hands on the damp table and instinctively lowered his head to rest upon it. There was a lull—but then two tripods were extinguished, and the sharp stench of stagnation was suddenly strong again; the pestilence of the Nile asserted its dominion over the temple. Choking on the breath of the river, Narkiss abruptly recovered himself.

To escape those odours of silt and decay he hurried towards an exit, where the distant gleam of water showed behind a colonnade. Fresher air drifted from the same direction, as if exhaled by the white flowers of giant magnolias that stood as if on watch in the night; and without knowing it, the child descended towards the Nile. Twenty blocks of malachite, loosened and leprous with moss, formed twenty steps that conveyed the Pharaoh there—and there, moving between a double row of sphinxes, crouching to part the soft hangings of lianas, the descendant of Isis—who was not at all astonished—clasped his hands together upon his necklace of emeralds, possessed by alarm and joy.

The descendant of Isis came to a standstill. He opened his mouth, but admiration strangled his cry.

There, in a wild extravagance of stems, leaves and umbels, was the heat of lust, the fever of sap, the swarming of life, the ferment of growth and all the expansive menace of a vegetation that was aggravated, superheated, triumphant, gargantuan and hostile: flowers thicker than clusters of dates, stalks taller than palms; translucent fruits like swellings of luminous sap, as bright as gemstones or figures of jade; serpentine creepers coiling about the spindles of every corollas and petals, hangings like showers of stars; whole fields of papyrus-grass spattered with pieces of the sky; calyces of unfamiliar form and colour, some of a metallic rigidity, others round and white; marvellous lotus-buds like the eggs of ostriches, haloed with enormous leaves ... and all of them writhed, drew themselves up in great disorder , intertwined and choked one another, joined together as if for flight, fled from one another, congealed like an indentation of bronze excised from the pale extent of the bleak swamp, a mirror silvered by the moonlight.

A few paces away, an old and crumbling portico cast its ruined silhouette upon the dead water; at that point, too, the centuries-old staircase of the sphinxes plunged into the realm of papyrus-grass and nenuphar water-lilies. The progeny of the charnel-house, their stems and calyxes displayed strange gleams of blueness within the shadows.

It was at this place, after the sacrifices, that the negligent slaves of the temple came to sink the mutilated corpses of the victims. Nothing was offered to Osiris but the heads and hearts of the immolated bulls; the god only required the virile parts of rams and prisoners. The remnants of the carcasses and cadavers were taken from the altar to the old staircase and there submerged in the mud of the river, so that the putrid waters were thick with blood. Flies and mosquitoes swarmed thereabouts in the daylight while frogs and vile lizards with tortoise-like heads lay in wait for them; at night, flights of bats and pale fireflies swarmed above the charnel-house ... and it was this ignominious display, this effusion of murder and pus that burst upon the divine dream of the little Pharaoh.

The charnel-house! He was aware of nothing other than the frightful breath of its vile decay. The charnel-house! The rotting carcasses of beached animals distributed throughout; the reptiles sleeping on the floating leaves; the snakes coiled about the long, excessively green stems, amid the suppurating tree-trunks and phosphorescent flowers . . . the child could no longer see them.

His eyes staring and dilated, the palms of his hands extended straight in front of him and the fingers splayed, the intoxicated Narkiss descended towards the water.

Narkiss was surrounded by the fragility of the irises, the femininity of the lotuses and the obscenity of arums whose amber phalluses darted forth from trumpets of ivory, lighting his way like flames, showing by turns the colours of jade, opal and beryl. Beneath the reflected light of the moon the fireflies seemed like jewels wandering in darkness, the reptiles on the lily-pads shone like so many enamelled designs. Lastly, there was the metallic resplendence of the Nile—and in that magical half-light, in the enchantment woven like a mysterious and moving tapestry out of shadows and water, corruption, flowers and foliage, the dazzled Narkiss saw one flower only: one unforeseen, unknown hallucinatory flower; one long and supple stem lustrous as a pearl, delicately balanced in a rhythmic movement, whose delicious calyx, designed like a face, smiled more broadly the further he descended towards it. He stared at it more fixedly with his human eyes as it came up to meet him.

This strange flower of the Nile had sprung forth at his approach, between the spreading leaves of the water-lilies and the silky stems of the papyrus-reeds. A flower? Was it not, rather, some divinity of the waters unknown in Memphis, which reigned over these trackless regions? Could a human being possibly dwell here in the water, within that mud, captive of the creepers and the reeds—some king's daughter perhaps, magically imprisoned there by demons . . . for she was sparkling with precious stones, as he was . . . jewels and flowers shifted along her pale thighs, sparks glistened against the skin around her neck—and, just like him, the creature appeared to be wearing a diadem made of three circlets of enamel connected by little lotuses of gold and scarabs of turquoise; just like his, the flesh of her right shoulder was bitten by a metal serpent whose twisting tail extended as far as her frail wrist; and her right hand, like his, seemed submerged beneath a glorious stream of rings!

Clearer than all the gems upon her brow and fingers, however, two immense eyes filled with life, as darkly blue as water at night, shone between her eyelids—and, without ever having seen them before, Narkiss recognised the staring and hypnotic eyes of the magical figure that rushed forward to meet him. The Pharaoh prostrated himself upon the steps and the descendant of Isis adored Isis herself.

In the muddy depths of the charnel-house, the flower with the human face continued smiling.

Then Narkiss got up again. With his hands joined together, his ecstatic gaze spearing the hallucinatory image, the Pharaoh leapt from the last step of the stairway of the sphinxes and dived into the marsh.

The carcass of a butchered ox, which was rotting there upon the paving-stone, pressed for one second upon the sole of his bare foot, oozing; a thread of rosy blood squirted on to the silt and a serpent disturbed in its sleep uncoiled. On the surface of the water, the nocturnal glory of arums and the nacreous splendour of the water-lilies was flooded with blue lights by the kisses of the great goddess.

※

The next day, at the first light of daybreak, the priests of Osiris found the little Pharaoh dead, engulfed by the mud in the midst of cadavers and the huge legacy of decay heaped up by the centuries.

Held upright in the mire, buried to the neck in the cesspit, Narkiss had been asphyxiated by the putrid exhalations of the swamp—but his head dominated the sinister flowers that were ranged around him in the form of a coronet. That charming flower with its bloodless and powdered adolescent face, its forehead mounted with a diadem of enamels and turquoises, protruded proudly from the mud—and on that dead forehead, night-flying butterflies were resting with extended wings, fast asleep.

Isis had recognised Isis; Isis had recalled to herself the blood of Isis.

Thus perished Narkiss, descendant of the great goddess and prince of the realm of Egypt, on a clear night in June.

The Princess aux Miroirs[1]

IN a cavern full of fissures and murky excavations, nameless and terrifying things loom up within the shadows: monstrous shapes creeping on all fours about the red-glowing embers and pestilential fumes of a brazier. Here and there, sculpted figures and the capitals of columns project from the stone walls of the vaults, for this is an ancient crypt that sheltered royal mummies in former times. It is not so much a cave as a sepulchre; its long mazy tunnels, where the shades of ancient Pharaohs still walk, are replete with a Millennial terror.

❈

Princess Illys had not been afraid of the mysteries of the cave, nor of offending its phantoms. She had crossed the desert without a moment's hesitation, in order to obtain the secret of a philtre that would render her imperious and fragile beauty imperishable from Numidian sorceresses. Fascinated and tremulous, still dazzled by the tawny glitter of the sands despite the long veils of violet gauze

---

1. "*Ouefs aux miroirs*" are eggs fried in butter, so the title lends itself to a much nastier metaphorical interpretation than the straightforwardly literal "The Princess of the Mirrors".

that she wore, she had descended into the hallucinatory realm of shadows.

And because the princess of Egypt, so frail and so nonchalant, had dared to do this, so too had her harp-players and flute-players—and, indeed, her entire retinue, all rustling with silks and bedecked with jewels, as befitted a young Oriental queen: a profusion of henna-tinted toe-nails, nimble fingers, bare breasts and slender necks, every torso and every knee gleaming with pearls, every pair of lips rouged. All the light, all the finery and all the gaiety of her young, sumptuous and futile heart was reflected there, in the green brocade of the eunuchs' costumes, in the fans of pink ibis feathers carried by eight Hindu princesses with throats encased by fine gold mesh, in the perfumes of the incense-bearers and the clinking of their little chains and the slithering of their long loose trains—like jets of water falling into basins—as they descended the marble steps. All that splendour, ostentation and magnificence went down with Illys into the shadows of the cavern.

Illys: radiant and irradiated beneath the pennants and the tall pikes decorated with tufts of fur of her Gallic guards.

Illys: helmed in gold and mitred in pearls.

Illys: like an idol dressed with turquoise pendants and strings of opals upon her temples and her nipples.

Illys: more beautiful than any creature that had ever been seen before.

Illys: surrounded by grovelling and seemingly-worshipful sorceresses.

Illys: standing tall in the middle of the staircase, on which her courtiers were arrayed in tiers.

Illys had enjoyed the ultimate vanity and the

sublime joy of imagining herself elevated to divinity, living for all eternity within the resplendence of her flesh and the glory of her beauty, exalted in all those watching eyes by Terror and Desire.

A heavy cloak with blue and amber eyes of sapphire and topaz had followed her feet from step to step, giving her the appearance of a jade Isis posed before the spread of a peacock's tail.

Intoxicated by her triumph, Illys had noticed neither the muted derision nor the eerily glittering eyes of the ragged sorceresses. Perfectly sure of her power, she had extended the great lotus encrusted with opals and beryls that served as her sceptre, so that they might kiss it. Then, calling her slaves forward, she had offered them the contents of her treasure-chests in exchange for the philtre of eternal beauty.

But the sorceresses had laughed, their eyes suddenly aflame within the shadows, as round and vitreous as the eyes of ospreys. Laughing like hyenas, the sorceresses had refused. That which she asked of them was not to be had for that sort of price.

Then, in spite of the cautionary remonstrances and whispered prayers of her astrologer, and in spite of the beautiful bare arms thrown imploringly and tenderly about her shoulders by her favourite slave Mandosia, Illys—completely possessed by obsession and desire—had promised to the witches that which their mouths of shadow demanded of her: one night of her life, in exchange for the herb that would conserve her youth forever.

Yes! one night in the life of a virgin princess, to be passed in their midst, in exchange for eternal beauty.

"Come and join us at midnight in the Libyan mountains," they had said. "There, amid the crags and the mastic-trees, on the high plateaux where even aloes wither and decay in the rare and excessively raw atmosphere, you shall pluck the magic herb that will preserve the youthfulness of your face and the loveliness of your figure against all change."

And before the mirrors that had suddenly appeared out of the shadows, Illys had stood, enraptured by vanity.

Illys: palpitating with pleasure at the sight of so many adorable images of youth and glory, so many teasing promises of an incorruptible future and imperishable power.

Illys: ensnared and imprisoned by desire;

Illys: the final female issue of a hundred legendary Pharaohs.

Although she was a princess of Egypt, Illys was a Christian, but she was somewhat forgetful of her baptism. She had promised to rejoin the Numidian sorceresses at midnight on the high plateaux of the Libyan mountains. And the sorceresses had laughed like hyenas, their eyes suddenly aflame in their earthen faces, as green and vitreous as the eyes of ospreys.

※

"But as you entered, Princess, something ghastly fled into the shadow, creeping on a fat and flaccid belly like some sort of gigantic toad."

"You always see chimeras! You live in mortal dread of attracting phantoms."

"Charmion and Oenoë saw it too! There were shrouds hanging in a corner, and the bones of dead men in a bronze vase. That's where the witches do their evil work. Don't go to this rendezvous, Princess, I beg you."

"But I have given my word, fearful Mandosia—and the word of a princess is more than that of a pretty slave. I will go."

"The gods protect us, then, for these women have an air about them that bodes ill. They reek of earth and death."

"Bah! They're desert women, the colour of sand. I won't change my mind. Look—see how the mountains fade into rose-pink fire at the horizon! The sky is as blue as turquoise. Ah, to have the power to adorn myself with the jewels of sunset! My beauty will never fade when I have picked the sacred herb. Every evening, as the sunlight dies. I shall be able to stand proud in this certain knowledge: *No one shall ever see me grow old.* But send my dancers away! They're whirling around like corn in a sieve, and their outflung dresses are humming like so many honey-bees. It's too enervating—and besides, that little Adysia is too beautiful; even the eunuchs are looking at her. I shall have her crucified some day."

Princess Illys and her little slave Mandosia are chatting as night falls. The bare flesh of the dancing-girls is scattered upon the clear blue shadow of the Egyptian evening. Dusk descends, as light as a puff of incense. Illys and her slave are talking to one another on the terrace of a grand palace built by the Ptolemies, whose walls are painted with green frescoes and decorated wit hieroglyphics telling of the loves of Memnon and the glory of Osiris. Dreaming sphinxes crouch in the interstices of a line of pillars. Garlands of lotuses are bound around each and every column, perfuming the night as they slowly wilt away. Their petals rain slowly down upon the cushions where the divine form of Illys is outstretched, and their soft touch makes her shiver beneath her veils.

Illys has taken off her jewels. With her elbow set upon the stone balcony she anxiously awaits the hour at which the moon will rise above the mountains of Libya and make the sands shimmer with its light. Then Illys will leave the palace and the environs of the city to rejoin the witches.

Below the terrace there is the sound of marching feet and the clash of weapons as the sentries make their first tour of the night.

"Chut! Don't make any noise, Mandosia. Keep quiet—don't attract the attention of the men. Is my cloak ready? My sandals? You shall accompany me as far as the city limits. How slow the moon is to rise this evening. This night will never end. Chut! You can talk now—they're gone, aren't they?"

※

Under an enormous red moon Princess Illys hastens across the sands.

The night is sultry and the infinite wilderness shines as whitely and as sadly as a plain of salt. In the distance, beneath the livid sky, the mountains of Libya look like a wall of camphor. It is a landscape of rare devastation and boundless distress. Here and there, the trunk of an aloe-tree extends like a desiccated arm, or a lump of rock emerges from the sand, the appearance of every such outline informed by disquiet.

Princess Illys almost regrets the folly that prompted her visit to the witches.

See how the moon enlarges itself, and the landscape with it! The desert is the colour of ash now, and the moon is a plaster mask set against a bitumen sky. Its cold, dull light pours forth like tears of mourning. At the horizon, the mountains are shrouded in funereal grey.

And see how the sand shifts and stirs beneath every step as unidentifiable creatures swarm within it: toads, dwarfs, infant crocodiles. No, the Nile is too far away for there to be crocodiles—but there are things that creep, things that crawl, things that walk and things that hop spasmodically; there are the stumps of amputated arms, cripples' crutches, legless trunks, even crabs' pincers! There are the round and fulgurant eyes of octopodes and the spineless backs of sinuous reptiles; there are the creased and scaly bellies of yellow serpents and the clicking bills of ibises. The entire desert is a seething swamp!

Illys, feeling as if she is being seized by claws, nipped by rows of teeth, licked by tongues and kissed by mouths, flees in panic.

When her haste only plunges her more deeply into the frightful moving softness of that satanic and bestial host she turns on her heel and instinctively throws her arms around the neck of a green jasper sphinx, which suddenly manifests itself, walking alongside her.

The sphinx whinnies like a horse as it immediately scampers away, rising into the air far above the seething, silent swarm—and the princess faints.

※

When she recovers her senses, Illys is on foot again, relentlessly drawn along the broken stones of a steep mountain path hewn from the living rock. She stumbles, because she is blind; her eyelids are sealed by a blindfold and a gag fills her mouth. Numb with terror, she is hurried along by two invisible companions, guided through the night and the unknown, towards she knows not what place of horror and suffering.

All of a sudden, there is a riot of strident jeering, menacing laughter, cracking whips, frantic cries and hoots of joy—as if the triumphant frenzy of an entire nation were aroused on night in order to seize its king—and the blindfold is removed from her eyes, the gag from her mouth.

Illys recognises—without ever having seen them before—the high plateaux of the Libyan mountain range. Within a circle of misshapen stones, above the stormclouds that cling to the skirts of the mountain, a vast ragged crowd is assembled around her, howling menacingly, swarming like serpents.

All the witches are here, their talons extended towards her and their eyes glowing like phosphorus: the witches of Thessaly, the witches of Thrace and the witches of Egypt; the sorceresses of Libya and the sorceresses of the Nile. There are French witches too, their white bodies sheathed in animal hides, and there are magicians from India, whose slender bodies are topped, like those of idols, with the heads and beaks of hawks and fowls. Some have bats set like flowers in their hair. Some are barking like dogs, others keening like she-wolves. Some have the trunks of elephants in the middle of their faces—long black trunks that curl around their legs to sniff the peculiar little death's-heads that are set in their genital regions, or which climb sinuously half way up the thighs of others, whose flesh turns white when little red vipers bite them on the knee. These have huge outgrowths of darkness on their foreheads, and within these dark outgrowths are enormous scarlet poppies, so fleshy and mobile that they seem vibrant with life.

This whole anarchic crowd closes in on the princess,

seizes hold of her, and drags her across the rocks and the precipices, the summits and the valleys—and Illys, half-dead, feels herself floating up and flying into space with them, into an inchoate pearly haze.

High above the palm forests and the snow-white peaks, the Sabbat whirls her around and around, thrice, again, and thrice more. Nude bodies—young and old, thin and stout, ugly and pretty, but all terrifying—zoom up before plunging hectically down, the jetting upwards again, all embracing one another and fornicating. Beasts fly through the air too. Owls brush Illys with their wings, monkeys tickle her, billy-goats butt her; a rat's tail grazes her, muzzles sniff her—and while she is whipped by vipers winged like cockerels, a thin-legged dwarf with an enormous head laughingly offers her his hand, and a strange sunflower. Far beneath her feet, on the other side of the wild stormclouds, riverside towns and forested valleys are sleeping calmly.

Now it is no longer a dwarf that is beside Illys. A monstrous crow takes her under its wing. It is wearing a priest's ceremonial robes and a bishop's mitre; a grimoire is clutched in one of is claws, from which it reads a horrible gospel in a croaking murmur. A white-eyed frog in a surplice swims through the air behind them, lost in ecstatic rapture. She has an escort of monks, who spread their frocks around her—but the monks are storks robed as capuchins, demonic penitents intoning satanic psalms.

※

Princess Illys woke up at dawn, in her bedchamber in the palace of the Ptolemies—but no mirror ever displayed her sinful beauty again. Her eyes searched in vain for her smiling face. Illys never recovered her reflection; she had left it at the Sabbat. The sorceresses of Egypt had tricked her, as punishment for her pride.

We must resist the temptations of magicians and attractive faces in looking-glasses.

CPSIA information can be obtained
at www.ICGtesting.com
Printed in the USA
LVOW10s0517170517
534668LV00002B/426/P

9 781943 813025